These stories are shocking, surreal and sensual.
They speak of experience, and a compassion that's nothing to
do with worthiness. Swinney has a distinctive voice and eye,
and she makes brilliant use of imagery. No-one is safe from
her dark, perceptive and occasionally painfully funny gaze.

– Cathy Galvin – writer and founder of
*the **Word Factory** and the **Sunday Times Short Story Award***

The Map of Bihar

and other stories
by

Janet H Swinney

Circaidy Gregory Press

Copyright information

Published June 2019
ISBN 978-1-910841-51-8

Printed in the UK
by Catford Print

Published by
Circaidy Gregory Press
Creative Media Centre,
45 Robertson St, Hastings,
Sussex TN34 1HL

www.circaidygregory.co.uk

For my Dad, John Harrison Swinney
an unschooled poet, who died when I was still a child.

Acknowledgements

Special thanks to Naresh Sohal, Cynthia Klein and Jolanta Woch who were my critical readers and a constant source of encouragement.

'Private Passions' was shortlisted in the Fish International short story competition 2011 under the title '21 Glebe Street' and was first published in *Barcelona to Bihar*, Earlyworks Press, 2012. 'Degsie's All-Time Runners' was first published online in 'The Feathered Flounder', and was longlisted in the Fish International short story competition 2011. 'Is It Sunday Yet?' was first published in *Significant Spaces*, Earlyworks Press, 2013. 'Leonardo's Cart' was longlisted for Best New Writing 2012 (USA), under the title 'Fat Chance'. 'Drishti' was first published online in *Joao Roque* literary magazine, Goa; *the Indian Review*, Assam, and *Out of Print* literary magazine, Mumbai. 'Internet Explorer' was first published in *Ways of Falling*, Earlyworks Press 2011. 'A Tadge to Your Left' was shortlisted in the Ilkley Literature Festival 2017 and chosen by Cathy Galvin to be published on the website of the *Word Factory*. 'The Map of Bihar' was first published in *Barcelona to Bihar*, Earlyworks Press, 2012; and then in *Best New Writing 2013*, Hopewell Publications USA, and was nominated for the Eric Hoffer award for prose. 'The Queen of Campbeltown was' first published in *The Ball of the Future*, Earlyworks Press 2016. 'Moving In' was first published in *Flight* online literary journal, 2016. It was a finalist in the Olga Sinclair short fiction competition 2015, and highly commended in the Bristol short story competition 2012. 'The Menace at the Gate' was first published online in the *Bombay Literary Magazine*, 2016. 'Washing Machine Wars' received a special mention in Fabula Press's 2017 Nivalis competition. 'Veil' was first published in *Recognition*, Earlyworks Press 2010. 'The Works of Lesser-Known Artists' was joint runner-up in the London Short Story competition 2014, judged by Cathy Galvin and Jackie Kay. It was first published in *Flamingo Land and Other Stories*, Flight Press 2015.

About the Author

Janet H Swinney was born and grew up in the North East of England, when packets of crisps still had blue twists of salt in them and pickled onions were considered a delicacy. She got her political education in Scotland and now lives in London. She worked in the post-16 education sector for many years, in roles ranging from teacher and trainer to inspector and consultant. For over forty years she shared her life with the composer, Naresh Sohal. She has travelled widely in India.

Janet had ambitions as a writer from an early age but, being from a working-class background, had no idea how to go about fulfilling them. After submitting work to the BBC's *The Northern Drift*, she was encouraged by the BBC radio producer Alfred Bradley. She abridged Dickens' *Dombey and Son* for BBC Radio Leeds. For this gargantuan effort she received a £30 payment, and no acknowledgement. (The work was never used). However, she regards this as one of the best formative experiences a writer could have.

Later on, she had some success as a journalist, writing features for the *Guardian, Observer (Scotland)* and the *Times*. In 2008, she was a runner-up in the Guardian's international development journalism competition.

Now, her focus is entirely on fiction. This is her first collection of short stories but there are others in the offing, and she is looking for a home for a play based on the stories of the much-loved Indo-Pakistani author, Saadat Hasan Manto.

You can find Janet at:

www.janethswinney.com

and

@janetsfictionaddiction

Contents

Private Passions

It was spring, but the sky was an undifferentiated grey and the buds on the trees in the park clutched themselves close. Archie McStriven looked round furtively. He wanted to get indoors, to keep any chance of human contact to the minimum. He poked his T-shaped key into the lock of the stair door and lifted the latch. He made for the bottom step, but the door leading to the back green was open and so was the door to the bottom flat. The darkie who had got the shop on the right was rummaging about with boxes, trying to drag stuff into what, presumably, was his storeroom. He looked up as McStriven approached. Even in the dim light let in by the back door and the window on the upper landing, McStriven could see an expression of greeting forming on the man's face. Underneath the hand-painted sign that said "No spitting" McStriven flexed his cheeks and collected saliva in the bowl of his mouth. He spat hard and achieved a good trajectory. The spittle smacked on the floor at the darkie's feet.

Satisfied, he sidled on up the stair, the sleeve of his snot-green Burberry sliding up the gloss paint wall. Darkies: he didn't like them. Who knew where they'd come from or what they were doing here? Running shops? Away tae fuck. Now he went up to Woodlands for his pies and rolls, where the old Polish gent ran the dairy. There the window was stacked with things you could recognise – wedges of red and white cheddar, slices of black and white pudding and a good selection of sausages. Not these boxes of limp and decaying vegetables propped up on the pavement, half of which he'd never seen before and didn't know what to do with.

He had time for the Poles. Their Air Force had done its bit during the war, stationed in Renfrew and Dunino. Some of them didn't want to go home afterwards. The Polish gent had strung Union jacks across his window, and stabbed others, on sticks, into the cheese. You knew where

1

you were with that. 'Good day, Mister Mac,' he would say whenever McStriven popped in in the morning. 'Very good, I think, but a wee bit cool.' Tried hard, you see. Darkies, on the other hand, you never knew what their game was. And as for their personal habits, you didn't know the first thing. You didn't want to know.

The flat was freezing cold. McStriven didn't notice. Cold was his metier. It didn't make much difference to him whether he was outside or in. He took a packet out of his pocket and lobbed his coat onto the stand. Without taking his muffler off, he went through to the living room.

McStriven still had a radiogram. He still favoured the vinyl. He also had a harmonium. They were ranged on either side of the vast 1930s fireplace his wife had persuaded him to install after he'd been made up to inspector, all lacquered oak and dark green tiles that had once been glossy. He turned the key on the pipe, applied a match and the gas popped on. He waited till the flames had suffused the bricks with orange, then turned them down to a mere blue flicker.

His fingers were still a bit stiff. He folded back the lid of the harmonium and considered ploughing through a few metrical psalms, but thought better of it. Instead, he thumbed his way through the tightly packed racks along the back wall till he found what he was looking for. He drew out *The Dream of Gerontius*, slid it out of its sleeve and placed it carefully on the turntable. It was the landmark 1945 recording with Sargent, Heddle Nash and the Huddersfield Choral Society. He'd gone to some trouble to get it, travelling on the bus down to England one weekend. And now he had the score. He ripped open the paper-clad packet, and sank into his threadbare chair as the needle settled into its groove. Head bent, his eyes roamed the staves hungrily as the phrases unfolded. He had his own misgivings about the Papish content of the text – Dora would have turned in her grave – but he could not resist the music.

At the end of part one, after the priest's invocation, he took a break. Truth to tell, and lofty sentiments aside, he was feeling a bit peckish. He went through into the kitchen, where he rattled some water into an enamel kettle and made a pot of tea. From the mildewed fridge, he took out a mutton pie in a cellophane wrapper, and unleashed it onto a cracked plate. He assembled the lot on a wooden tray which he took back into the living room. He sat with the tray over his knees and consumed at his leisure, savouring the strong tea and the droplets of cold mutton fat that adhered to the roof of his mouth. With careful adjustment, one could be persuaded to moderate the temperature and the consistency of the other.

He awoke with a jolt, as the crockery skidded to the floor and a cold patch of tea made itself known on his trouser leg. The room was many shades gloomier. Shifting the debris of his dinner to one side with his foot, he got up, shuffled through the layers of newspaper that littered the floor, went to the radiogram, and turned the volume up. Time for part two. As he resumed his seat, an unsettling gurgle made its first strange pronouncements in his gut.

~

Craig was a high flier. He was on his way up. Thanks to his aptitude for financial modelling, he was blasting his way up the departmental hierarchy at the Royal Bank like a Soyuz rocket. *And* he'd landed Penny, she of the long legs, neat frame and earnest expression, mother so wealthy she behaved like minor aristocracy. Despite Craig's origins on a Lanarkshire housing scheme, the mother had agreed to the couple marrying and had paid for the whole Highland clamjamfrey last summer up in Pitlochry. Penny herself was starting to make a tidy sum from her mother's personal indulgence, a business shipping artefacts from Hong Kong and flogging them, at a vast mark up, to folk in the West End. Life was full on. Every evening the pair of them went running, every weekend they went climbing up north and at Christmas they had bought a load of gear and gone skiing in Courmayeur. They were currently considering investing in a villa on the south side, but if Craig got his next promotion – and no reason why not – it would be the big move east.

Now Craig stuffed his hand up Penny's jumper and tweaked a nipple. 'The old guy's giving it some tonight.' Penny's eyes opened wider with half-kindled interest. She lowered the magazine she was reading. A chorus of some size was, indeed, going full blast upstairs. 'Come on. Let's go and give it what-for ourselves.' Penny giggled. Craig looked at her like an eager mastiff. He was difficult to resist, but she was rather interested in the article she was reading on interior design in villas along the Amalfi coast. He grabbed her wrist. 'Or we could just do it here.'

They made short, sharp work of it. Penny didn't manage to get her jumper off and Craig wasn't interested in helping her. They mangled magazines and kicked over the coffee table. The chorus subsided as they reached conclusions. Dazed, they cleaned their teeth quietly and went to bed.

At two am, his penis was at her belly again, knocking for entry. It wasn't Penny's best time of day, but she wasn't clear in her own mind yet about the distinction between conjugal rights and forced entry. She made much of being deeply asleep, but Craig crouched over her insistently, nudging and pawing, the aggressive stubble of his beard scraping over her breasts, until she felt obliged to give him her attention. He'd picked up a few ideas, of course, about what was required of him, and had probably tried them out on enough women to think he was on the right lines. So after some peremptory foraging, she let him in.

And actually, if she closed her eyes and twisted her pelvis to and fro, ignoring the way he had pinned her arms above her head, things became interesting. Craig went at her pneumatically, as though he had a road to dig and was working to a timescale. He hung on, digging, digging... Ah yes, and there it was, the sharp intake of breath that showed he had engaged her attention. Penny was not hugely demonstrative, but she was responsive. At last she yelped and moved beneath him with a shudder. He made one or two more thrusts for victory, gave a gruff shout then fell on top of the vanquished.

~

McStriven has had to adjourn to his bathroom. He is sitting on the cracked wooden seat of the Victorian toilet. He has made several attempts to get to his bed, getting up and wrenching at the chain, and then sitting down again almost immediately. He hunches with his arms folded across his lower abdomen as a stabbing pain shoots to and fro within his entrails. Beads of cold sweat stand on his neck and forehead, even though a freezing draft is sifting through the window. It is not in his nature to call out, but 'Oh!' he groans sotto voce. 'Oh!'

~

On the second floor, Shona lay on her back and looked hard at the ceiling. Tommy was huge and silent beside her, his back turned towards her in the dark. These days, it didn't take much to wake her. She hadn't had a sound night's sleep for several years. She felt her scalp creep above her ears before she actually heard the sound: 'Whoo! Whoo! Whoo!' like a bicycle tyre being inflated. For a moment she couldn't think what it might be.

4

Then she recognised it: they were at it again. It was the sound of the athletic, hard-as-nails bitch who lived upstairs achieving an orgasm. And once she'd heard it, she couldn't not hear it. At first, it seemed prurient to be listening. Why would she listen to someone else's sex life? Good luck to them! They weren't long married, let them make hay. But then, the sound of their sex life was the only sex life she had herself these days. And despite herself she found it erotic.

She'd had two babies by Tommy, but he'd never once brought her to orgasm while he was inside her. Felt his natural charisma should suffice. It was an honour to be fucked by his swaggering, bumptious, rakish-looking good self. And now he didn't come near her at all. She pursed her lips. The bastard was taking his pleasures elsewhere. In the back bedroom with the student to be exact. A lump of anger filled her throat. When she confronted him, he didn't even bother to deny it. What was the harm? he said. She was a grown-up lassie who knew how to take care of herself – nothing would come of it. The implication being: unlike Shona who had fallen pregnant at the first possible opportunity. Thus he avoided the point altogether. Tears gathered at the outer corners of Shona's eyes, then trickled cold across her temples and into her hair.

And how could she compete with the student, a young woman with glossy hair down to her waist who'd come all the way from Lytham St Anne's with her A levels to study literature. Shona had done an SVQ in Social Care at her local FE college and had once toyed with the idea of working in Childcare, but now she had weans of her own, she would as soon knock them over the head as look at them.

'Literature?' Tommy had asked. 'What literature? Whose literature? No good coming here with your Wordsworth and your Keats. Effete bloody pansies. Shallow as shark shite.' He'd fixed the student with a provocative glare and immediately she was hooked. Shona could see which way things were heading. And that was all the opening he needed for an extensive discourse on Hugh MacDiarmid and the other guy, whatsisname, Grassy Gibbon.

That's the way Tommy had always been. It was a sport with him. And with all his friends, for that matter. Many a time she'd sat with them in *The Keys*, and inevitably one of them would start spoiling for a war of words. And always the same subjects: politics, history, books, but most of all politics. It would be Maxton this, Maxton that, and Tommy would yell, 'Did he, fuck!' and bring things round to John MacLean, the Bolsheviks' consul in the UK, and what the British Government did to him. She'd been proud of him, so animated and so well informed. She'd sat with cheeks flushed and a dopey smile on her face while they'd gone at it hammer and tongs. Now she realised that she had not been part of their circle at all, just a tolerated ring-side spectator.

~

The woman upstairs was still sounding as though she were approaching a sneeze. Shona raised her nightie and smoothed her hand over her belly. Not bad, despite the two kids. Her pelvic bones still stood higher than the soft cushion of flesh they embraced. Probably the smoking that did it. She slipped her hand between her thighs and worked at herself gingerly. Was there a glimmer of pleasure there? The woman upstairs gave a yelp. The man groaned. Tommy stirred and turned to face her. The moment evaporated. No, there could be no pleasure in her pain. She was pathetic. She turned her back on Tommy, and waited wearily for dawn to happen.

~

McStriven is still on his perch. But only some of the time. He thinks he must have blasted the entire contents of his alimentary canal into the bowl, but still the malaise grips him, wave after wave, and when it does, he doesn't know which end of himself to point at the porcelain.

~

At five, Tommy woke and went into the kitchen. Shona wondered if he would detour via the student's room, but no, she could hear him in the kitchen making his piece. Shortly afterwards, he closed the main door quietly and went off down the stair to his job on the Blue Trains.

~

Asha stood behind the counter, swaying slightly on her feet. She was desperate for Prakash to get back from the cash and carry. She needed sleep like a junkie needs a fix. Her eyes felt as though they'd spent the night in a jar of achar, and her feet ached with the cold, two pairs of woollen socks making no impression at all on her circulation. Thankfully, the new baby was asleep in a banana box under the counter.

She'd had the shutters up since six thirty, taken delivery of the rolls and the papers and set out the vegetable boxes, removing the yellowed leaves from the outside of the cabbages, and lopping the tops off the leeks. She'd also filled the gaps in the shelves with cans of mince and horrible-looking stew. Cow, it might be. A few early morning workers with grey, pinched faces came in, grabbing their papers and fags and flinging their money onto the counter. 'Smile,' Prakash would say, 'whether you like them or not. Say something to them. Make them feel they want to come back. We need their money, even if it's just a few coppers for their newspaper.'

But how could she smile? Life here was so hard. And what could she say, other than 'Seventy pence, please.'? At the reception centre, Prakash had been the first to put his hand up when they'd asked for volunteers to come to this place. 'Are you mad?' the others had looked at him. 'Going all that way?' They all wanted to go to London. Everyone thought they had a relative or knew someone in London, someone who would help them get their hands on some of the capital's indubitable riches. Prakash was under no illusions, or maybe he was just naive. 'Look,' he said, 'I'm sick of sitting here behind this fence cooking one chapatti and one brinjal on a flame. It makes no difference where we go. Same-same. It's all our Mother Country. I want to get on and start doing something with my life.' And so they'd been dumped on the outskirts of town, among broken houses and broken people. If it hadn't been for the local minister who had found Prakash a job as a motor mechanic and some of his congregation who had brought Asha old cardigans, worn out shoes and a misshapen blanket for the cot, God knows what would have happened. After a couple of years of it, when they were down to their last window pane and had saved almost every penny Prakash earned, they had managed to squeeze a loan out of the bank and moved here.

Now, though, they both worked: a joint enterprise, every day of the week, from first thing in the morning till last thing at night, whether she was pregnant or whether she wasn't. She went nowhere and knew no-one. She didn't understand how anything worked here. Neither of them did. And that was how baby number one had ended up in the freezer cabinet, a beautiful, beautiful little girl with masses of hair and eyelids like pistachio shells. The first, vicious winter at the shop had polished her off. They were caught in a dilemma. They thought she should be buried, not cremated, because she was so young, but they weren't sure. And where would they bury her, even if they were right? They could hardly put her out in the back green. There was no informed person to consult, so they wrapped her in a length of sari cloth, then fastened her in a plastic bag, and there she lay in the freezer under the strawberry Mivvies and frozen sprouts waiting for a time when they could get proper advice from a pandit.

~

McStriven is dying of thirst. But he cannot get up to reach the handbasin. His freezing body is locked in a seated position. The cold has got to him at last. His knees are numb, and his shoulders and neck creak with the smallest of movements. Now an excruciating pain tears from the centre of his chest down his left arm. He cannot bear to lift his ribs to breathe. His anal sphincter is open, but his body has nothing left to offer up. He needs help, but he knows no-one will come. No postman, no neighbour. Over the years he has actively discouraged the lot of them. Now he'll have to face things on his own.

~

The student had long since departed to lectures, throwing Shona a pitying look as she went. Shona sat in her housecoat on the gargantuan sofa they had bought on tick. She rolled herself another fag and poured herself a glass of William Low's cheapest whiskey. Her loneliness filled her like a silent sea. How had she got into this situation; how could she get out? No solution presented itself.

The little one was bawling, while the toddler was battering around the room with a plastic horse on a metal trolley. To and fro he went, over the bare boards they'd been meaning to strip for ages. She'd not yet managed to get the pants on him. The noise was deafening. 'Shaddap!' she shouted. He carried on, pausing briefly only to squeeze out a turd from between the cheeks of his bottom. Leaving the roll-up on her lip, Shona went and placed the latest Olivia Newton-John on the turntable. She sank back onto the sofa and waited for the music to move through her, to bring some sort of internal relief. As Rory racketed past her one more time, she fetched him a hefty clap on his backside. He took no notice. *Slow learner*, she thought. She got up and turned the volume up.

What they said about drowning your sorrows, it didn't work the way you expected. She always hoped for amnesia. But, as usual, after she had listened to the track several times over, her sorrows had distorted and billowed out of all proportion, like the gown of a diva dragging her under, and she wept openly and noisily in full view of the child.

~

From eight till about half nine there was a steady stream of customers. Asha's hands moved automatically to and fro across the counter, twirling paper bags and dropping coins into the till. 'First?' she said, or 'That all?' Weariness pervaded her every cell. Prakash's voice was constantly in her head, 'Speak to them! Speak to them!' but she could not make her eyes engage with those of any of the people she served; she could not make her facial muscles move into any sort of greeting.

Most customers were housewives, wanting rolls and milk for their breakfast. But there were also pensioners. As far as Asha was concerned, pensioners were a despised class of persons, like that chap upstairs who only ever looked at her in the worst possible way. Most only ever wanted a couple of bread rolls or a stick of butter. She would be standing here till the Equator frosted over if that continued to be the volume of their sales.

She was serving one now, an old woman with a woollen hat and a small shaggy dog on a tartan string. The dog was snuffling with interest around the biscuit packets on the bottom shelf. 'Oi!' Asha wanted to say. 'No dog in shop. Dirty thing!' but she couldn't organise the words quickly enough in a way that would do the trick.

There was a small carton of crowdie and two Dairylea triangles on the counter between them. And two pairs of hands. 'How much?' the woman asked nervously. Asha looked hard at the hands. Two of them were small with translucent flesh through which you could see the veins, and crooked fingers with carbuncular knuckles malformed through hard work. The others were long, brown and well-formed, with fingers almost the same length as each other and fingernails the colour of Persian roses. But which were whose? Asha stared at the hands for a long time, like a scientist observing an experiment. If she commanded her hands to move, which ones would shift? She simply did not know the answer. Panic rose within her. 'How much?' the old woman asked again. Asha shook her head. 'Just take.'

The bewildered woman departed, taking her dog with her. Asha stayed, looking at her velvety hands on the counter. What the hell was happening to her? She was neither asleep nor awake, neither present nor absent. She had entered a state of unreality where she could exercise no influence on anything around her. Not like a sadhu, or any of these elevated people who spend hours in meditation. She was, she thought, "undead", a living person with no life.

A howl of protest filled her head. At first she couldn't be sure whether it came from without or within. But then came the scuttling of feet, and the sound like a boulder rolling across a tilting deck. Back and forth it went across the ceiling, round and round, this way and that, no fixed pattern, stopping and starting, its unpredictability making it all the more aggravating. Then, inevitably, there was the song, the same one the woman played endlessly, day after day. *Fizzerkel*, the female singer squalled, *Let's get Fizzerkel!* The baby under the counter started to scream. 'Prakash,' shrieked Asha, 'where are you?'

~

McStriven is breathing his last. Who can tell whether it's as bad or worse than he feared. His mouth is open and so are his startled eyes. Columns of sinew are all that is left of his neck. A final rush of pain carries him off. His trousers are still round his ankles. His rigid body, bent like an allen key, keels over sideways. His skull hits the pine panelling, just below the dado rail.

~

Penny was first back to the flat. They didn't run for pleasure: it wasn't a social exercise. They ran, as Craig put it, 'to get as fit as fuck'. He had already lapped her twice in the park, and she had left him to finish off with a few more rounds. She had had a shower and was bending over the hand-basin in her knickers, trying to insert a contact lens when he crashed into the bathroom. He tore off his kit. His hard flesh was pink with freshly oxygenated blood. Rivulets of sweat coursed through his hair and down his body. He was cock-a-hoop. 'Best time ever!' he crowed. His penis stood in front of him as tall and arrogant as the Wallace monument. 'Yeah?' she said. 'Yeah! Now let me at you!'

He came at her from behind. Tearing off the lacy frill, he prised her open and thrust himself into her hard. The contact lens that had been perched on one finger dropped into the drain. 'Wait!' Penny exclaimed. She put out a hand to steady herself on the steamy mirror. He thrust hard into her again. Her pubic bone banged against the edge of the basin. 'Ow!' She was about to protest further when he whipped the belt from the

10

dressing gown hanging nearby, jammed it between her jaws and yanked her head back. If she had not been so shocked, she might have seen her anguished face reflected in the mirror.

'Get with the programme!' Craig yelled.

Neither of them was in a position to notice the ribbons of tar-coloured liquid dribbling down the walls above the toilet.

Penny had no intention of getting with it. In a moment she had made her mind up on the subject of conjugal rights. She was very, very angry. She writhed and twisted beneath Craig's controlling grip. Tears of frustration ran down her cheeks. Regardless, Craig continued to drive home.

Suddenly, there was a sound like a shotgun going off, and then a tremendous crash. The room was filled with clouds of dust. Craig fell out of her and stepped back. Penny hung over the basin in relief. Their own toilet bowl was shattered. On top of it sat another one and on top of that, the old guy, like some ancient arachnid. Gallons of brown liquid poured through the gaping hole in the ceiling. The stench was foul.

Penny had never felt so humiliated. She struggled to cover herself with the dressing gown. Craig stood perplexed, his clammy body streaked with plaster dust.

~

Prakash had had a terrible day. First he'd had trouble getting his full quota of stock at the cash and carry, and then the ancient van had broken down in the middle of the Cross and he'd had to take a heap of abuse until a doctor had finally helped him get the vehicle off to the side of the road so that he could figure out what was wrong. Then, when he'd got back, Asha had been in a very peculiar state of mind.

Now people were gathering on the pavement outside the shop. Something had happened upstairs. The police were the first to arrive and then the paramedics. It took a while for the situation to unfold, but it seemed it was the elderly fellow from the top floor. Prakash inserted a paan into his mouth, and chewed thoughtfully while they all waited. Among the small crowd he noticed the woman from the first floor flat, all puffy eyes and blotchy face, a skimpy horse tail of hair tied high up on her head. She had her two kids in tow, one on her arm, the other hanging on to her leg, both grizzling as usual. There was no sign of her man, the one who was the train conductor. The other couple were also there, the tall chap looking grim and self-important, a protective arm round his wife's shoulders; the woman looking upset and cowed. Asha was still in the shop, standing silent and statuesque behind the counter. Prakash thought of her fondly. This had been such a weird day. When this was all over, he thought, they would draw the shutters down early for once, and he would make sweet, sweet love to her.

At last, the medics came out, bearing their parcel on a stretcher. You could make nothing out, of course: the elderly chap was all trussed up. It wasn't like back home, where you could verify with your own eyes that someone had lost an arm or received a fatal blow. Here, you had take the word of some unknown person. The two men threaded through the murmuring onlookers in a businesslike fashion. Prakash found himself in prime position. As the bundle passed, he spat, 'Fetoom!' A bright plaque of scarlet expectoration hit the ground.

~

It was spring. There had been early rain, and weak sunshine now grazed the buildings, investing the air with a sense of optimism. Alec parked his small green and orange van at the end of the road. He didn't like people to know that he was coming. He eyed the parade of shops and then his clipboard. Aye, that was it: Asha Stores, one of six places in the area he'd be visiting today. Pound to a penny this'd be the source of the problem. He checked the job sheet again. Pies and bridies. 'Here we go again,' he thought. He'd have to get them to turn their freezer cabinets out of course.

Degsie's All-Time Runners

Degsie – don't ask – drew himself in, flattening his fur against his ribs, and squeezed through the tall privet at the top of the allotment.

He'd had a good night up on the railway lines. An almost full moon had come and gone amongst billowing clouds. There had been ample opportunity for springing in and out of the shadows onto unsuspecting prey, and he'd made considerable headway into a family of voles living unobtrusively in a ditch. There'd been plenty of opportunity for sexual antics too. The grubby female with the black patch over one eye put in an appearance when the moon was high. They took a few steps around each other, and then set to with a screeching that tore the neighbourhood apart. Later came the slender mackerel tabby with the pretty white feet – a lower key, but equally satisfying affair.

Towards the morning, the moon paled and made its exit. The undergrowth became dank; a reluctant glimmer felt its way between the branches of the crippled elm trees; a few birds stuttered nervously their nests – the start of another dingy autumn day. Degsie shook himself. He wanted to get indoors. He slalomed between the last of the Brussels sprout stalks, and padded along one of the ridges where the potatoes had grown. He scrabbled up onto a fence post, dropped down into the lane, up again onto a wheelie bin and down into the blind woman's yard.

~

Degsie had had many live-in arrangements over the years, but the best was the one he had now. His long, smoke-grey fur with the cream undertones was very high maintenance, but made him hugely attractive to humankind. A pair of pale, button-like eyes gave him an air of wide-eyed innocence that added to his appeal. Children and pensioners fell upon him with oohs and aahs, failing to notice that he was, in fact, a menacing muscle-bound meatball. For a while he'd lived with Dennis, a barber, who

13

called him "Choo-choo". Life in the barber's shop could be good, snoozing all day in a sun-soaked leather chair, and being cosseted by the customers. But Dennis was a bit too fond of groomings that featured latherings and unctions. And he took "Choo-choo" to the vet far more often than "Choo-choo" would have liked. Ultimately, Dennis developed an allergy to hair. He became so depressed that Degsie found his own mood and appetite deteriorating. So one evening, after closing, while Dennis was moping over a back number of *Harper's and Queen*, Degsie did a runner.

Some time after that came Steven, a small boy who hated school. Degsie made friends with Steven on a demolition site where he was hiding to avoid number lines and vectors. He followed him home to reconnoitre. The place looked promising, so he introduced himself. There was a mother, a father and a grandmother. The mother regarded him with suspicion, and made it clear he was on probation. But shortly after his arrival, Steven stopped wetting the bed, so Degsie was allowed to stay. Things went smoothly for a while, though the atmosphere in the house was never entirely comfortable. The father would give Degsie a scoot up his furry arse with his workman's boot every now and then; the mother ignored him altogether, and grandma individually hand-counted the pieces of Go-Cat into his bowl as though they were gold nuggets. But Steven had a large room, and once he was back at school, Degsie could spend long hours lolling undisturbed on his bed. And then, Steven genuinely cared for him, so when he came home, they played together till bedtime or until some parental intervention overtook them.

It all went wrong during the summer holidays. The pair of them had been out all day wriggling through the undergrowth. At teatime, Steven suddenly grew flushed and breathless. He dropped his drop scone. The doctor was summoned. By the time he came, Steven was stretched out on the sofa and was in serious difficulty. The doctor probed beneath his shirt and placed a stethoscope on his chest. 'He's having an asthma attack', he said, and looked round the assembled group, the mother, the father, the grandma and, lastly, Degsie. 'For Goodness sake!' he said, 'He's allergic to the cat. Get that thing out of here!' 'That blessed cat!' shouted the mother. 'I knew it!' Degsie felt himself seized by the scruff, so tight he himself could hardly breathe, and in no time at all, his paws were hitting the unforgiving surface of the yard. He could hear Steven inside crying and choking, 'No, no! Let Smo-okey stay!' So he got up on the water barrel and started wailing himself in the hope that it would make them change their minds. But it didn't. When the back door slammed that night, he was locked out of their lives for good.

Now, after careful surveillance, he had ended up in a quiet cul-de-sac where only pensioners lived. He had a "distributed" lifestyle, spending part of his time in the home of the blind woman, and part with the woman next door. The women lived alone, and never spoke to each other. Neither knew that Degsie was a resident of the other's house. All that either woman required was the occasional exchange of body heat, and a bit of chest rattling that they construed as affection. Degsie was happy to oblige for, on this basis, he could extend his lodging indefinitely, enjoying the comforts of both homes.

~

As Degsie sat outside the blind woman's door, he heard an alarm bell ring. Great! That meant breakfast was on the way. The blind woman's day was entirely regulated by alarms of one kind or another. A clock radio got her out of bed at six in the morning. Then came a bell in the kitchen for breakfast time. An electronic peeping in the living room foretold the arrival of the district nurse, and a cuckoo clock with a daft wooden bird announced dinner time. And so on, throughout the day. Next door, it was an entirely different matter. There, the elderly resident had a more laissez-faire approach. Sometimes, the driver of the Social Services bus would have his mouth letter-boxed to the front door at noon bellowing, 'Aw, ha'way, Miss Thornton, we're all waiting for you', while Miss Thornton would still be deep beneath the duvet, in a fleecy suit and two pairs of angora socks, clutching a packet of chocolate digestives that she had taken to bed the night before.

Degsie had concluded that it was better to start the day with the punctilious Peggy, the blind lady, and then to move round to her profligate neighbour in the early afternoon. His usual practice was to stay with Miss Thornton until the evening. Generally, he sat on her lap, while she watched the telly until that blasted programme *Countdown* came on. There were certain sounds that just made Degsie's claws curl. And one of them was its oft-repeated catchphrase – 'Bee-baa, bee-baa, pum-pum-pum-pum'. Determined to avoid this, he would disappear into the hatbox on top of the wardrobe, leaving only his tail out to remind her of his presence.

Sometimes, he would look in again on Peggy, just to see if there were any kippers on the go, but just as she was an early riser, so she was an early sleeper and, if your timing was worse than hers, could be encountered manicuring her dentures. Rather than risk this, he usually just made his way up the allotments to see what was doing in the pigeon lofts.

On this particular morning, when Degsie shoved his head through the cat flap in the uPVC door and wriggled into her house, Peggy was already in the kitchen, at work with the can-opener. He sprinted towards her and wound himself in figure eights around her stick-like legs. 'Why, hello, Samson, is it a nasty day out there? You're all wet. I hope you've not messed up my stockings, mind.' Peggy manoeuvred some fishy substance into a tin bowl for him with a fork, and placed it on the floor. Degsie eyed it critically. Bog-standard fare, and a modest portion, but it would do to be going on with. If he made a racket afterwards, he might get some biscuits.

After breakfast, he crept up onto the back of an armchair. He closed one eye and with the other watched Peggy feeling her way round the room. She was forever tidying up: wiping down surfaces and wringing out cloths, smoothing out runners and plumping up cushions. She even polished the television screen regularly, though she could barely see it. Today, he watched her folding away tea towels that had been drying in front of the fire, a tartan one with writing in the middle and another with a red stripe border.

He was woken from his dozing by the electronic beeper. Peggy was sitting in the chair beneath him. He could see pink avenues of scalp between the tight white bales of her hair. She sat bolt upright. 'Aye, time for the nurse, Samson.' She got up and turned the knob on the gas fire up several notches: 'I divvent want her to think I'm starven in here.'

In due course the nurse arrived. It wasn't the usual woman, thin Pam, with the cold shaking hands, who pretended she didn't smoke: it was a short, plump woman with dark hair and a bossy manner. Her glance scoured the living room. Degsie took an immediate dislike to her. He moved swiftly to the armchair opposite Peggy's and flattened himself into the cushion.

'Have you got a clean towel for nursie?'

'Aye, top left hand drawer.'

The nurse went to the sideboard and pulled out a towel.

'Your man, Mrs Blake?' She nodded at a framed photograph that stood on a crocheted mat.

'Aye, that's our Ernie. Been gone a long time now and all the bairns ha' moved away.'

The nurse spread the towel over her knees, propped up one of Peggy's legs and began changing the dressing. Degsie averted his gaze. He didn't care for the smells either of the wound, the dressing, or the lubricant on the nurse's latex gloves.

The nurse worked briskly. She kept up a stream of small talk about people and places Peggy didn't know, and trotted out admonishments that she was too old to need. 'Now no scratching, and no fiddling with the safety pins.' Once both legs were dressed, and Peggy's stockings had been hoisted again, the nurse peeled off her gloves. She made a few notes on a chart and popped it back into her bag.

'And who's this?' she said, her eye falling belatedly on Degsie.

Who dae yer fuckin' think it is? purred Degsie, *Sandy Claas?* The nurse looked at him sourly.

'Aye, that's our Samson.'

'I won't stroke him: I'd have to wash my hands again.'

Please yer fuckin' sel. Degsie stretched his lips over his teeth to show that any advance would be unwelcome anyway.

After the nurse had gone, the two of them sat and looked at the fire for a long time.

'To tell you the truth, Samson, I think she's getten one of these on a bit too tight.' Peggy twisted one of her stockinged feet about to try and bring freedom to a ferociously strapped leg. 'And another thing is, she's wore me out.'

Degsie joined Peggy on her chair and waved his tail under her nose. Peggy moved her hand along his back, the carbuncles of her knuckles bouncing along the knobs of his spine. 'Aye, you and me, Samson, we've getten used to each other, but strangers is another matter. I tell you what: I think we should treat ourselves to a cup of tea.'

Peggy pushed Degsie's bottom and he dropped down onto the floor.

While Peggy tottered into the kitchen and felt about for the kettle, Degsie sauntered into the bedroom and got up onto the windowsill. When Peggy said "a cup of tea" that usually meant she would warm a little bit of milk for him and drop a Malteser or two into it to melt. He stretched out a hind leg and started nosing through the fluff in his groin. As he worked methodically to and fro, he looked like a cat with serious intentions, but all the while he was thinking fondly of the gaggingly good treat that lay in store.

Suddenly, without forewarning, a large wheeled beast turned into the street. It trundled past numbers one to three and stopped, plonk! in front of his window, entirely blocking out the light. It had a grey cylindrical body and a trunk that lay over its back. Degsie froze with his leg in the air. His eyes hardened like beads. He hoped fervently that the beast could not see him through the net curtain. A man climbed down from the creature's head. He took two metal rods and heaved up the drain cover at the edge of the pavement. He unhooked the animal's trunk so that it moved about freely, and then plunged it down the hole that had been revealed. He gave a shout. And immediately the beast let out a mad roar of pain.

Degsie toppled backwards off the windowsill, shredding the net curtain as he fell. With difficulty, he righted himself. He shot across the living room, executed a hand-brake turn to get into the kitchen and sprang onto Peggy's chest. By now, the gas kettle was screaming. Peggy toppled backwards. She fell hard onto the work surface next to the sink, and folded in half like a piece of cardboard packing. 'Oof', she said as she slid to the floor. Degsie still clung to her cardigan. And he stayed there with his legs like rigid tent poles while the kettle continued to scream and blackcurrant jam flowed out of Peggy's head.

After a bit, the kettle stopped its din and made small explosions instead. Degsie released his hold on the cardigan and tiptoed to the bedroom door. The grey beast had gone. He crept under the blue valance of Peggy's bed hoping for security, but the chill near the floorboards drove him out. The house was possessed by the ticking of its many clocks and the hissing of the gas fire, but there was an absence of Peggy. He went again to the kitchen where there was a peculiar smell from the cooker. The jam was no longer flowing from Peggy's head, but a large black patch had appeared at one temple and spread around one eye. Her mouth was open in a taut and breathless "O".

Degsie stood still, only his tail twitching. He weighed up the situation. Time, he concluded, to cut his losses.

~

18

Getting into Miss Thornton's house was an altogether different kettle of fish. No cat flap here. Degsie had to go round to the front street, leap onto the bedroom windowsill and wail plaintively until he could prevail upon Miss Thornton to get out of bed and let him in. Or he could wait by the back door until she came out to shout for him. Today, he preferred to wait by the back door.

At last he heard the chain being undone. A sliver of a pyjama-ed Miss Thornton appeared at the door. 'Delilah! Delilah!' she called. Degsie shot past her into the house. And yes, that was the one drawback to being Miss Thornton's lodger: despite all evidence to the contrary, she fondly imagined he was a sweet, unsullied little girl cat. She followed him into the living room and gathered him up into her dressing-gown. 'By Jove, you're quick off the mark today. Have those nasty tom cats been pestering you again?' She inspected his eyes and ears for signs of molestation. 'If I could get my hands on those dirty beasts...' She took him into the kitchen and dropped him on the counter. 'But I tell you what I've got will cheer you up.' She set out an old wooden chopping board and a knife with a blackened blade. 'Hmm, nice little bit of lamb's liver.' She brought out a plastic bag from the fridge and slit it. The liver slithered like a jewel-bright blancmange over the chopping board. 'See?' Degsie nearly wet himself. This was what made gender-bending worthwhile. Miss Thornton carefully chopped the delicacy into cubes, slid it into a murky pan, and set it to simmer. Degsie stalked impatiently up and down the work-surface fluffing his pantaloons. At last he had the delicacy in front of him on the floor. He ate with total dedication, not noticing Miss Thornton fry up bacon and egg for herself. Eventually there was nothing left to do but nose the dish around the floor and then look up pleadingly, even though he was full to the gunnels.

The two of them sat, replete, in the armchair in front of the telly. Degsie cast up a coquettish glance whenever Miss Thornton tickled his chest. They watched the news and then racing from Chepstow. A comforting after-fug of frying drifted through from the kitchen.

Just as the horses entered the turnstiles for the two-o'clock, there was a knock at the back door. It was Jackie, the home care assistant.

'Sorry, I'm a bit late, Miss Thornton. Ee, are you still not dressed?'

Miss Thornton looked wrong-footed.

'I think you'd better go through and change your clothes.'

Miss Thornton got up reluctantly. It was soft going, and she wanted to see whether King's Own Regiment would come through strongly.

'Have you have had your dinner?'

'Couldn't wait any longer.'

'I'll just put it in your book then, shall I?'

Miss Thornton trotted off into the bedroom, while Jackie went to the sideboard drawer and took out an exercise book. 'What did you have?' she shouted.

'Bacon and egg.'

She pencilled this in next to the date under a long line of 'egg and bacon', 'bacon and egg', scribbled her name then dropped the book back into the drawer.

'I've got your pension.'

'What?'

'I've got your pension and your shopping.'

'Wait a minute.'

Jackie switched off the telly and swiftly pocketed the small china figurine that stood on the cabinet. She stepped back to the sideboard. From elsewhere in her jerkin, she pulled out a pension book, some cash and two small Kit Kats and dumped them on the surface. She took one of the Kit Kats, stripped it and broke off one of the logs. She winked at Degsie, tossed him a bit, which he gobbled immediately, and stuffed the rest into her own mouth.

Miss Thornton reappeared from the bedroom in a battered skirt and baggy jumper. She glanced at the telly to discover that she would never know the fate of the King's Own Regiment.

'Look, let me count it out for you. There was seventy-eight pounds twenty-five due. The shopping came to eight pounds ninety-five. I got you some Granny Smiths like you asked. I could only get one Kit Kat though. Then I paid the paper bill. That was seven pounds seventy-five. And you still owed me dad twenty, remember, for mending the garden gate. That leaves thirty-one pounds fifty-five.'

And Jackie spread the items out in descending order: six fives, a one pound coin, a fifty pence piece and a five pence.

Miss Thornton looked at them slowly. 'Say that again.'

'Pension seventy-eight twenty-five; shopping eight ninety-five; papers seven seventy-five; gate twenty. There, see. Thir-ty one, fifty-five. Now where shall we put them?'

Miss Thornton still stood looking uncertain.

'What about your brown purse?'

Miss Thornton nodded.

Jackie quickly found the purse and made a show of inserting the notes and the coins in their proper places. 'OK. I'll put the purse in the top cupboard next to the fireplace. Now don't go letten anybody else get their hands on it. All right? You know where it is then?'

Miss Thornton nodded again.

'Sure?'

More nodding.

'So I'll be off then.' Jackie ruffled Degsie under the chin, and whirled across the room. 'Tomorrow,' she said over her shoulder, 'I'll get the hoover out and give the place a going over. All right?'

The door slammed behind her. Then the gate thudded. Miss Thornton sat down heavily in her chair. She pressed her fingers to her brow. 'Now what did she say? Shopping eight pounds ninety-five... Mind that seems a lot...' She sat silent for a bit. Then she got up and went to the sideboard. 'Let's have a look in the purse.' She opened first one drawer and then the other. 'Why where is it? Where's me brown purse?'

For a long time Miss Thornton went foraging about the house. Degsie could hear her clunking cupboards in the kitchen and shunting drawers in the bedroom. He hated all this fidgeting about. Eventually, she came back empty-handed to her chair. It was getting dark and rain was starting to rattle against the windows.

'Let's have some light, eh?'

Miss Thornton switched the telly on. It was the tail end of *Murder, She Wrote*, and dangerously close to the start of *Countdown*. Degsie stretched himself across Miss Thornton's chest and gave a yawn.

'Time for your snooze?'

Degsie hopped down from Miss Thornton's lap, nudged open the door of the spare room, and ambled over to the corner by the front door where he relieved himself copiously and luxuriantly on the carpet, augmenting an existing bog of peppery piss. One thing about being Miss Thornton's lodger: you didn't have to go outside for anything when it didn't suit you. Feeling much the lighter for his effort, he bounded up effortlessly onto the top of the wardrobe, slid open the lid on the hatbox, jumped inside, and pawed the lid back again. Only his tail dangled casually outside, like a fur stole left at the opera. In a matter of moments he was fast asleep on the crushed velvet that lined the box.

Bloody hell! His eyes popped open in the darkness. Thump! Thump! What was that? There was somebody at the front door. Only officials came to the front door. He whisked his tail quickly inside the box just as Miss Thornton flicked the light switch on.

'Who's there?'

The letterbox lifted, and a voice clucked.

'It's Julie Jenkins, Miss Thornton.'

'Who?'

'Mrs Jenkins. Your psychiatric social worker.'

Silence.

'Remember? I'm from Social Services. I can show you my card if you like.'

Miss Thornton grudgingly pulled back the bolts.

'Ee, mind, it's nice to get inside. What a day.' The social worker stepped in off the street, shaking her bedraggled hair. 'I was just driving across from Philly when suddenly it started to pelt down. I...' There was a sharp intake of breath. 'Ooh! Have you had an accident, Miss Thornton?'

'Eh?'

'Have you had a bit of an accident? It's all right. You can say.'

'I was watching the telly.'

The voices moved into the other room.

'How've you been keeping, then?'

'Canny.'

'Shall we have the light on?'

The living room light didn't work any more. It had become Miss Thornton's practice to sit into the evening with the room illuminated only by the flickering light of the television set. When she couldn't stand the otherworldly ambience any more, she went to bed.

'What's happened here?'

'Missing part. The girl was going to get it.'

'What girl? Oh you mean the home care assistant. Well it's not her place to do that. She should've reported it. How long has it been like this?' There was an unintelligible murmur.

'Well, that's ridiculous. That should've been sorted out weeks ago.'

The conversation ebbed and flowed. Inside the box Degsie's ears turned to and fro like satellite dishes as he strained to get the gist.

22

'That lass has got my purse,' Miss Thornton complained.

'Now are you sure?' said the other woman. 'That's a serious thing to say.'

'She takes my money, and spends it down on Newcastle Quayside. And she's had things away out of this house to sell down there. She doesn't play fair by me.'

'Now, Miss Thornton, I think you've just got a bit confused. Where have you looked for your purse…? Well, let's try again.'

There were some scufflings and bumpings while the two of them rummaged around.

'What about this cupboard next to the fireplace?' said the social worker. There was a "poink" as the catch freed. 'Look, here it is. And it's got your money inside it. One of you must have put it here for safe keeping.'

There was an eerie pause and a muffled sound Degsie had never heard before, then the social worker's voice again, this time lower. 'Now, don't get upset. It could happen to any of us, and often does. There's no harm done. But I think what we should do is have a cup of tea and a bit of a chat.' There was an interlude where water thundered into the kettle, the fridge door went "whumpf" and teaspoons jangled in cups. Then the social worker went on:

'I doesn't help, you know, that you've been living in the dark. No wonder you're going to bed at the wrong time and missing your appointments at the day centre. And it doesn't do you any good to be on your own so much. You really should make an effort to go there for the company. Which reminds me, how're things with your neighbour?'

Miss Thornton's cup came down with a clatter.

'Her? I wouldn't give her the time of day.'

'Ee, Miss Thornton, she's just an old lady like yourself. And it would be nice for you to just to say hello now and then.'

'Let me tell you,' bellowed Miss Thornton, 'her and me are nothing alike. She's a thieving auld beggar.'

'She's blind, Miss Thornton.'

'Ah, man, you know nothing. She's had things off my line.'

'What things?'

'She's had my Rabbie Burns tea-towel and my crocheted mats.'

'Now when could she possibly have done that?'

'When that ignorant husband of hers was alive.'

23

The social worker was at a loss. Eventually she tried a placatory tone and a change of tack. 'The other thing is: I'm a bit worried about your health. You seem to be having problems, you know. Maybe it's because you're not keeping regular hours...' There was a pause. 'What do you say?'

'I do wonder, sometimes,' faltered Miss Thornton. 'I do wonder if I've got things quite right. They keep changing. I think they're one way and then they're another.'

'That's what I mean. It can't always be easy...'

'Sometimes I just can't quite remember what I did, or where I did it.'

'No, exactly. So what I'm thinking is: I know a place. I think we could get you in there. Just for a few days. You can see how you like it, and while you're in there I'll get your light mended.'

'Will it be all right?'

'It's very nice. You can have your own room, and you'll get all your meals. They do a lovely Sunday lunch.'

Miss Thornton hesitated.

'Can I take me Tom Jones records?'

'Yes, and the Vienna Boys' Choir as well, if you like.'

'Is this it, then?' said Miss Thornton slowly.

'It's just for a few days. Really. And then we'll see how you feel.'

There was another eerie pause, and a sound like a balloon deflating. Then the social worker said, gently: 'I'll just make a phone call then...' There followed a minute tapping sound, then: 'Hello Jenny, Julie. One bed... Uh huh... emergency admission... might: might not.... Confused... Yes, dementia, some paranoia... incontinent as well... No, single... Uh huh... I can bring her straight down myself... No, no next of kin... I'll just pop her in the car... See you in a bit then.'

The social worker switched off her phone.

'You'll need to pack some nightclothes, Miss Thornton.'

'What about me cat?'

'Your cat?'

'Yes, what about Delilah?'

'What cat, Miss Thornton? I've been to visit you quite a few times now, haven't I? And I've been all round your house. If you had a cat I would have seen her, wouldn't I? Or a least a litter tray or some cat food. But I haven't.'

24

'She's in here every day.'

'All right, I tell you what: you go and put your nightclothes in a bag and I'll have a look round for the cat.'

'But while I'm away?'

'Don't you worry. I'll get the light fixed and I'll see to the cat.'

Miss Thornton shuffled through to the bedroom. The social worker came back through the spare room and opened the front door. Degsie lifted the lid on his pillbox and peered out. He saw the writing on the wall. In a minute, the house would be locked up and empty, except for him. He would be trapped inside. He slid down the wall like a shadow. Outside the front door, the social worker was busy in her car, the door open, her ample bottom in the air. Degsie sidled past and scuttled across to the other side of the road, where he hid beneath a gasfitter's van.

The social worker went back into the house and escorted Miss Thornton out. She sandwiched the elderly woman into the front passenger seat. The lights in the house went off. The door was slammed. The little car made off up the street. It was still raining, and Degsie's arse was in a puddle. Now what? Two homes lost in a single day. That was some going even for him. He stretched out, first front legs and then hind, and gave himself an all-over shake. Nothing for it but to head up to the pigeon lofts and see what succour was available there. Tomorrow, he would start the search for a home all over again.

Is It Sunday Yet?

Any moment now the phone would ring and it would be Effie with her inevitable question.

Barbara needed to get a move on. They'd been out last night, and she hadn't had time to do the vegetables or prepare the roast. It was pork. After all these years she could just about get the crackling right. She slit the hide with a Stanley knife, and rubbed salt into its wounds. She considered the marmalade alternative, but decided against it. She smeared the floor of the roasting tin with fat, stuck the roast on top, sprinkled it with sage, covered the whole lot with tin foil and stuffed it into the oven which had already been on warp factor five for far too long.

She paused for a swill of coffee, then started peeling carrots.

~

They'd gone up West, one of their rare excursions. To the opera. Not *Turandot*, not *Madam Butterfly*, not anything you might conceivably get your ears around. No, bloody Wagner. Geoffrey's choice. *Das* bloody *Rheingold*. Of course, you had to indulge him these days. It was really his trip out after all, and she was but the handmaiden. It had taken an age to organise. All the usual faffing on about disabled access, transport arrangements to and from, and so on. No matter what people told you, there was always something that went adrift. Really, there was no alternative but to check things out in person, but she didn't have the time to do that.

She finished the carrots and started on the greens.

The thumping on the floor began. Bugger! She'd been hoping he would doze a bit longer after the previous day's excitement. She decided to ignore it.

They'd had a long debate about whether to eat before the show or after it. In the end, they decided that as they would be going home by taxi

26

anyway, they would eat afterwards in the Italian restaurant next to the theatre. Well, that had worked out well. A brilliant plan that had foundered somewhat in its execution.

She filled a cafetière and left it to stand.

Oh yes, you could, as they claimed, get in through the folding front door, but then the tables were organised in such a way that you couldn't get the wheelchair through. People halfway through their linguini and cannelloni had had to be disturbed, their bags and parcels moved, so that they could reach the table that had been reserved for them. The looks they got were less than friendly.

Geoffrey selected a Chablis from the wine list. Once he'd got it in his clutches, it wasn't long before he started on about production values. She shot him and his glass a warning look, but that made matters worse.

'The whole m-mis en scène was ridiculous,' he harrumphed.

She had to agree with that. The Rhine maidens were lowered onto stage in three tanks of water. They cavorted about in bondage gear like a cross between pole dancers and swimmers who'd lost their synchronicity. Some male designer's fantasy, no doubt. You couldn't concentrate on the music for wondering whether the maidens would surface in time to sing it.

'And that business with the g-ods and giants, in their automated cr-anes, was totally pre-pos-terous,' he continued, glaring as though it had something to do with her.

'Yes, it was,' she said. 'I think I've seen something like it before in a science fiction film. How's your mozzarella?'

He swept his hand over his plate, ignoring her question. She sighed. In the old days, before his stroke, they would have been able to laugh about such things. But now he was angry with everyone and everything, and he was embarking on one of his rants.

'Another t-uh-riumph of style over sss-ubstance', he declared.

She agreed with that as well. If only he didn't keep menacing her across his food as if it were all her fault. He was getting louder and louder.

In fact, from her point of view, the whole performance had been a disaster. After scene one, she was terminally lost amid the relentless squalling. On reflection, she would rather have spent the evening with her hand jammed in the car door. The interval couldn't come soon enough and, when it did, she spent most of it queuing for the toilet. At the last minute, she got back to her seat to find Geoffrey fuming. Someone had managed to melt a great gobbet of their Ben and Jerry's choc ice all over the rug that covered his legs. She spent most of the second half pondering on a line in the programme that mentioned that 'Freia's golden apples had kept the gods eternally young', and wondering just exactly how that might work.

The waiter cleared their starters and brought their mains. Barbara had to cut up Geoffrey's pollo all'aglio for him, a fact that he resented, and he fixed her with a look of utter hostility as she handed back his plate. 'Perhaps you should settle for pasta next time,' she said, merely on the basis of objective assessment.

'I'll have what I d-damn well please,' he snapped and stabbed viciously at a chicken morsel.

Then came his own *leit motif*, the one about Bayreuth. Ah yes, how many times had she heard it? Nothing could compare with the Sh-Sholti performance of 1983. That was when the first wife had still been around. Geoffrey raised his voice to an insistent braying so that people at the nearby tables could have no doubt that he'd witnessed Doris Soffel, in person, as Fur-ricka, and had known from the off that she had a great career in the m-m-making.

Barbara absented herself mentally for a while to wonder how wife number one might be faring now in her apartment overlooking Nice's Promenade des Anglais. No emptying of catheter bags, or teaching remedial English three days a week for her, she supposed.

As Geoffrey became more animated, saliva accumulated at the side of his mouth that no longer worked and slid down his chin. Fashionably attired people were looking at them askance. 'Napkin!' she whispered. She didn't want to offend him by leaning across the table.

'Wh-what? Oh!'

As she'd derailed him momentarily, she took the opportunity to make another kind of point:

'What about poor old Freia?' she said. 'Yet another case of horse-trading over a woman. No say in her own fate at all. Same the world over, it seems.'

Geoffrey shot her a withering look. 'Do you know what?' he said. 'You're just a one note b-loody samba. Here I am ter-rying to convey something about the nu-nuances of Christa L-Ludwig's performance as E-Erda, and all you can do is make some ha-half-baked political point that purr-pa-passed its sell-by date in the Ay-Eighties.' It seemed quite a thoroughly baked and nicely risen political point to her, and as valid a way

28

of looking at the world as it had been when she first grasped it, but she lapsed into silence.

They were on dessert now, and Barbara was a dessert kind of person, but looking at the sorbet shimmering in its glass with its Chinese gooseberry perched on top, she suddenly felt weary, very weary. She excused herself, and went to the toilet. She had a damn good cry over the hand basins. Looking after Geoffrey was like being handcuffed to someone serving a life sentence. If only she could end it all now, one way or another. Him or her. Preferably him. Life was so wretched, and might go on forever. If only she could run away.

At the end of the row of basins was a small casement window held open on a stay. She opened it further. It looked onto a dark court full of extractor fans and ventilation ducts. In her present state of mind, it looked extremely attractive. If she hitched her skirt up, she might just be able to get out through there. Why not? People left relatives in worse places; supermarket car parks with the labels cut out of their clothes, for instance. She was just looking for a period of grace, time to get home, get some things packed and make herself scarce. Someone could return Geoffrey to his solitary splendour and to the mercy of Social Services in a few hours time.

She got as far as getting a knee up onto the sill, and ripping her tights. At this moment, a slender young woman in a beige coloured shift entered the washroom. She looked at Barbara suspiciously, groomed her long, dark hair in the mirror, adjusted her jewellery and, without saying a word, left.

Barbara knew she was making a fool of herself. It wasn't hard to see as farcical an older woman trying to make a getaway through a lavatory window. Worse still, she was acting on impulse, without proper planning. Maybe tomorrow, in the cold light of day, she could really think about what her escape might require. She adjusted her skirt, washed her hands and face and went back to the table.

Geoffrey had slumped forward towards his pannacotta with fig confit and seemed immersed in the logistics of eating it. His wine glass was empty. He looked up at her with a bleary eye. Who knew whether or not he sensed what she'd been up to? They took their coffee in silence, him grimacing but not complaining out loud about the fact that it was nearly cold.

And then she wheeled him out onto the pavement where it immediately began to splash with rain and where the taxi they'd ordered failed to materialise. At last she managed to organise one that was willing and able to take them to the south of the city. As they sat in the back of the cab, with the wheelchair clamped to the floor, Geoffrey stretched out his good arm and took hold of her hand. 'Come on, Old B-Boot,' he said. 'L-let's go home.'

~

She was just about to start on the crumble when she heard him shouting. She couldn't decently put it off any longer, so she took the coffee through with the papers.

'Morning,' she said.

'Late,' he snarled.

'Been busy,' she answered, 'and I'm expecting Effie to ring soon.'

She examined the contents of the catheter bag. They were very dark.

'Looks like you've been drinking Guinness,' she said.

'F-fuck off!' he answered.

She got him cleaned up, and poured his coffee. 'There's a good article in the supplement on land-grabbing in Ethiopia,' she said.

'Wh-what would you know?' he muttered.

'Right, then,' she said, and went back into the kitchen to finish the dessert.

She was busy rubbing the butter into the flour when the phone in the hall rang. She rushed out and grasped the receiver in a hand clogged with crumble:

'Hello?'

'Is it Sunday yet?'

'Yes, Effie, It's Sunday. You can come over now.'

Effie was a friend she had inherited from her mother. She didn't even know what 'Effie' was short for – Euphorbia, Euphemia, Euphrasia? The two elderly women had been in the same sheltered housing complex and, as Effie had no relatives, Barbara had invited her to join them all for dinner every Sunday. It had become routine for Effie to take Geoffrey for a circuit or two round the park while Barbara and her mother stayed and chatted in the kitchen. Barbara's mother had died several years ago, but Effie continued to turn up every week and the practice continued.

The trouble was: late onset dementia had started to encroach on Effie's intellectual wherewithal. Although she could find her way between her flat and their house as reliably as a bloodhound following a scent, other parts of her memory were as full of holes as a net curtain that's been dragged through a thicket. Every day, sometimes several times a day, she would ring to ask 'Is it Sunday yet?', and Barbara would have to explain yet again that no, it wasn't, and how many more days there were left to go.

As the dinner was as fixed as it was going to be, Barbara poured herself a very large Martini and stepped out into the garden through the French windows. She had fifteen minutes to herself before she had to think of going in to get Geoffrey into his chair, and about another thirty before Effie would appear on the doorstep.

It was a gorgeous day, one of the best they'd had so far this summer. The sky was clear and the sun brilliant, and it looked set to stay that way. The lawn was like velvet, and still sparkled with dew in the corners closest to the house. Barbara wandered out across the lawn to inspect the borders. She'd finally managed the knack of planting in drifts. The snub-nosed heleniums looked magnificent against the spindly counterpoint of the verbena; the crocosmia had shot forth a startling blood red mist against the fence, and even the agapanthus had deigned to bloom, producing constellations of deep blue stars all along the border. At the top end of the garden, hollyhocks were opening their trumpets in slow succession, allowing bees to cruise dreamily in and out. She sighed contentedly. Gardening was her solace. Back-breaking work it might be, but it was never a chore, not like marking homework or changing catheter bags. The earth set its own pace. It embraced you as a careful attendant, accepting your ministrations on its own terms. In return, it breathed peace into you.

A lawnmower purred across a neighbouring lawn, and she could hear the pop of tennis balls from the nearby park. She looked back at the house, surveying their joint estate. Well, Geoffrey's really. She loved it here. This stone-built villa, with its gabled upper storey windows, and Mrs Proudie, with its broad blooms the colour of ecclesiastical purple, thriving on the wall, was the most she could ever dream of in terms of a home. Geoffrey's editorial salary had covered the down payment and the instalments on all of this. His early retirement pot had paid for the French windows and the conservatory. Her own modest earnings merely contributed to the running costs. She took a deep slug of Martini. Was she really prepared to give all this up?

An escape plan would mean continuing to work long past retirement age, spending yet more days helping confused, demoralised and generally alienated youth with the intricacies of spelling. It would mean downsizing. It would mean living somewhere so small that you would barely be able to have a shelf of books or a single rack of CDs. It would mean a return to the galley kitchen where pans had to be stacked on top of one another, and looking around furtively when you came home late at night and were on the point of putting your key into the door. She had grown-up children living in foreign climes and doing well for themselves. She didn't know whether she could go back to such a restrictive lifestyle. Slowly, reluctantly, she went back into the house.

Geoffrey effed and blinded as she rolled him to and fro on the bed to get him into the sling for the hoist. He'd always been forthright, but it was amazing how, since his misfortune, he'd managed to personalise so much of his invective. She tried to turn a deaf ear; she tried to reassure him as she went about the business of securing the harness, and manoeuvring the arm of the appliance over his chair, but despite her many years as a school teacher, it still needled her.

She'd become pretty adept at operating the hoist single-handed, but there was always a moment of uncertainty as Geoffrey hung in mid-air, like goods of lading on a quayside, waiting to be lowered, and the chair tipped back as though it were preparing to do a runner. At this point, his abuse rose to a crescendo:

'Come on, you f-fucking idiot. Get a move on! What d'you think I am, a s-sack of potatoes?'

'Thankfully, not, my darling,' she said, winding him up still further.

At last she got him settled, with his feet properly organised on the rests, and the sling carefully stowed. She shoved him through to the living room, positioned him near the window and thrust a hefty whisky and soda into his good hand.

She'd just finished setting the table when the doorbell rang. A scrawny Effie stood in the porch. Despite the weather, she wore her usual shapeless knitted hat, a bedraggled cardigan, support hose and a pair of derri boots.

'Gordon ready?'

'Geoffrey. Yes, he's ready,' said Barbara. She watched the two of them set off, and closed the gate after them. Strangely, they were having the sort of coherent conversation that she and Geoffrey seldom seemed to have these days. Geoffrey was commenting on the state of the pavement, and Effie was describing how the country lanes round about used to be filled with dog rose.

~

Barbara had disposed of the travel and financial supplements and was a long way through the literary review when she realised that time was getting on. She checked the clock. A quarter to two. They were normally back by now. The roast was hissing and spitting in the oven. She couldn't really leave it much longer. She got the vegetables on, helped herself to another Martini, dispelled any niggling concerns and sat down again to see who'd been shortlisted for the Costa prize. She hoped Norma Sunderland was in the running. Her tale of bizarre goings-on in a northern coastal town had been an excellent antidote to southern introspection.

After another quarter of an hour, her anxieties resurfaced. She took the roast out and left it to stand. It was singed round the edges: she had buggered the crackling again. It crossed her mind that Geoffrey and Effie might have got lost, but this was unlikely. The pair of them were the dream ticket: one sound of mind and the other sound of body. Geoffrey issued instructions from the chair, and Effie followed them. Plus, Geoffrey knew the area very well. She stepped out into the garden. It was now blisteringly hot, probably the one memorable day of an unremarkable British summer. Perhaps they'd stopped for a drink somewhere. Or maybe...could they have been attacked, say, by bullies in the park? But that didn't seem very likely either. Not round here.

She went back into the house, slumped back down on the settee and closed her eyes. She tried to think: was there anyone she could ring or anything she could do? It was definitely too early to phone the police, and probably too early to contact the warden at Effie's sheltered accommodation. If she left the house to look for them and they came back while she was out, then that would create more complications. No, she'd better sit tight for a little while longer.

~

She awoke with a jolt. The light was different and the room was cooler. There was absolute silence apart from the click of the clock. A frisson of alarm ran up between her shoulder blades and into the back of her head. What the..?

Suddenly, the phone rang. She shot out into the hall. A voice that she didn't recognise was on the other end. 'Are you Mrs. Grainger?'

'Yes.'

'I've got a man here who says he's your husband.'

She set off round the avenues, took the cut-through between the high fences and emerged into the convoluted warren that was the new housing estate. All the houses were detached or semi-detached and were set on their own turning circles or in minor cul de sacs. All had carriage lamps on the porch; white fascia boards and downpipes, and low walls around their gardens. At number thirty-one, the up-and-over door of the built-in garage was open, and in the cavern that this revealed, she could just discern Geoffrey in his chair, in the far corner, facing a battery of hosepipes and ladders.

The man who had phoned her was waiting for her. 'We found him here when we got back from Leisureland,' he said. 'Said he'd been here all afternoon. He was in some state with himself – still is – and completely out of puff. We couldn't get him into the house to give him a cup of tea, so he's just had to have it out here in the garage. We put lots of sugar in it.'

'I'm really grateful,' Barbara said, 'I just didn't know where he'd got to. I take it there was no-one with him?'

'Nope, not when we got back. Completely on his own-e-o.'

Geoffrey looked absolutely all-in: rattled and frayed round the edges. He sat silently in his chair, humiliated, defenceless and unable to meet her eye.

'Let's get you home,' she said. She could see the man whose house it was sizing her up, sizing them both up, wondering what sort of deranged menagerie he was dealing with. How the hell was it possible to lose someone in a wheelchair? She wasn't inclined to enlighten him. She slipped the brake off and manoeuvred the chair awkwardly to get it out from its corner and facing onto the street.

'Thanks again,' she said, as she pushed it down the slope. 'Thanks for your... er... hospitality. And thanks for phoning me. I was really worried about him. I was getting ready to call the police.'

They were halfway home before she asked: 'So what happened, then?'

'Sheee buggered off!' he proclaimed. 'That ha-halfwit buggered off. That's what ha-happened! I kept telling her: 'Go l-eft. No, l-eft. But no, she wouldn't. Did just what the heh-hell she liked. She h-had me everywhere: over h-hill, over dale. I don't know how many times we went through the purr-urr-ark. And then she took us out through the wr-wrong gate. I kept saying to her, "Wh-what are you playing at? Are you d-deaf, woman? G-go the other way," but she didn't take any notice.'

They moved on a little distance, then Barbara started to laugh.

'Wh-what's so bleed-bleeding funny?'

Barbara could see it very clearly. Geoffrey had hectored Effie half to death, and she'd become more and more confused. In the end, when she'd had enough of it, she'd simply parked him up in that garage where she wouldn't have to bother with him further. Out of sight, out of mind: problem solved. Sure enough, when they got back to the house, Barbara rang the warden at the sheltered housing complex, and learned that Effie had been at home for most of the afternoon watching *The Antiques Roadshow* on the television.

As Barbara put Geoffrey to bed that night, he asked her: 'W-were you really g-going to ring the police?'

'Of course,' she said. 'I thought they might need to get the helicopter out to do a neighbourhood search.' She didn't mention falling asleep.

~

The following morning, she got up late. By the time she took his tea in, he was back on form.

'Where the f-fuck have you b-been? I have n-needs here, you know.' He pointed to the bag.

'Yes, sorry about that,' she said.

After toileting, she got him into the sling and started to move the hoist out away from the bed.

'Not like that, you cl-clumsy bitch!' he yelled.

Barbara took her thumb off the control button, allowing Geoffrey to hover gently in space.

'Well? W-well?'

Barbara stood unflinching.

Geoffrey flung himself to and fro, exacerbating the motion of the sling and amplifying his own panic.

'C-come on, come on! Wh-what's your f-fucking game?'

'Not very fond of this, are you?' said Barbara. She folded her arms, and took her time before continuing.

'Look, you poisonous old bugger, at the risk of sounding like a vicar, I'm going to tell you something: we're in this together, and from today, we have a new contract. I'll undertake to take care of you, but in return you have to treat me civilly. If you can't do that, then there'll be more of this...' She put the control pad down on the bed, and moved towards the door, leaving Geoffrey caught like a spider hanging in his own web.

'And,' she looked back over her shoulder, 'see that fixed-term bond you've got? You're going to cash it in, withdrawal charges or not, because I'm going to resign today and we'll need some living expenses.'

After a couple of hours, while she was preparing some exercises on suffixes for her afternoon class, the phone rang. It was Effie: 'Is it Sunday yet?' 'Yes,' said Barbara cheerfully, 'from now on, Effie, it's going to be Sunday every bloody day. Come on over.'

Leonardo's Cart

Of course, there was absolutely no way he was going to get in through the school gate without encountering them. And there they were. Hanging about where Lavinia Close bumped into Partington Avenue. Bending branches and kicking things. Creating an enemy presence. Which he ran slap bang into.

'Hello, Fat Boy,' sneered Tyrone, leader of men, an elegant black boy with immaculate cane plaits and insolent gaze, no uniform required. His henchmen flowed across the road, creating a wall that Sunil could not pass. Ellis, undernourished, and with electrocuted hair, jabbed him in the chest. 'Fat Paki!'

The others joined in: Spig, a black lad the same age as Tyrone, but less stylish, and Keats, a white waster they'd picked up from another school. They started elaborating the chant: 'Paki! Fat Paki! Piggy Paki! Piggy porky Paki!' They nudged him backwards down the road.

'I'm not a Paki. We're from India.'

'Listen to 'im!' they laughed. They started shoving. Tyrone deftly got him down. 'Fuckin' porky Paki!' They got hold of his ankles, pulled his shoes off and threw them into the trees. His trousers tightened in his crotch as they dragged him along the ground. His blazer was up round his ears and burned in his armpits. Somehow, gravel got inside his underpants. Nearby, someone closed a garden gate. Sunil was conscious of heeled shoes clicking along the pavement just as Keats landed a kick in his ribs.

They rolled him over.

'What the fuck is this?'

'He's wearing a girl's shoulder bag. Fuckin' Paki queer!'

Sunil cursed the day his parents had insisted on buying him a leather satchel because he'd done so well in his exams.

They got the satchel off him, and threw the contents around on the ground. They found the plastic multi-purpose drawing tool he'd just ordered from a magazine. They got it out of its box and stamped on it. It made a noise like a cap gun firing. Spig and Keats delivered another kick apiece, burying the toes of their boots deep in his peachy buttocks. Several streets away, the school bell rang.

'Shopping time!' called Tyrone. 'Leave 'im!' And the gang disappeared.

Grix was on yard duty. One of the new teachers they had who seemed to think he was working for a merchant bank. He eyed Sunil up and down. 'Late again?' he asked. It was more than his new, pale suit was worth to start an investigation.

Sunil caught up with his mate, Bevan, in the corridor. 'Tyrone and crew again?'

'Yes.'

'You've really got to do something about that.'

'Like what?' lisped Sunil hopelessly.

The day didn't get much better. In the morning it was double French, which was only *comme si comme ça*, followed in the afternoon by PE where ritual humiliation was compulsory. There were ropes that you were supposed to climb on like a lemur, and bars that you were supposed to hang from like a bat. All esoteric mysteries to him. He got out onto a horizontal bar, well above the ground, hoping to acquit himself just once without shame. He rested on the bar, on his groins, his legs outstretched, and grasped it with both hands. Then, he folded himself into a ball and set himself in motion, pivoting slowly round the bar. It was a first for him, and a flush of success started within his chest. But before it could engulf him, he realised he had lost all sense of which way was up, and didn't know how to get down. He screwed his eyes shut. Fear scuttled from his brain to his bowels and back again. There was only one way out of the situation: he released his sweating palms.

The crash attracted a small crowd. The teacher came storming over. 'What have I told you,' he roared, 'about what you must do before descent?' 'Straighten your legs,' muttered the crowd. 'You're an idiot, boy!' he bellowed. 'What are you?' 'An idiot, sir,' said Sunil, from his foetal position, his nose scraping the perfectly sprung floor.

His knees wore blue caps. He sat on the bench in the changing room, nursing them and swearing quietly. His thighs quivered with nervous exhaustion. If only he didn't resemble that fat bastard of an uncle of his, the one in Hoshiarpur with the ice cream factory. 'Well done, dough ball,' laughed the athletic elite, messing up his hair, as they stamped past him on the way out.

~

Sunil and his brother Ravi shared a room at the back of their terraced house. They had bunk beds the width of parcel shelves, a navy-blue shag pile carpet and a wardrobe made of contiboard. They also had duvet covers with pictures of footballers on them – though neither of them gave a toss about football. You could put these down to their mother's attempts at racial integration.

Even though he was four years older than his brother, Sunil still occupied the top bunk. Beyond the dark wilderness of their garden there was a tangle of rough ground and then a tall wire mesh fence that stretched away to left and right, enclosing the massive car manufacturing plant where his dad worked. Off to the left were the assembly shops, and a canteen block. Slap bang in front of their terrace was the depot, where cars were lined up like dormant sheep. Railway lines ran into the yard from the right.

Sunil spent ages observing this scene from his bunk. He was familiar with every model of vehicle, and could spot every new radiator grille and reconfigured headlamp at a distance. But even while he noted these things, he kept a keen eye on the assembly shops, waiting for the moments when the doors rolled back and vehicles fresh off the production line were nudged out from the inspection bay into the yard. And he waited on high alert for the clang of metal or the whirr of machine belts, because then he got a whiff of a kind of labour where you produced something of value that you could actually touch. What he loved above all, though, was the sheer expanse of the yard, the infinity of cars hinting at a distant place where life would be a far better thing. Not forgetting, of course, that once his dad's shift had started, he was penned behind that fence and they could all breathe easily for a while.

After his rubbish school day, Sunil lay on his belly and kept watch till long after his brother had gone to sleep. When it got dark, powerful sodium lights snapped on, turning the compound into a Lucozade-coloured oasis, and flattening the vehicles into eerie two-dimensional shapes. At about midnight, a loco hauling eight transporter wagons trundled into the yard, its engine throbbing. It idled to and fro for a bit, and then the driver got down and went away for a cup of tea and a fag. Sunil sank his teeth into one of the pea and potato samosas he had brought up from the kitchen. When he'd polished it off, he wiped his fingers on a footballer, and settled down for another stint of watching.

Once, briefly, the door of an assembly shop slid back revealing a lozenge of hot light, allowing the clank of machinery to bounce into the wide night sky, then closing again as though on a private party. Later, a fox with a tail like a broken panhandle skittered erratically across the yard, disappearing from view under a family saloon.

At 2am a couple of men emerged from the canteen block. They sauntered up and down the rows of vehicles, pausing now and then to refer to each other. Finally, one of the men got into the car at the head of one of lines, started the engine, drove it round in a wide, lunatic arc and brought it up onto the transporter wagons. The second man followed suit. They continued until all eight wagons were full, both top and bottom decks, with the cars perched at precarious angles. Then they disengaged the connecting plates and walked back in the direction of the canteen, sometimes giving each other a shove or a kick.

About an hour later, the loco driver put in an appearance, and put the engine through its paces. The engine protested at high pitch and then, subsiding into a steady put-put, slowly nudged the transporters out of the yard. Satisfied, Sunil fell asleep.

~

The following day was Saturday. They all crept around the place like cats, as it was their father's day off. Ravi had hidden himself somewhere with a puzzle book and Manisha, their older sister, was in the bathroom doing something that involved a lot of steam.

When Sunil came down to the living room, his father was sitting in kurta pyjama watching *Shree 420* for the umpteenth time. A can of Kronenburg hung from the fingers of one hand even though it was barely ten o'clock. A fag with a long stack of ash dangled from the other. In the kitchen his mother, in the dingy cotton suit she reserved for housework, was deep frying pakoras. Every time Raj Kapoor swung round a tree or sang a lyric from a moving vehicle, his father would click his tongue and sigh, 'Hai, hai, what talent!'

While Rafi and Lata continued with *Ramaiya Vasta Vaiya*, Sunil's mother beckoned him into the kitchen.

'What's happened to your school uniform?' she hissed.

Sunil shrugged.

'Don't give me that. It's in a terrible state. I don't know how you expect me to get it clean.'

'It was an accident.'

'What sort of accident could a person have to get their clothes into this state?' His mother swept another load of pakoras out of the karahi and deposited them on a kitchen towel. 'Your pants actually have a split in them. Do you think I'm some kind of dhobi or something? Do you think life's not hard enough as it is,' – she jerked her head in the direction of the living room – 'without…?'

His father cleared his throat menacingly.

Sunil lowered his voice. 'It was an accident.'

His mother shook the pakoras onto a tea plate. 'Here, take these through.'

Sunil balanced the plate on the arm of his father's chair and returned to the kitchen.

'Have you been fighting?'

'No.'

'Then tell me. What's going on? What kind of trouble are you in?'

'Some boys pushed me down. It doesn't matter.'

'Some boys? What boys?'

'Just some boys. They hang about outside the school gates.'

'What are they doing there? Why do they pick on you?'

From the living room his father erupted: 'Aray, ji! Am I trying to watch this film or what? Can't I get any peace in my own home?'

'He's being bullied, Prakash. Sunil's being bullied. I'm trying to get to the bottom of it.'

'Come in here, boy,' his father called. Sunil and his mother stepped into the living room. His father turned down the volume on the telly a notch, and screwed his cigarette end into an ashtray. 'What's all this?'

'He says some boys are picking on him. They must have been rough with him, judging by the state of his clothes.'

His father looked him up and down disparagingly. He raised his fists. 'Then fight back, boy. Don't let them have it all their own way.' His mother clicked her tongue.

'They're bigger than me, and they're rougher,' said Sunil. 'They know how to fight.'

His father narrowed his eyes as he felt for another cigarette.

'Are they black boys? I bet they're black boys.'

'A couple are.'

'Huh, those black people. They're the same everywhere in the world. No bloody good. You should stand up for yourself and show them who's who.'

Sunil was saved any more of his father's helpful analysis by the appearance of Manisha, flushed and scented like a steamed dumpling. His father put his arm round her waist and pulled her onto the pakora-free arm of his chair. 'Ah, here she is, my little Hindu goddess.' Manisha smiled coyly and tugged at her split ends. Everyone in the house, except her father, knew that to her friends and teachers she was already known as Mandy and that she was planning to have her long hair cut into a bob at the first opportunity.

That afternoon, Sunil walked all the way up to the high street. In the key cutter's and cobbler's he bought a rucksack. It was made of rust coloured rip-stop nylon with grey straps, and he liked it very much. It took nearly all the money he'd saved since Christmas. Then he crossed over to the charity shop. With his last £1.50 he got a book about Leonardo da Vinci's machines. He placed this carefully in the rucksack and walked home feeling well contented.

Up in his bedroom, he extracted the book and put it on one side. He took out a black permanent marker and drew a four-legged design, on the front panel of the rucksack. Ha, bloody ha. No more bloody Muslim Paki. Hindu, Hindu, Hindu! That would show them. He sat back and admired his work. Then he drew four dots, one within each quadrant, just the way they drew them on temple walls, to confirm the position. Satisfied with this, he turned his attention to the book. He was particularly taken with Leonardo's design for a self-propelled cart, the engine comprising a combination of leaf springs, cams and cog wheels. He opened an exercise book and copied out the diagrams in pencil, shading them carefully. He'd been wondering if automotive engineering might be something he could get into in the future.

~

On Sundays they often drove round to Wembley, where his father performed at weddings, engagements and birthday parties. It was another source of income. This Sunday it was an engagement party. Sunil was grateful that he was devoid of any form of musical talent, for while he sat and had his Frosties in the kitchen, Ravi was already seated on the rug in the front room and was being put through his paces on the tabla. Manisha, on the other hand, would have to sit on stage at her father's back later on and pick steadily at the tanpura. Behind closed doors Ravi executed some boinking with the tuning hammer, then set up a steady, but complex patter. Every now and then, Sunil could hear his father's booming interpolations: 'Teental! Teental! How many times? Ninth beat empty!' There would be a pause while Ravi got a smack round the head, and then they would resume.

After a bit, it was their father's turn to practise. One of the best, classically trained singers of northern India, he had never given up this ritual. Despite the booze and the fags, his voice was still in excellent shape, deep brown velvet at the bottom and a light sweetness of touch at the top. He ran up and down a scale in bharavi mode like an athlete on an escalator and then, summoning Ravi's support, began on a precisely ornamented performance of an early morning raag.

At one o' clock, they all assembled at the front door in their best dress. Sunil wore his western-style suit made from a shiny material that puckered at the seams when he sat down, while his mother was clad in a nylon sari in an eye-watering shade of citrus-yellow. His father, no longer the couch potato, was resplendent in raw silk kurta and pyjama, with embroidered front panel, while Ravi wore a smaller version of the outfit, with the addition of a cute alpaca waistcoat his mother had made for him. Manisha, meantime, shimmered in a pastel coloured salwar chemise that would look good under the lights. Prakash loaded the instruments and a Persian carpet into the boot of their old Ford Escort, then they packed themselves into the interior, Prakash put his foot to the floor, and they bombed round the North Circular to the appropriate meeting hall.

There were already many people queuing for food when they arrived. Others were milling about, gossiping. Women with children were beginning to form seated rows on the floor. Sunil saw which side his paratha was buttered on, and joined a queue for food at once, while his mother went off in search of friends. The performers moved down the hall to see to the business of setting up.

The throng grew more intense, and the noise level rose. The soon-to-be-betrothed couple appeared, flushed and proud, while the self-satisfied parents flapped to and fro. More people sat down. Children ran about, got their feet in food trays and were scolded. Sunil eyed up the fare at the buffet, piled his tray up high and took up a place towards the back of the gathering, next to an elderly gentleman he didn't know.

Eventually, when most people had been fed, the din had settled to a steady roar and condensation was streaming down the windows, a series of discomfiting explosions and whines erupted from the sound system. Sunil looked up from wiping the last of his dal from his tray with a roti and found that up on the platform, seated on the Persian carpet, his father was ready to sing.

Prakash brought his hands to his chest in the practised gesture of greeting. The hubbub died down. He squeezed the harmonium into life and began with a ghazal by Sahir Ludhianvi: 'How many dreams you dreamt, my love, how many songs I sang'. Ravi rattled away diligently at his side, and Manisha, a smile fixed on her lips and a thin veil of hair falling over her shoulder kept the tanpura humming steadily. Every now and then, to emphasise a rhythmic complexity, Prakash held down the keys with his right hand and jerked his left one to and fro, finally flinging it into the air with a flourish. 'Wa, wa!' chorused the older people in the audience. As it was a bad case of unrequited passion – common in the world of ghazal singing – every now and then he tilted his jaw at an angle and raised his eyes to the ceiling, imploring Love to relent.

Twenty minutes passed, and then half an hour. The people behind Sunil were talking. Prakash began a ghazal by Jigar in the more classical style of Begum Akhtar. He took a note and bent it downwards. Then he began a slow and meandering tour of the lower basement of his voice. Ravi rapped pointedly on the larger drum with the flat of his fingers and then, applying the heel of his hand, followed his father down into the basement. At the front of the hall, several small children broke loose from their parents and galloped about. Sunil shot a look behind him. A huddle of uncles and fathers in their suits and socks were muttering about property development. Behind them a group of young men in brightly coloured bandanas, who had not seated themselves, were joking with each other and bouncing up and down as though they were on springs. Only the elderly man next to him continued to wag his head and murmur 'Wa, wa!' under his breath.

44

Prakash climbed out of the cellar at last, allowed Ravi an interlude of his own and brought the ghazal to a poignant conclusion. Applause ran raggedly round the hall. Some women got up and adjusted their clothing. Children were taken off in search of ice cream. Prakash held up his hand to forestall further activity, while Ravi dusted his palms with powder. 'And now,' Prakash rumbled into the microphone, 'a work by the beloved master, Faiz Ahmed Faiz.' 'Aah!' sighed the audience. The women sat down again.

It was another plaint of the lovelorn. 'Let there be romantic monsoon clouds,' Prakash crooned, 'and let there be wine!' Not far in, the audience showed renewed signs of restlessness. The words were lost on many of them, and those who understood perhaps shared the sentiment. Chatter surged across the hall like an electric current across water. Prakash redoubled his efforts at ornamentation, working the harmonium bellows steadily. Ravi tossed back his head and brought the heels and finger tips of both hands down on the drum skins like the hooves of galloping horses. Manisha held fixedly to the drone. But, gradually the word, 'Dance!', emerged from the crowd like a political slogan.

Appearing from nowhere, the father of the bride-to-be mounted the platform, edged his way forward and grasped the microphone positioned in front of Ravi. Then, jumping on the pause at the end of a phrase, he stretched out his arms and applauded the performers. The musicians stuttered to a halt. 'Thank you, Bedi-sahib,' he said into the microphone, 'for such a wonderful performance. We are honoured indeed.' The audience helped him out with polite applause. 'But now we have something that will appeal to young and old alike: Amarjit's Bhangra All Stars!'

From behind Sunil, the young men charged forward with a tremendous waft of aftershave and testosterone. Some banged dholaks and others waved sticks. They yelped with high spirits. The audience cheered. On stage, the musicians quickly rolled up their carpet, gathered up their instruments and, without bothering to bow, climbed down.

On the way home, no-one dared to speak. Prakash had the window rolled down and spat phrases out as he chopped into other people's lanes, and overshot traffic lights. 'Bloody bastards – come all the way to England – what for? All they want is peasant life. Why didn't they stay in the fields – bloody pots and bloody sticks? No culture there, no culture here. I told him, "Shove your bloody money. Shove it so far up your arse no-one will ever see it again." "Aray, ji," he said, "Don't spoil the day for the young people." "Brother," I said, "Who's spoiling what for who?"'

At home, their mother sent them up to their rooms with cheese and tomato toasties. 'And don't come down,' she warned. Sunil and Ravi huddled in their room. Ravi tried his puzzle book and Sunil turned his attention to Leonardo's design for an armoured tank. But their father rolled around the house like a thunderstorm. Doors slammed and things fell over. There was thudding and shouting, and feet thumping up and down the stairs and the occasional profound sigh. When it got to bedtime, the boys were too afraid to go out to the bathroom, so they peed out of the window and decided to forego brushing their teeth. Ravi slept under his bunk and Sunil wrapped the footballing quilt around his head as though he were expecting mosquitoes.

The following morning it was quiet, and not much sign of disturbance: one or two ornaments missing, but no broken glass. Their mother was in the kitchen as usual, scrambling eggs and singeing toast. There was a purple patch round one of her eyes and she was not inclined to speak. When Sunil asked her where his tie had got to, she answered him slowly, holding an arm across her midriff. Sunil noticed that one of her front teeth was broken.

'Has dad gone to work?' he asked.

His mother indicated the ceiling. 'Asleep,' she said.

~

Sunil set off for school with the new rucksack. He got in through the school gate without any problem. Things were looking up. After break it was a double session of Design and Technology. The teacher, Mr Griffin, was a bluff, phlegmatic man touching sixty who, despite appearances, had not quite reached his sell-by date. Under his watchful eye, they filed into the workshop. Tyrone, who was on his last warning before expulsion, had shown up and was behind Sunil in the queue. He tugged at the rucksack: 'Hey, man. New kit!' Sunil dragged his shoulder away and tumbled into the room. He took up his place alongside Bevan at a bench near the front. The pair of them had chosen a project brief that involved designing and building a child's toy using an eccentric cam. They were still at the design stage. Sunil carefully set out his pencils, rulers and squared paper along with the exercise book in which he did his own drawings. He'd been thinking he might show the teacher the self-propelled cart. He turned to Bevan to discuss his thinking on the cam.

At the back of the room, Mr Griffin was trying to help Tyrone make up lost ground. 'Got a car, Tyrone?' 'Er... my brother has.' 'Does he do any work on it?' 'Yeah, he keeps it sweet.' 'Ever heard him talk about the cam or the cam shaft?' 'Yeah. I heard him.' 'Well what do you think the cam is?' Tyrone's briefly kindled interest began to fade.

'Dunno.'

'A cam changes one kind of motion into another, and that can be useful in a lot of ways...'

Tyrone got half out of his seat.

'See him, sir. He's a Nazi.'

'You've got an awful lot of work to catch up here, Tyrone. Let's have some concentration.'

'He is sir. I seen him this morning.'

'Let's get back to cams and your brother's car. In a car the profile of the cam is pear-shaped. Let's think about why that is.'

'I seen it on his bag. A bloody big Nazi sign, a swastika.'

'I don't think so, Tyrone. And no swearing. Now I think you can work this out: why pear-shaped?'

Tyrone scraped his chair back. 'Go on, sir. Have a look. I'm not havin' you on. He's a Nazi. Shouldn't be allowed.'

Normally, Mr Griffin would have carried on, coaxing Tyrone to the point where it would dawn on him that he actually knew something. But the words 'Nazi' and 'swastika' stopped him in his tracks. He'd had a close encounter with the 1st Panzer Division in the Ardennes in 1940 and he didn't want any more of that malarkey. He turned on his heel and strode down the room: 'Bedi! Bag!' Reluctantly, Sunil put his rucksack on the table. And there it was. Mr Griffin traced one of the legs of the design with his blunt forefinger.

'What's this doing here?'

'It's a Hindu symbol, sir.'

'Hindu symbol, my arse, sir,' shouted Tyrone from the back of the room. 'He's National Front.'

'I've told you, Tyrone: stop swearing. Well?'

'It is, sir. That's how we do them. The Nazis did them tilted at an angle.'

Mr Griffin scratched his grisled scalp. He couldn't see why a brown boy would flaunt a swastika: on the other hand he didn't want to be accused of turning a blind eye to fascism. Mentally he thumbed through the school's anti-everything policies and realised he was out of his depth. 'Up,' he commanded Sunil. 'Headmaster's study! The rest of you: work!' He drew Sunil up by the collar and hustled him out of the room. The exercise book was knocked to the floor and got trampled on.

'Yes!' cried Tyrone gleefully, knocking over a chair to celebrate. Tables turned.

~

Even after a lengthy detention, Sunil was still the first one home from school. Ravi was at a friend's house and Manisha had gone to netball practice. The rucksack had been confiscated. Wearily, he put his naked books down on the draining board. His mother was still standing next to the sink, as if she hadn't moved since morning. Sunil was about to ask for a Coke when he realised something was amiss.

'Don't go upstairs,' she said.

'Why?' Even without the bag, he still had homework to do.

'I... I...'

It seemed she had been crying, maybe still was crying. There were snail trails down her cheeks, and underneath her nose something a bit gummier. As her mouth opened and closed, her bluish-brown lips twisted in a way that reminded him of writhing earthworms.

'Something's happened, beta...' she managed to gasp at last, and a great burbling sob jumped out of her mouth.

'What do you mean?' Sunil said. He wished she would get on with it. Then he might be able to say something about whatever it was, and the thing would be over.

His mother braced herself on the edge of the draining board to control her shaking.

'Your pitaji's... upstairs... He was...'

'He was what? What's the bastard done now?'

His mother clicked her tongue in distaste, distracted briefly by the swear word.

'Well?'

'It was me. I... I...'

The back of Sunil's neck began to prickle.

Without taking his shoes off, he turned on his heel and thumped up the stairs to his parents' bedroom. The door was ajar. He thrust it open further. There was his father on the bed in a tousle of bedclothes, one of his arms cast wide across the pillows, his mouth open and his eyes rolled upwards, as though he were frozen at the pinnacle of song. Ribbons of white flesh hung from his feet and ankles, revealing dark red meat beneath. Sunil gagged in revulsion.

He thundered down the stairs again.

'Mataji? Is he...?'

His mother was making a dreadful girning noise that he really didn't want to hear. Eventually, she stopped and nodded:

'Bilkul buggered.'

Sunil goggled at her. 'What happened?'

'He wouldn't go to work. Stayed in bed and started drinking as soon as you'd gone out. Had me fetching cans for him all day. Shouting foul things, about those people yesterday, about me.' She paused and wiped her nose on her dupatta. 'By this afternoon he was flat out. I knew what he'd do when he came round.'

Sunil nodded. He was familiar with the pattern.

'I was dreading, dreading, so much dreading.' His mother broke down again. She pressed her dupatta to her swollen her eyes. '"Dear God," I thought, "surely this was not what you had in mind for me?"' She stopped.

'So what did you do?' Sunil said softly.

His mother gestured at the stove, where the glistening karahi stood askew and empty. 'God forgive me. I heated oil in it. I tried to pour it on his chest, but all too heavy. It slopped out on his feet.' She paused for more weeping. 'I thought, "Aray! Aray! He's going to wake up and then he'll kill me! And he did wake up. He roared and roared – like a tiger – but he couldn't get up...' As her voice trailed away, Sunil could see the shadow of hideous images passing across her face.

It crossed his mind to rush to her and give her a large and comforting hug, but he was locked to the spot, confounded by the enormity of what she had done.

'Now what to do?' his mother wailed.

Sunil breathed hard. Yes, what to do? This was well outside the realm of normal problem-solving, and the consequences of not coming up with a good solution were beyond consideration. He went through to the living room where he sank into his father's armchair. Sitting with his elbows on the armrests and his finger-tips together, he suddenly felt like a designer taxed with producing a new prototype. He thought hard for some time.

'Don't worry,' he said, at last. 'I've thought of something.'

The pair of them went up to the bedroom. Sunil had a towel and an Iceland carrier bag. He wrapped his father's feet in the towel and then pulled the carrier bag on over the top. They fastened the bag in place using a nylon cord from the rotating drying rack that stood out in the garden. It was hard work, so once they'd finished, they paused for a cup of tea and his mother brought out marshmallow biscuits. Something occurred to Sunil at this point and he checked his watch. He went upstairs again, bent his father's legs to a right angle at the knee and propped them up with the bathroom stool. Then he came out and shut the door.

He waited by the front door until Manisha came home.

'Upstairs. Into your own room. Put some music on. Don't look out. OK?'

Manisha looked at him quizzically, but didn't protest. She didn't care what was going on. It suited her to be on her own in her bedroom.

It was already dark when Ravi came home. Sunil primed him, but didn't tell him the detailed story. Ravi's face crumpled in distress, but Sunil forestalled any howling.

'I need your help tonight. Really important that you don't blow it. Just do everything I say. Right?'

Ravi looked as though he might be about to have diarrhoea. 'Right,' he gulped.

~

Sunil kept watch at the bedroom window. The floodlights were on in the yard and a thin drizzle was falling like needles. At about half nine, he went downstairs and rummaged about in the front room till he found the cutters that his father used for trimming the strings on the tanpura. He went down through their neglected garden, and clambered over the rotten fence. He battered his way across the rough ground, the brambles tearing at his clothes and the couch grass causing him to stumble. He chose a spot on the perimeter fence that was between two lights but not too far away from their house. Then, working quickly, he cut out three sides of a sizeable rectangle from the mesh. He checked that he would be able to

50

bend this back, then secured it temporarily using fasteners from his mother's freezer bags.

Back in the house, he roused Ravi.

'OK!' he said.

They got their father off the bed and bumped him down the stairs. They dragged him through the living room and out through the kitchen door. Now it was time to lift.

'Lift!' he commanded.

Ravi did his best at the leg end, while Sunil grasped his father under the arms. They could barely get their father's backside off the ground.

'Move! Move!'

Two or three inches at a time, they staggered down the garden until they reached the fence. Sunil had underestimated this obstacle: they were not going to be able to lift their father over it. With all the force he could muster, he plunged his foot into one of the crumbling planks and then another. He paused briefly to see if the neighbour's light came on. It didn't. They were OK. They were through.

After this, they took an armpit each and dragged their father through the undergrowth, his knees still in the air. Every few feet, Ravi needed to stop. 'My fingernails are bleeding,' he complained. His frightened face was wet with rain. But Sunil felt a strength he had never experienced before. 'Get on with it!' he insisted.

At last they got as far as the perimeter fence. It had taken them an age. Sunil looked at his watch. Almost eleven o'clock. They had to get across the rails and back before the engine arrived with the transporter wagons and blocked their way. He surveyed the vehicles parked on the far side of the track and picked out a saloon. 'Right, we'll go for that one.' Methodically, he undid the tags on the mesh he had cut earlier. He laced his fingers through the grille and yanked it back. Then he ducked through the doorway he had made, stepping out at last onto forbidden ground. The rain had stopped, leaving puddles like bottomless black holes in the cement. The railway lines gleamed like polished silver. The place had the atmosphere of the seaside when the tide is a long way out.

Together, they dragged their father headfirst through the fence. They bumped him across the railway lines and hauled him as far as the designated car. Sunil got the rear passenger door open and, between them, they tried to get him up and in. But this was impossible. For the first time, Sunil began to panic, but he forced himself to reappraise the situation. He squeezed into the car himself, placed his arms in a lock round his father's ribs and then, giving an almighty heave at the same time as Ravi gave a push from below, got him up onto the seat. They turned him to face forwards, and fixed his bent legs behind the front passenger's seat. He fitted perfectly, his head snug against the headrest, his torso barely altering the contour of the seat. Sunil scrambled out over him, and closed the door as quietly as he could on the smell of fresh vinyl. Then the two of them scuttled back to the fence.

Sunil sent Ravi back into the house. He fixed the mesh back in place and then waited, crouching in the long grass. In the distance he heard the whine of the locomotive. At last the engine nosed into the yard, trundling its transporter wagons right past him, and stopped. The driver climbed down, smoothed his hair, pulled on a cap and made off to the canteen.

Back indoors, a dirt-stained Ravi had fallen asleep on the lower bunk. Sunil pulled his cover over him, and resumed his watch. As expected, at about two o'clock two men appeared. Opening the window a little, he could hear the tiny sound of their voices. An engine started up, and then another. The first vehicles broke away from their columns. They sped down the yard, performing elaborate arabesques as they went. At the last possible moment they turned, then clanged, first one, then the other, onto the ramp at the end of the last wagon. They bumped through all eight wagons and then stopped. There was a pause, then the men walked back down the ramp whistling and chatting.

And so it went on. Bit by bit the columns grew shorter, the wagons got fuller, and the men came closer to the car in which Sunil's father sat. The rain still glittered on the windows of the vehicles and Sunil hoped that this would obscure their view. The moment came. Sunil held his breath. One of the men approached the car. He opened the door. At the crucial moment, his mate called to him. There was a brief bit of badinage then, still preoccupied with the joke, the driver slid inside. Another momentous pause, then the engine fired and, in no time at all, the car was up on the top deck of the eighth wagon. The man got out and walked down the ramp. Sunil could barely believe it. Still he didn't move. He waited until the last few vehicles had been loaded and the men had disappeared. At a quarter to three, he was still at the window. He watched the engine driver return to his cab. He waited with fists clenched while the locomotive

52

rehearsed its objections, then slowly pushed its freight, including one Shree Prakash Bedi, out of the yard.

~

In the morning, his mother had her case packed. She was on the phone: 'Look Bibi, it's absolutely urgent. My mother is very ill. Please could you ask uncle to bring me a ticket to the airport. I have the money. It's no problem...Batcha theek hai. They're staying with a neighbour.'

Next she rang the car plant. 'It's my husband: he won't be in for a few days. He has gastric problem...' She put the receiver down.

'You know it's for the best, beta. You they can't do anything to: you're too young, but me they can lock up for ever. Don't worry, I'll send for you. All of you.'

Sunil nodded. Yes, he did understand. It would be a problem solved and he and the others would just have to put up with whatever the consequences might be. Maybe she would send for him, and maybe he wouldn't go. He had never felt better, never felt so proud of having accomplished something.

By the time the others came down for school, their mother had gone. Sunil explained the position. Ravi was a mess. He leaked a lot and wouldn't shut up. Manisha was furious with everyone and everything. She shouted and wailed and vented her wrath by kicking the settee. Sunil could see that he was going to have to take matters into his own hands.

'Look, both of you. You're going to have to pretend that nothing has happened. You can't cry, go moping about, or saying anything to anyone. For Ma's sake. If you let the cat out of the bag, she's done for.' He puffed up his chest and glared. 'If you even give a squeak, you've got me to reckon with. So you,' he gave Ravi a clip round the ear, 'can cut that whimpering out. And you, "Mandy",' he twisted his hand roughly through Manisha's hair, 'better not breathe a word to any of your stupid girlfriends.'

He finally got them off to school, telling them that he was staying behind to clear some things up. He opened a Coke, spread a cold paratha with raspberry jam, sat down in front of the telly and put his feet up on his father's pouffe. Things were going to be a bit different round here from now on. He started watching a programme on the design of the linear motor. He wondered what Leonardo would have made of that.

~

Lewis Thorneycroft stood on the down platform of Oxenforde station glancing at the *Daily Mail*. The morning was grey and water dripped heavily from the trees opposite. Suddenly a diesel engine with car transporters in tow pulled noisily through the station. As the last wagon passed him, he noticed a man sitting very erect in the rear seat of one of the cars with his arm up in a stiff gesture. He thought it might be the Duke of Edinburgh.

Drishti [1]

Satish sits in his high chair with his spindly legs wound round one another in garudasana. He is wearing the uniform the company provided him with eighteen months ago: scarlet shorts with yellow stripes down the sides, and a blouson jacket that is far too big for him in the same colours. He also has a pair of goggles, picked up from a market stall, and a large canvas hat. The jacket has the word "drishti" inscribed on the back, and when he'd first put it on he'd been pretty damn proud of it. At least someone else in the family besides his mother had managed to get a job. Now, the jacket is beginning to show signs of being too long in the sun, and alongside the yellow stripes that run down the sleeves there is another one in a sort of bleached tapioca colour.

From his perch, he scans the bay. It's still too early in the day for much to be going on. The European women might be up, but they'll be at their yoga classes, or taking long, complicated breakfasts that might feature cigarettes in the beachfront cafés. As for the Indians, well God knows what they'll be doing – knocking up a day's supply of parathas probably. They don't usually appear until nearly midday. The tide is just on the turn, licking voraciously at the foreshore; undercutting the beach, and leaving great creaming scallops of froth behind it as it slides back into the ocean. The sky is clear and the sun is already warming up, but the breeze is a little stiffer than you would normally expect for the time of year, making the flags on the marker posts flap briskly. Out in the blue bay, the surface of the water is covered with raised white eyebrows.

Two white men come down to the water, one young, one not-so-young. Father and son possibly. They compete with each other, swimming in towards the shore through the breaking waves. The older man is

---

[1] Drishti – 'focused gaze', 'focal point', 'look-out', 'vision', 'discernment'

holding his own until a larger wave smacks him on the back and drags the pants off him. And that puts an end to that. Satish clicks his tongue. This is an error of judgement nearly all bathers make: they mistake the beauty of the sea for beneficent good nature. Still, this is what justifies his being here.

He watches another man in checked pants playing Frisbee by himself. Is that really possible? He looks around for a dog who might be serving as the man's sparring partner. None to be seen. The man flicks his wrist and throws the plastic dish high into the air so that it circumscribes a parabolic arc, turning back upon itself some distance away. The man then jogs towards it at a steady and none-too-athletic pace and catches it as it nears the ground. Hai, hai! How sad. No playmates.

Having inspected his surroundings, Satish now turns his attention to his fingernails and, in particular, the one on the thumb of his left hand which denotes his membership of an obscure Vaishnavite sect. He has been cultivating this carefully. It now extends about an inch beyond the end of the digit, and is varnished a bright red. He likes the kudos the thumbnail brings him, marking him out as an insider in some clandestine group. He enjoys the look of wariness that crosses local people's faces when they spot it. He likes the way Europeans recoil and then grow curious.

It was Dhirendra who'd got him involved in the whole business. Dhirendra is also a drishti, some years his senior and full of savvy. He says little about himself, but he rides a Kawasaki bike that his meagre wage doesn't justify; wears a black t-shirt with the sleeves ripped out, and has a snake tattoo that starts by his ear, and curls down over his bicep.

Dhirendra is the kind of guy who mooches about the town of an evening, usually outside the loudest bars and wine shops. He's on good terms with a remarkably large number of people it is important to know – bar owners, bouncers, security guards at posh residences and so on. After the power goes off at eight, he puts the bike into a low gear and trundles round the dark streets with the headlamp off, seeing what unusual goings-on he can uncover – fellows entering houses that are not their own; home-made hooch being transported in three wheelers; girls disposing of unwanted babies in garbage bins: that sort of thing. These days, Satish is often a passenger on the pillion, as Dhirendra roams the drinking dens and eateries and follows solitary women scuttling to get home after work.

Their meetings with their guru take place a couple of times a week. A handful of them cram into the small room he rents on the upper floor of a down-at-heel building. The form is this: the guru waits until they have all paid their respects, and then recites some scriptural homily, which he expounds upon, emphasising its supernatural properties. In no time at all, they are immersed in astral projection, the manipulation of auras, the casting of spells and all manner of other siddhis. Satish is already beginning to discover the lure of being able to menace someone just because you can, and is interested in learning more.

The guru is an excellent story-teller and, often, as he brews up some potent concoction for them all to drink, he also brews up tales of the remarkable things he has witnessed in the far-off pilgrimage places of the land. They ponder these at length, hoping to learn from them what they might apply in their own lives to right wrongs and reverse ill-fortune. Then, as they lie back on their divans, he summons favoured ones, presses a kumkum-covered thumb to their foreheads, and issues them with charms and mantras to assist them in their endeavours. Satish has already received a beginners' mantra from which he hopes to graduate if he recites it often enough. 'Submit to me, mere bachche,' the guru says,' his eyes glittering alluringly, 'then whatever you desire, all is coming.' Satish experiences a clenching feeling in his lower entrails.

Close inspection of the thumbnail reveals that the cuticle has started to grow back over the half moon and that he's amassed a considerable amount of grime under it as a result of the oil change he helped Dhirendra perform on Sunday morning. Obviously some routine maintenance is required. Dhirendra has informed him that the nail will enable him to give female personages a good time. He has difficulty envisaging how, but he is loath to give up on the possibility before he's had a chance to try it out. One thing, though: the nail is certainly a bloody big nuisance when it comes to using his cell phone.

In fact, he has two cell phones: one brick-sized one in a plastic bag that he is supposed to use for making calls to the emergency post in the main resort – this he keeps strung up on the metal frame of the canopy that shelters him from the sun – and his own, more slim-line affair, which he keeps in the pocket of his jacket. He takes out his own phone, and opens up *Grand Theft Auto, Punjab*, which he downloaded at the week-end, but hasn't had a chance to try. He looks at the opening screen shot –

conveniently, the canopy means that he isn't troubled by reflections – and is just gearing up to start, when he notices the distinctive figure of Miss Mango Slice making her way along the shoreline.

Miss Mango Slice is the love of his life though she doesn't know it. He calls her that because she always wears a yellow blouse and a concoction of yellow and orange shawls and skirts that he can't quite fathom. And today, as usual, she has a red leather hat with a wide brim jammed firmly on her head. She makes her way towards him in a leisurely but purposeful manner, with her big basket braced on one hip, and her sweeping brush trailing from her other hand. He can't take his eyes off her. He admires the way she paces herself. She works long hours, mostly in the hot sun, criss-crossing the beach systematically until the job is done. He struggles to think of what he might say to her once she gets close to him. He settles for a small joke:

'Found any gold today, Miss Mango Slice?'

Miss Mango Slice looks up at him solemnly from beneath her hat. She waves her brush back in the direction from which she's come and tells him that the Russians were fooling about late last night and had left beer bottles stuck in the sand just below the high water mark. Satish clicks his tongue to show he shares her outrage. 'Idiots,' he says. 'Some kid could've got hurt.'

Miss Mango Slice is way below him socially. Poor though his family is, his mother would be horrified if she knew that he entertained thoughts of a relationship with a refuse collector. Miss Mango Slice is older than him too. That's easy to tell. He doesn't even know if she's married, as she wears none of the usual markers. However, as he looks down into her laconic brown eyes, and notes the jittery earring that plays against her neck in the breeze, like a bunch of keys inviting entry, he knows he just doesn't care.

Miss Mango Slice puts down the tools of her trade. She places a hand to her forehead and points out to sea. She asks him some question. Satish doesn't follow what she's saying at first, nor does he follow her gaze. Instead, he studies the elegant extension of her arm, the subtle angle of her bent wrist and the languid unfurling of her forefinger. He melts with desire. At last, he gathers his thoughts sufficiently to explain that, even with the help of the binoculars, he can't see whose boat is standing to beyond the horizon. Miss Mango Slice smiles sadly. 'Ah,' she sighs. She gathers up her things, and drifts off again across the sand, showing him an excellent pair of pink heels and long, narrow, well-formed calves. Now it is his turn to sigh. Aam sutra! How he thirsts for her, and how hopeless that craving is. What can he ever do or say to displace in her affections the fellow who labours on the other side of the horizon?

Grand Theft Auto, Punjab is really disappointing. He has been looking forward to something that is authentically Indian, with over-laden trucks parmping their horns, meandering cows, and tractors chundering towards you on the wrong side of the carriageway. Yes, OK, the designers have factored in a few Indian vehicles – a Mahindra Scorpio, a Tata Jeep – but otherwise, the streetscape is undeniably American. He fiddles with it for a little while, doing his best to build up a bit of speed on the keys with his nuisance nail and his other thumb, then gives up in disgust.

Things are livening up a bit. A pallid girl comes and unfurls a towel in the shadow of a fishing boat and takes out a book. Satish examines the long slope of her breasts before they disappear into two scallops of bright pink bikini. The girl has a dog with her. It digs itself a trench alongside her, and settles down with its tongue hanging out. It looks as though it needs a book to read too. Then groups of Indian businessmen escaping from their hotels, and one or two families escaping from hum-drum domestic life start to arrive. The sea turns jade green in colour as the sun climbs higher in the sky.

Six businessmen unpack a cooler box full of Kingfisher. They disport the glossy bellies that overhang their shorts with a certain amount of pride, as evidence of the conscientious effort they have already applied to the consumption of alcohol and to the pursuit of the good life. Each of them has a compensatory stoop to offset the belly. Conversing loudly, like dowagers at a cocktail party, they dangle bottles of beer from limp wrists, as though it's too much trouble to drink it, and finger cigarettes it's too much effort to smoke. Perhaps they're discussing sales figures, or maybe the women they had the night before. Satish watches them with distaste. They're like a shoal of puffer fish with nowhere to go. He despises their indulgent behaviour, but covets the wealth that makes it possible. The men begin a disorderly game of kabbadi and are soon out of breath. More alcohol is taken.

Satish digs under his thumbnail with a toothpick for a bit, and then gets back to his phone. He opens up *Extreme Riptide*, a body-boarding game. This looks more promising. He plugs in his earphones, and ties a scarf round his head to protect his face from the reflected midday sun.

Beneath his hat, and above the scarf, only his shades are visible. *Extreme Riptide* is an altogether more interesting proposition. As Rory Riptide, you can get out on the waves, and learn to pull all kinds of tricks. The better you get, the higher you score. When you move up a level, you are rewarded with a new board. The visuals are pretty good, and the soundtrack has a pumping bass under a compelling guitar riff. You get a real sense of being on a beach on Australia's Gold Coast. He grasps the principles quickly, and sets to with enthusiasm. As before, though, the jutting thumbnail cramps his style. Eventually, after due persistence, he manages a score of five hundred and twenty eight and feels pleased with himself.

Suddenly, it occurs to him that he's thirsty. He glances at his waterproof watch. His shift should be coming to an end soon, but there's no sign of Dhirendra who should be replacing him. He tries him on his cell phone. There's no answer. He leaves a message for him: 'Hey, bhai, where are you? Get your cool ass right down here. I've got something to show you.' He knows Dhirendra isn't easily impressed, but he gives it a try anyway.

A group of European women drop their sarongs on the beach and launch into the water. They're followed by two young men. Most amuse themselves diving through the waves, but soon three of them are well out beyond the surf line, the two young men treading water, and one of the women doing a very commendable crawl. A party of Indian lads arrive, on high octane for the day. One of them is in a wheelchair. His mate is pushing him. The wheelchair doesn't look anything very modern, maybe a cast off from a hospital department. Anyway, even though the crippled guy wears red leather gloves and snazzy trainers at the ends of his shrivelled legs, it's clear he isn't going anywhere fast. His mate heaves and shoves, but he can manage to move his cargo no more than a few centimetres at a time. The rest of the party runs shrieking into the water. The friend can contain his enthusiasm for the sea no longer. He leaves his wheelchair-bound comrade in the rough, his chair tilted forward in a nosedive towards the sand. The guy in the chair adjusts his spectacles philosophically with a leather-gloved hand. He has very dark skin. Perhaps he's been left out in the sun more than once too often. 'You and me both, bhai,' Satish thinks bitterly.

Things are getting too complicated in the water. The Indians are thrashing about in the zones reserved for the whites. Of course, they

60

haven't troubled themselves to find out what the flags signify. The browns are supposed to go between the red flags right in front of him, whereas the whites can go in the areas on either side, marked out by red and yellow flags. Beyond that are areas where you go at your own peril, as nobody is guarding them. On the drishti training course, it had been explained that Europeans generally know how to swim and have a better idea of how to handle themselves in the water, whereas Indians, on the whole, are hopeless. This was why there were separate zones. Satish wonders about his own situation as a dark-skinned man. What should he do if someone were to get into trouble in the white-skin area? Is he just supposed to stand at the edge and shout? He doesn't feel the course fully addressed this matter. Anyway, things are getting chaotic and he needs to do something about it.

Reluctantly, he puts his phone aside and climbs down from his chair. He stalks to and fro along the beach, blowing his whistle, and waving his arms at the errant Indians. If they notice him at all, they look back at him uncomprehendingly. He keeps at it for several minutes, effecting some minor change, and then gives up. The tide is ebbing fast, so while he's down, he takes the opportunity to move the flags further down the foreshore, and wheels his lookout post forward. He reorganises the surfboard and his float and climbs back up again.

Dhirendra really ought to be here by now. He tries phoning him again. Still no answer. He elaborates the message he has already left, trying to sound upbeat rather than anxious, which would be really uncool.

At last, Rory Riptide performs a competent series of basic manoeuvres, and Satish accumulates a score that allows him to move up to intermediate level. Yay! He still needs to get his left hand technique sorted out though. Things are still far too slow using the thumbnail, and his rate of inaccuracy is far too high. He tries a few rounds using his forefinger, and another few using his pinkie, but no go: Rory crashes repeatedly into the water. Advanced aerial manoeuvres are going to be an impossibility if he can't gain any greater mastery than this. He adjusts his sunglasses, furrows his brow and applies himself with fevered concentration.

Suddenly, a stillness descends, as though something has stopped. The sun is at its zenith. The white woman has finished churning to and fro across the bay; the reader and her dog have gone for lunch; the young men have trundled their friend away, and a pleasure craft has whisked the businessmen off to a drinking paradise in another bay. Miss Mango Slice is nowhere to be seen. The whole place is in suspended animation.

Satish stops playing. He is desperately uncomfortable. His mouth is dry and his belly is rattling. He is gasping for a drink of water, but there is no-one he can ask, and he can't leave his post. If anything were to go wrong while he were away, he would be in deep trouble. He tries Dhirendra's number again. This time there's a mumbling voice.

'Where the hell are you, bhai? I'm frying to a potato chip here.' More mumbling. This time he makes out the words, 'Fuel tank leaking.'

'Are you stoned? Or more?' There's a belch followed by a scream of laughter at the other end. Shit! Satish ends the call.

He's stuck now, torn between loyalty to his friend and seeing to his own pressing needs. If he phones HQ for relief, it could make trouble for Dhirendra. It wouldn't be the first time he hadn't turned up for work. In any case, the roster is pretty tight and it would take them an age to find someone to replace him and then to get them here. He decides to sit out the first part of the afternoon in the hope that Dhirendra might get his head together, realise the spot he's placed his friend in and eventually turn up. It's a fond hope, he knows, but he's short on ideas. He's furious about being exploited, but he has more than a sneaking admiration for Dhirendra's libertarian attitude.

The sky whitens with the heat. Two hawks drift out from the palm trees that line the beach, and soar out over the sea, first one taking the lead and then the other. Four dogs prance down to the water's edge. After a dancing a brief quadrille, two of them suddenly plonk themselves down in the waves to cool their balls. Satish sits in his spindly chair like a scorpion roasting on a stick. There's only one thing he can do to take his mind off the situation: he sets about persuading Rory to learn some new tricks.

It's about a quarter past two. He's just completed a particularly satisfying game where he's managed to get Rory to carve for ages along the barrel of a wave and emerge unscathed when he notices some activity along the foreshore. It's Eddie Carvalho untangling the kite-boarding kit his nephew brought back from Dubai last year. There are few bathers around now, but Eddie's noticed the lively breeze, and come down to the beach to see what business he can drum up. He's caught the interest of one white man, a tall chap with the minimum of hair and the maximum in shorts, who's sniffing around waiting for the kit to be assembled. Eddie gets the stuff organised, and appears to offer some instruction. Satish gathers from the shrug of the white guy's shoulders and the flap of his hands that he's brushing this aside. Maybe he has some experience of kite-boarding already, or maybe he thinks there's nothing an Indian can tell him he doesn't already know. He flounders about a bit in the shallows, and then – whup! – there he is, up on the board and off.

Satish watches him stutter out across the bay. He starts cautiously at first with a straight run out and a straight run back. There's a stiffness in his body that those who are fluent in water sports no longer have. His bent-leg stance suggests someone who is trying to avoid sitting on a spike. He carries on with the straight runs until he gets the feel of it. Then he starts on arcs, modest ones initially, tacking round one side of the bay and then back. Then he tries the other side. Same again. Little by little, he increases the size of the arcs. Once or twice, he loses control of the kite and it collapses into the sea. When this happens, he stays in the water for a while, thrashing about. Then he manages to launch the kite again and, as it creeps into the sky, he is hauled from the waves to resume his quasi-seated position. The guy may not be as proficient as he would like to think, but he's dedicated. As there's no sign of imminent danger, Satish gets back to trying to get Rory to back flip out of the lip of the wave. It's very frustrating: the nail makes him so much clumsier and so much slower than he needs to be. Rory topples off his board once again.

The next time he looks up, the white guy is performing a lurching series of figure eights. The bulging kite twists and turns above him, sometimes turning red, sometimes blue, against the ocean. A handful of stragglers have come down to the water's edge to watch him. A European with a vast zoom lens on his camera is trying to follow the action. Satish wouldn't mind being able to perform such feats himself. There's no point in even thinking about it, though. Where would he get the money from? Unless...?

'Submit to me, mere bachche, then whatever you desire, all is coming.'

Satish wavers momentarily, then gets back to his game.

By late afternoon, the guy is still at it. The sky is now the colour of a dirty dish towel, the sun hanging like a molten eye at its centre. The face of every breaking wave is chromium plated, and the surface of the sea an incandescent sheet of beaten metal. The man and his kite are visible only in silhouette. The stragglers have gone. The breeze has strengthened, fixing the flags on the poles at an unwavering horizontal, and sending scarves of sand snaking across the beach. Only Satish remains, wilting in his canvas tabernacle, and Eddie, pacing frantically to and fro along the shoreline. The white guy has been out there for far longer than he has paid for, with the most valuable asset Eddie possesses.

It is evident to Satish now that he is stuck here for the double shift. The sides of his throat cling together through lack of water, and he feels sick with hunger. The backs of his eyes ache. Once he gets out of here, he will have to reassess his allegiances. He looks out to sea briefly. The guy on the kiteboard is careening out towards the horizon at a tremendous lick. His figure is so small that Eddie waving to him from the beach must be totally invisible to him. What the hell is he playing at? Is it some kind of off-shore smuggling ruse? Is he expecting a delivery of gold nuggets to his generously proportioned shorts?

Satish considers what he would do if the guy got into trouble now. While further up the coast at the larger resorts, the lifeguards have a Sea-Doo at their service, he has only a battered surfboard with a bent fin and a load of running repairs along the edge. Even if he were to paddle like a fan set on turbo, there's no way he could make it that far out. Let the fellow carry on to Djibouti if that's what he wants, then he'll have only himself to answer to.

But, at the last possible instant, before disappearing over the horizon, the kiteboarder changes course. Slowly he grows in size. Mercifully, despite the offshore winds, he manages to execute a change of direction, and starts heading inshore. Satish breathes a sigh of relief. The guy will be back on the beach in a matter of minutes. He attacks intermediate level again, plugging his headphones deep into his ears so that he gets the full benefit of the soundtrack. He is determined to get to advanced level, where you have to avoid obstacles, like rocks and buoys, before his double shift is over. At least then he'll be able to say he's done something worthwhile with his day. And he can shove that right up Dhirendra's groovy ass.

But the kiteboarder has his own agenda. He decides to take a complicated route back to the shore. Instead of setting his sights on Eddie, he veers towards the slew of rocks that are the outliers of the headland on the northern side of the bay. Eddie dances an apoplectic dance on the edge of the beach. Not even the locals go near this shoal of rocks because of the treacherous currents.

Satish frenetically dabbles his keyboard, trying to get Rory to perfect an air roll spin.

The kiteboarder weaves erratically in and out of the rocks. Sometimes only his kite is visible as the rocks grow larger; sometimes he is visible too in the feisty gaps in between. There are strange hesitations in his line of progress, odd moments when the kite hangs in the air and nothing seems to happen, and others where he bounces forward in what appears to be a surfeit of enthusiasm. Eddie has his fists to his mouth and is holding his breath.

Satish's thumbs jiggle frantically up and down above the keypad. Every now and then, he bangs his feet on the top rung of his chair to help him pull off a trick.

The kiteboarder is now tearing towards the headland proper. It's not clear that he can avoid the wall of rock. Suddenly, the billowing kite jerks and pivots several times on its lines, then both it and its human freight are lost to the gaze of any observer. But only Eddie is watching, and he drops to his knees in despair.

Satish battles on furiously, tapping and clicking, the driving guitar riff swelling repetitively inside his ears. Success is within his grasp.

Then, unannounced, the kite appears above the headland, its shape like a curl of potato peel or a clipping from a fingernail. It cruises in stately fashion behind the stand of palm trees that crown the headland and then, freed from its human cargo, and as though bidding goodnight, disappears finally from view. Eddie lets out a yelp.

Satish fouls up with the thumbnail, and it skids right off the keypad. Rory executes an ungainly pirouette and takes yet another tumble. Satish swears and looks up. He yanks the headphones off and observes the empty ocean.

Like someone returning from a lengthy journey, it takes a moment for him to connect. Shit! Now he really is in trouble. He looks fixedly at the nail and then at his phone. Nail, cell phone. Nail, cell phone. 'Submit to me, mere bachche, then whatever you desire, all is coming.' Somewhere behind him, up beyond the fringe of palm trees, he hears the faint but familiar cackle of a motorbike. He stands on the top step of his chair and, mustering all the strength he can, flings his cell phone far out into the surf.

Internet Explorer

'I can't call you that,' said Evelyn.

'Why not?'

'Because we have an equal opportunities policy here. If I'm caught calling you that I'll be for the high jump.'

'But I've always been called Porky.'

Pork. On the other side of the room, a young woman in a black hijab that narrowed her face to a triangular sliver wrinkled her nose in distaste.

'Surely you have another name.'

'I have. But nobody ent gonna call me that. I'm Porky because my old dad had a pork butcher's for years over in Camberwell.'

'Ah well, that's different, I suppose.' Evelyn twiddled her pen nervously on the enrolment form before writing something on the page.

'My brother was called Pinky. And he was an' all. A right ole Pinko. Always out on the picket line, till he didn't have a job no more.'

'Your brother sounds like a very worthy citizen,' ventured a gaunt man with horses' teeth and an elderly blazer. 'I myself was a member of the Indian Workers' Association when I first came to the UK.'

'And you are?' said Evelyn, flicking through her forms.

'Sonny Rosario.'

'OK, Sonny. Thank you very much.'

Evelyn continued round the group until she had the names of everyone and a little bit of information about each of them. Meanwhile, they were busy sizing her up. She was lanky, with a pastel pale skin, almost flat shoes and a bit of a dark moustache going on. What saved her from drabness were an unruly cascade of black hair and breasts like globe artichokes, slung across a narrow frame. Her deep, dark cleavage was a place where Porky, and probably several other members of the group, lost himself in thought for an unconscionable amount of time.

The course, Evelyn explained, would help them to overcome their fears about IT. She had written what she called the intended learning outcomes up on the board. They included *Switch on the computer and log-on*, and *Send emails (with and without attachments), Perform basic calculations using Excel* and *Carry out an internet search*. Despite her assurances, it all looked pretty daunting. Porky curled his toes in his velcro-fastening shoes. He was beginning to wonder if he'd come to the right place.

Then they all had to say something about why they had signed up. Ursula, in a wheelchair and attended by a carer, was researching her family history. She'd been at it for years, apparently, and had got as far as she could without getting access to some documents on the internet. Ursula had lank grey hair, and one of her spectacle lenses was misted over. She had developed the knack of holding her head on one side so that her decent eye could get a good look at the world. Just how interesting could her family be, Porky wondered.

Shazan, the young woman in the hijab wanted to 'better' herself, and perhaps get a job. Porky didn't think much to her chances – what with the headscarf and that. Hardip, a broad, shy bloke in denims and a checked shirt confessed he was a builder who couldn't keep his books straight. Mabel, a large, African-Caribbean woman wanted to keep in touch with her family. Mabel's hands shook while she rehearsed the whereabouts of her familial diaspora. Obviously, none of the bastards wanted to keep in touch with her. Ephraim, a thin leathery guy who looked as though his shirt was still on the rack, had been sent along by another tutor who was teaching him English. To be able to get a job in the UK he needed to pass a Citizenship test. The English tutor had suggested that learning IT might help him with this.

Then there was Sonny. Negotiating the foibles of his teeth, Sonny carefully explained that he talent-spotted young performers of classical music and launched them on their professional careers. He wanted to be able to use email to keep in touch with orchestral managers and concert venues worldwide. As he finished, he leaned back in his chair, revealing a slight paunch and the piece of hairy string that held his trousers up. It was clear that no-one, not even Evelyn, believed him.

Porky got straight to the point. He told the group he had a growing suspicion that there was a whole world he knew nothing about. 'It's like sitting in the coal hole with the light off,' he said. 'No matter what you watch on telly, it always ends with: "Visit our website, w w w." You can't even give money to charity without doing that.'

By the end of that first session, they had done pretty well. They could all switch their machines on, and use the mouse to get around the screen and open up Internet Explorer. They'd been shown how to conduct a basic search, and had looked up the college website. On the way home on the one five six – he couldn't manage the walk any more – Porky felt well pleased with himself.

~

Barrie came round that night with a bag of groceries. He went straight into the kitchen with them. 'Did you have them burgers, dad?' he shouted.'

'Yeah,' said Porky without interest.

'What?'

'I said "Yes!"' yelled Porky.

Barrie came through into the living room, where Porky was sitting in front of the telly with his feet up on a pouffe watching *The Dog Whisperer*. Barrie was a stocky young man with go-faster tattoos on his upper arms, and a fast food belly that loomed above his cargo pants.

'Only, I've just brought some more, but there's still a packet in the freezer.'

'Ah,' said Porky. He was eyeing the Dog Whisperer who was working his magic on a crossbred Doberman with teeth in every orifice.

'And there's sausages in there that have seen better days.'

'Is there?' said Porky. He wanted to see what happened when the Doberman got put in with the Whisperer's own pack.

'You have to watch out with these things, dad. You don't want to end up poisoning yourself.'

'Yeah, yeah. I know.'

Porky really didn't want to debate the pros and cons of sell-by dates. He snapped the television off.

'Whatchyou do with the kids today?'

'Took 'em up Trafalgar Square.'

'Oh yeah?'

'But it wasn't the same as when you and mum used to take me. Now the place is full of fucking fencing, and a bloody stupid statue that looks like shelving from IKEA. Not a pigeon in sight. We had to take the kids to an effin' ice cream parlour. You should've seen the fancy prices. Me and Tanya couldn't afford nothing for ourselves.'

~

The next time they met, Evelyn said: 'These are your individual learning plans. You need to write on your form exactly what it is you're here to learn.'

'Er,' said Porky, sucking on his biro. 'I don't know exactly what I'm here to learn. I'm waiting to find out.'

'It's like this,' said Evelyn: 'You're all going to do the same basic things, but you'll have your own special reasons for wanting to do some of them. Remember? Sonny said he wanted to be able to email people in the music business. That's the sort of thing.'

It was at this point that it became clear that Mabel couldn't read and write very well. She had started to sweat copiously over her form. Porky took advantage of Evelyn's gentle concern, and the fact that her back was turned to him, to write *Pigeons* on his form. He then inserted *Ken Livingston* and *pigeons* into his Google search engine and waited to see what would come up.

He sat next to Ephraim during the break. They were in the library's spanking new cafe with drinks that were made in a machine and piddled into cardboard cups.

'Pigeons sweat on the inside,' said Porky, kicking off the conversation and thinking mildly about Mabel.

Ephraim looked at him without interest: 'Oh?'

'Yeah. They release water vapour into their lungs and expel it to bring their temperature down.'

Ephraim grunted and twiddled his fingers. You could tell he was longing for a cigarette.

'You'd be amazed at the number of diseases pigeons can get: one-eyed cold, canker, feather rot, rickets. It's only feral pigeons you have to worry about infecting humans, though, like the ones that Ken banned from Trafalgar Square.' Porky became aware of Ephraim's boredom.

'Do people race pigeons back home then?'

Ephraim shrugged his narrow shoulders inside his dingy polo shirt. 'Nope.'

'What, never?'

'Nope.'

'Ah,' said Porky. He looked at Ephraim thoughtfully. He was very much his own man, what with that distant look and his reluctance to speak. He had dressed in all the right sort of things to pass himself off as an acclimatised westerner – jeans, trainers etcetera – and yet he looked wrong in them.

'How's Citizenship?' asked Porky.

Ephraim shrugged again.

'What's it all about then?'

'We been doin' about Em Pees.'

'Oh yeah? Don't you have them back home, then?'

Ephraim shook his head.

'You ent missing much, mate. Bunch of wankers.' Porky reflected for a minute. Maybe this wasn't the most constructive thing he could have said. 'Whatchyou doin' here, anyway?' he asked.

'War back home,' said Ephraim. 'Many years. The government is weak.'

'Oh,' said Porky. 'What they fighting about?'

'Same as everywhere. Everyone wants to be the big shot.'

'Whatchyou do back there, then?'

Ephraim scrutinised Porky closely with a mean eye, then looked around cautiously. He lowered his voice. 'Vigilante', he said.

Porky played with the word slowly in his head, reminding himself of newsreels he'd seen on telly.

'What,' he said eventually, 'You mean you...?'

Ephraim drew his fore-finger across his throat and made a noise with his glottis. 'Yeah,' he sniggered. 'Lots. Dogs didn't go hungry after we bin through a village.'

Porky could think of nothing to say. He felt out of his depth. In silence he followed Ephraim back into the classroom for the second half of the lesson.

~

Porky had really got the bit between his teeth on the pigeon front. It was a sunny afternoon, and the sunshine dispelled the curious unease he had felt since Ephraim's revelation, so he did something he had never done before in his life: he went and joined the library proper. This meant he could sit at the computer for about forty minutes at a time before it was someone else's turn. During two forty minute slots he discovered that racing pigeons had been used during both World Wars for carrying messages. The Germans had commandeered over a million from the Belgians in the First World War, as they were the best going. The Americans and the British had their own Pigeon Services. The birds flew all sorts of missions and thirty-one of them ended up getting outstanding service medals.

It was as he had suspected: a whole new world was waiting in the ether. It was like being in a mystery mansion with an infinite number of doors. Every time a page clicked open, more treasure was revealed. Excitedly he pressed on door after door. On he went greedily, page to page, link to link, faster and faster. His craving for door-opening could not be satisfied: he was hooked. By the end of his second session, he was conversant with every detail of basic loft design, and a whole lot more. When the assistant came to tell him his time was up, and that a sixth-form student was waiting for his place, he could barely recognise her as the woman who had given him his log-in details. Outside, the high street looked like a foreign country.

~

Porky unlocked the door and stepped out onto the minute balcony of his ground floor flat. There was a clothes frame there that he used occasionally and a broken armchair that no-one could be bothered to nick.

Of course, he wasn't best placed being on the ground floor. No-one flew pigeons from the ground floor. He considered the possibility of flying them from the drying area at the top of the building, but it only took a moment to realise that washing and bird droppings don't mix. He wished he could be like the Dutch fanciers, with a house of his own, and a loft built into the er, loft. But the fact was: he hadn't lived in a proper house throughout his entire married life, and he wasn't likely to get one now. No, he thought wistfully, the idea was not a goer.

~

The group grew into a comfortable accommodation with one another. Porky and Shazan were usually the first to arrive. Sonny could turn up at any time, having walked all the way from his digs in Crystal Palace. Hardip was sometimes delayed by work. Mabel would arrive panting, weighed down by shopping bags. Ephraim slipped in like a shadow and departed the same way. Ursula sometimes didn't arrive at all. If either her taxi or her carer didn't turn up, she was stuck. If they turned up late, she was effing and blinding by the time she was delivered into the room.

They were all pursuing their own line of study now. Evelyn was the guiding presence who moved between them, offering a pertinent question or a piece of useful information. Porky enjoyed the sense of having a woman around the place again, generating a warm scent of cosmetics mixed with body odour as she wafted past you. It reminded him how much he missed Irene. You could tell Hardip felt the same. Every time Evelyn neared him, he stirred uncomfortably on his chair, like a bear on a boulder. It turned out his wife had recently left him with two small kids to look after.

Porky gradually developed an affection for Mabel. It began on the day he clocked that one of her bags was always intended for Shazan, a bag of vegetables that she could take home as proof that she'd spent her morning shopping. Money changed hands of course but, all the same, he was touched. Yet though he liked Mabel, he didn't fancy her. No matter what the task, whether to open a new document, or convert something into a different font, her first response was to sweat. The fact that she was endocrinally challenged was a turn-off. Still, Porky contemplated the vaguest possibility that she might be a kindly home-maker who could see him through his later years.

They were all developing talents and skills they didn't know they had. One of these was screen flicking. Porky turned in his chair one day to find Hardip looking at pictures of what he could only describe as totty.

'Whatchyou up to then?'

'It's a matrimonial site,' said Hardip, blushing. 'Look, if you like.' He scrolled through some images:

'Nisha – "I am happy-go-lucky person who loves playing pranks." 'At thirty-two, I don't think so,' said Hardip. He scrolled on:

'Groovy – "I have a bright personality and live a very modern life style. I seek a like-minded partner who is mentally stimulating, and who can respond to my..." Ball-breaker,' muttered Hardip. He pressed his finger on the mouse again.

'Ooh, what about her?' said Porky. A heavily kholed woman peered from beneath a curtain of unrealistically black hair. 'Rami – "I am a very social creature, but I very much enjoy my own space as well."'

'Well, she's playing the field, ent she?' said Hardip, 'You can't tell nothing from that.'

72

'So what *are* you looking for?' asked Porky.

'None of them says what I want to hear.'

'Which is?'

'I make first class pooris, love kids, like a damn good jiggy-jig and am a grade one accountant,' Hardip tittered.

At this point Evelyn approached. With a flick of his finger, Hardip brought up the inevitable spreadsheet, and Porky returned to his pigeon researches.

~

'For Chrissake, Dad!'

'What?'

'There's a onion in this freezer!'

'So bloody what?'

'What's a onion doin' in the freezer?'

'I bleedin put it there.'

'What for?'

'I had a plan.'

'What plan?'

'Never you mind. It doesn't matter.'

'Don't let me think you can't look after yourself.'

'Or?'

'We'll have to start thinking about a home.'

Porky felt as chilly as the onion.

~

They were about half way through the course.

'What we're going to do today,' said Evelyn – it was one of those days when her moustache was absent and her cleavage removed from view, so you began to wonder if you might be dealing with a doppelganger – is have a look at your individual learning plans again and review how far you've got. If you remember, I asked you all to tell us about something you've been working on.'

They turned their chairs into the room and sat facing one another, their arms folded, feeling exposed without their computer terminals.

Shazan went first. She made a brief PowerPoint presentation about the top oil producing nations worldwide; moved on to a consideration of prices at the pump in the US, the UK and Iraq; made reference in passing to the cartel of oil producers in the States, and concluded with a proposition about British foreign policy. Her slides included snappy bar charts and graphs and a number of colourful maps. When she finished, there was silence.

'Any questions?' asked Evelyn. There were none. 'You've done so well, Shazan, I think you should be preparing to get onto an Access to Higher Education course. Do you know what that means?'

Shazan shook her head. 'It means you should be preparing to go to university.' Shazan glowed and sat down, Hardip whistled. Ursula said, 'Well done, gel!'

There was no Mabel. She had flu. Sonny was next under the spotlight. He explained that he could now send emails with attachments. He read out an email he had drafted: 'Dear Maestro, I will be arriving in Vienna on thirteenth inst. with an exceptional young violinist who has recently left the Academy with highest distinction. I beg you most ardently to make some space in your schedule to hear her. Yours, most obliged, Sonny Gunaratna Rosario.' Sonny's slightly antique turn of phrase made you wonder if after all he was, as he claimed, descended from a minor Indian royal family.

'So what next?' asked Evelyn. Sonny hadn't thought about that. Evelyn pressed him. Reluctantly he conceded that he might be persuaded to learn how to book tickets online, though he was wary about letting blighters of unknown background and dubious credentials have sight of his banking details.

'Good,' said Evelyn, scratching this hastily on his form. 'What about you, Hardip?' Hardip gave a jumbled description of how he had attempted to enter the last six months of his accounts onto a spreadsheet, and how it had all gone badly wrong. Evelyn rubbed her finger thoughtfully across the place where her moustache had been: 'You're starting to get a hang-up about this, Hardip. What's the problem?'

Hardip shifted uncomfortably on his chair and looked at the floor for a long time. 'I don't like it,' he said at last. 'I'm no good at it.'

'He wants to look for a wife to do it,' chuckled Porky. Hardip looked at him half in resentment, half in gratitude. And so it was agreed that Hardip would work on drafting a profile of himself that he could post on a matrimonial website.

When it came to Ursula's turn, she proclaimed that she had unearthed a new relative, a great-uncle who'd gone logging in Canada and disappeared without trace, abandoning his family.

'OK. That's fascinating. Very exciting,' said Evelyn slowly, tapping her pen on Ursula's record sheet. 'But you've spent a lot of time delving into that 1911 census now. I think it's time to move on. What about using Word to keep a learning journal, or...? Ursula glared at her with the glittering eye of the obsessive: 'I'm nowhere near ready yet,' she breathed. 'I have to find out what happened to the family.'

Ephraim read out an assignment he'd prepared for his Citizenship course. He'd taken the trouble to print out typed copies which he passed around the group. It was brief, to the point, and he'd made a stab at getting some punctuation into it: 'In this England,' it went, 'there are; laws to protect people who Have come from Other countries. So we can Get jobs and maybe a flat and Vote. There are laws for women, as well. So they can get jobs and Divorced. These are Good laws that make everybody equal. But to me women can Never be like men. A man should beat a woman if, She annoys him. So the laws are OK but what's the point.'

'Pisshead!' muttered Ursula.

'A sound analysis, my man,' smirked Sonny.

'Get on, there!' said Porky.

'Hmm,' said Evelyn. 'What line of work are you thinking of going into, Ephraim, once you've got your certificate?'

'Care. My tutor says there is always lots of jobs for assistants in care homes.'

'Right. Good choice. But you'd better think carefully about the fact that a lot of the people who live in care homes are elderly women. They're not going to take too kindly to your views.'

'I won't tell them,' said Ephraim.

'Better not,' said Evelyn. 'OK then, I'll put down that you're progressing on to a Social Care course, and need to learn how to write reports. Next: Porky!'

Porky had made no preparations. He simply opened his mouth and waxed lyrical about pigeons. 'These days people mainly keep three different types of pigeons,' he said, 'long-distance or racers – that's mainly what we have here in the West; high flyers or tipplers – people over in India and Pakistan like them, and fancy pigeons – and that's a case of "if you fancy them you keep them"! Racers have to be trained before they can do long distances. Some of the best can do about eight hundred miles. One of the biggest races every year is from Barcelona, so if a pigeon went the wrong way, it could end up in North Africa!'

'Erm,' said Evelyn.

Porky pressed on: 'But I've got to tell you about fancy birds. There's pouters and fantails, and tumblers – they can flip over backwards while they're flying. There's Lahores – they're amazing. They've got these really crazy feet – two fans made up of feathers. And Bokhara trumpeters – they look like two washing up mops having a... I mean, one on top of the other...'

Evelyn cut in: 'That's good, Porky. You've learned an awful lot about pigeons. I think we can safely say you've learned how to do an internet search. Now what about moving on to something else?'

Porky was taken aback. There was still a hell of a lot of ground he had to cover.

'Are you on Direct Payments? You could learn how to use Excel to keep track of your cashflow.'

Oh, no. He was going to head that one off at the pass. He shook his head vigorously. Only last Wednesday he'd come across the website of an Armenian chap, Yovnan, who kept the most spectacular array of fantails and tumblers. He wanted to know a whole lot more about that.

'We have to think about what you're going to go on to after this. We have to think about your progression on to a more advanced course or into something socially useful. What did you have in mind, Porky?'

Porky shrugged. He was sixty-seven. His idea of progression was keep out of the home on Daggert Street that smelled pungently of wee with a none-too-subtle bouquet of Glade.

Evelyn noted his disgruntlement. 'All right,' she said, relenting, 'what about learning how to download pictures of your favourite pigeons, and including them in a presentation that we can all see?' Porky brightened at once.

~

'Barrie,' wheedled Porky, the next time Barrie came round. 'I bin thinking.'

'Oh yeah?'

'See your little garden?' Barrie and his family lived in a tiny terraced house at the foot of Runnymede, built in the eighties, all mod cons but no room to swing a cat.

'Yeah.'

'And you know how the kids have always wanted to have a pet, but Tanya wouldn't let them…'

'Yeah, no point with both of us out at work all day.'

'Well, how about we get a few pigeons and build a loft at the end of your garden?'

Barrie was silent.

'I could get fancy birds, white fantails maybe. The kids would love 'em, and they don't need much flying.'

'An' who's going to buy them?'

'I could do that. We only need a pair to start with. I could come over in the mornings to see to 'em after you've gone to work. And I could come over again in the evening, clean them out and' – Porky felt a sudden rush of blood to the head – 'have my tea.'

Barrie thought for a moment. 'OK,' he said. 'I'll speak to Tanya about it.'

~

The following week there was still no Mabel and no Shazan either. They'd just got their noses stuck to their screens, when there was a commotion outside the door. A man in a sports jacket and a white, high collared shirt was thumping on the glass. He was carefully turned out: closely trimmed hair, neat beard and wire rimmed specs – a man of conservative appearance who, on this particular occasion, appeared to have completely flipped his lid. Evelyn unfolded herself from examining Hardip's screen and went out. She attempted to engage the man in conversation, bending towards him – she was taller than him – in a placatory fashion, but he was having none of it, and continued gesticulating. The plate glass was thick and they couldn't hear everything, but phrases like, 'What business…?' '…ideas into her head…' '…western values…' '…wife and mother…' drifted through. They were clear now that it was Shazan's husband, and that her scheme had been rumbled.

'Poor git,' said Ursula. 'That'll be the last we see of her.'

As the library's security staff bore down on him, the man waited till the last moment then ricocheted off into the book stacks.

~

Tanya had said yes. And then added, 'As long as the thing doesn't look a flamin' eyesore.' Gleefully, Porky joined Barrie in his beat-up little car in the evenings and they trundled round the better streets, delving into skips and hauling out bricks, ply, lengths of four-be-two and refrigerator shelves. What was in short supply was sheet metal and tarp. And they needed a strip light, but that would have to come from Wickes. The kids, meantime, were on the lookout for anything that would serve as drinking pots and a nesting bowl.

Porky's preparations of his PowerPoint presentation were well advanced. He'd learned how to do bullet points, and fancy scripts and he could make the words appear a line at a time – with sound effects like a Gatling gun if he wanted. Evelyn had shown him how to make the script large and not too fancy, so that everyone would be able to read it. Best of all, he'd learned how to save pictures from the internet and import them into his presentation. He was busy reviewing these during one of their sessions when they got a visitor, a large woman in a light-coloured trouser suit and a bottled tan. A look crossed Evelyn's face that reminded Porky of a cat coughing up a fluff ball.

'Ah,' – she got up – 'remember I told you we may be having a visitor. Well, she's come to look at me, not at you. Just carry on with what you're doing. Of course it was all horseshit. The woman sat at a work station, donned the smallest pair of reading specs that Porky had ever seen, extracted a pen from a handbag the size of a stuffed hog and started scribbling at once on a sheaf of papers. At intervals, her eyes darted rapidly round the room, sizing each of them up, like a hawk on a hunting mission. Evelyn continued discussing with Hardip how best to present himself to a potential bride. Hardip faltered. His suggestions became increasingly lame. A conversation that five minutes ago had entertained them all as they'd eaves-dropped on him now sounded completely inane.

The woman summoned Evelyn and, in a stage whisper, requested their individual learning plans. Evelyn handed them over. The woman devoured these with the coruscating vigour of Nitromors stripping paint off doors. Then came more pointed whispering.

'The inspector would like to talk to you now,' Evelyn announced, 'without me present. There's nothing to worry about. Just answer her questions and tell her what you've been doing.'

It was like setting a trap:

'Have you enjoyed your course?' the inspector smiled, peering over the top of her spectacles.

'Yes,' they chorused.

'And how do you like your tutor?'

'Bloody good,' said Ursula. 'Nothing's too much trouble for her,' added Hardip. 'She explains things good,' said Ephraim. 'You're never afraid to ask,' said Sonny.

'And what have you learned while you've been on the course?'

That was harder.

'I have made significant progress,' ventured Sonny. 'I am now able to communicate with distant persons via the medium of email. I find it a considerable boon.' 'And I'm doing Powerpoint,' threw in Porky.

'And what about the rest of you?' the inspector pressed further. 'What would you say you've gained by coming here?'

'Friends,' said Ursula, 'And I've found a second cousin once removed – in Saskatchewan.'

'I've got a meeting to discuss programming at the Cadogan Hall,' said Sonny.

'And I'm getting a pigeon loft,' said Porky.

The woman appeared to weigh this up. Then she fixed her gaze on Hardip: 'Hardip, isn't it? According to your plan, you were working on Excel. Isn't that right? How did you get on with that?'

'I...'

Porky rushed to his rescue: 'Hardip done best of all. He's got a date. With the love of his life.' He managed a camp falsetto: "Sandip – I can be a bit shy but I'm a loving personality. My interests include Hindi film music and cooking. I am easy to get along with and I'm just glued to family values. My favourite pastime is Excel spreadsheets."'

They all laughed.

'Seriously, though,' the inspector laughed too – she'd got into the spirit of things now, and they were warming to each other a bit – 'Is anyone going on to college, or to a job?'

They all looked at Ephraim. 'Yeah,' he said grudgingly. 'I got a place for that.'

'And there was Shazan,' added Ursula, 'She was bloody brilliant, but she's left.'

The trap shut.

~

Evelyn was visibly shaken after the session.

'What did the woman say?' they all wanted to know.

'She said not enough of you had achieved all the course outcomes, and not enough of you were going on to further education, training or employment.'

'The woman is deluded,' declared Sonny defiantly. 'Ask the wrong question and you get the wrong answer. The woman is a soulless functionary of a small-minded governing class. The Naxelites were right to dismiss such people.'

'Even if you're right, Sonny,' said Evelyn, 'what she says still matters. Once my bosses find out, the course won't run again, you can be sure of that.'

~

Porky was very excited, despite the disturbing impact of the inspector's visit. After class, out in the main concourse, Sonny had shown him how to send an email. And so, Porky had sent his first ever message...to Yovnan. He didn't say much, just hello and something about how much he admired his birds. He guessed from the captions on Yovnan's photographs that his grip on English was a bit rudimentary, but if he got a reply – big if – and depending on how intelligible it was, he might ask some questions.

He lay on his back on his orthopaedic bed. He had printed off his favourite pigeon pin-up and stuck it on the wall of his bedroom. It showed a pair of Yovnan's fine white and brown tumblers, elegantly poised in gentle fellowship, in their cage, deep in snow. The two birds bore as much resemblance to London pigeons as Concord did to a Hercules transporter. The light reflected from the snow gave them an ethereal quality, the darker feathers of their mantles and tails softened to the colour of rock rose, their Persil-white breasts suffused with a subtle glow. The pair stood meek, but alert, as if waiting for instruction from one whom they respected. Porky was awed by the beauty of the birds, and struck by the humanity of the man. Someone he didn't know, in a land that he knew nothing about, had taken the trouble to hand rear these birds and care for them, day in day out, no matter how harsh the weather. Surely that was something worth knowing about and understanding?

~

The group met one more time. Mabel returned, her bouts of perspiration replaced by a chesty cough. Ursula read them a letter she'd just received from her second cousin once removed. She emphasised the bit where he mentioned his jacuzzi. Hardip – in a suit for once – told them he was in with a chance, and would be meeting the lady of his affections for a second time later that day. And Porky gave his presentation. 'Those birds are too good to eat,' said Ephraim, which Porky took as a sign of approval. 'You come a long way, boy,' said Mabel. Porky beamed at her. She was immediately thrown into a fit of wheezing and obliged to look away in confusion.

Even Evelyn, in a demure skirt and waisted jacket, had something to report: she had an interview for another teaching job on the far side of town.

As a farewell gesture, Sonny treated them all to a meal at the Officers' Club where they stuffed themselves with naan, chicken makhni, aloo ghobi and several different kinds of chutney even though it was barely twelve o'clock. Sonny himself had bought tickets online, and was off that night to the Venice Biennale.

~

As Porky plodded across the green from the bus stop to his flat, he felt he was making a new beginning. Tonight, he and Barrie were going to make a start on the foundations for the loft. Then – you never knew – today might just be the day he would hear from Yovnan. Later in the afternoon, he would go back to the library to check. What's more, deep in the pocket of the padded jacket Tanya had got him in the market, was a small slip of paper, and on that slip was Mabel's phone number.

A Tadge To Your Left

He wasn't an old man, but he wasn't fanciable either. There wasn't one of them who would have volunteered to have anything to do with him. Chalky, the Maths teacher, on the other hand, or Thumper who taught music...

~

Someone forced open the grudging back door and swore. The thing had a habit of swelling in the rain.

~

No, he was about thirty or forty. Neat, innocuous, straight up and down. Shit coloured trousers and a snot-green shirt. Spectacles that sat at the top of a long nose that he blew frequently on a khaki handkerchief. A wide, formless mouth with a moist lower lip. Straps of oily, no-colour hair plastered across the top of his head. Sometimes he wore a lab coat that made him look like a storeman in the Co-op. He'd only been there a couple of weeks when he got his nickname – Hooter.

~

She stirred in her bed. It was only Derek. Home late after a long shift at the Caterpillar factory.

~

Hooter taught Biology. Fittingly enough, she thought, in retrospect. He was good at his job. Organised. Systematic. Expected the same of them too. They started writing up their experiments properly, and producing neater diagrams. A big improvement on the chaotic woman who had swept through their class on supply the previous term. Then their work had degenerated into inconclusive scrawl and enigmatic illustrations.

Spug, one of the lads, had preferred to execute his visuals on the surface of the lab bench with a compass. Over the weeks of that Spring term, his etching edged towards the gas taps then flamboyantly circumvented the sink. His rivals were filled with envy and his admirers with adulation. Margaret wondered what would have happened if Spug had ever deigned to speak to her. They all eagerly awaited the day when he would get his come-uppance, but when he was finally discovered, all the supply teacher said was, 'You're in the wrong class. You should be doing Art.' It was the Sixties after all.

No, Hooter wasn't like that. He didn't have to do much to instil discipline, and with him, you felt that if you just followed his game plan, you would have a good chance of passing your exam, and might even get a decent mark.

~

Derek stumbled heavily on the stairs. If he thought that by kicking off his boots at the back door and coming up in his socks he wouldn't disturb her, he was badly mistaken.

~

But the thing about Hooter was the lab store. The lab store was a walk-in room off to the right of the roller board. Hooter was always needing things fetched from the lab store. And whatever it was – scales or bell jars, beakers or flasks – it was, regardless of risk to life or limb, always stored on the top shelf. And whatever it was, it always required a girl to get it down.

He started with Shelagh. Not surprising really. Shelagh was a plump cushion, with soft brown hair and sleepy eyes. She was an expert in bending the school's dress code to her own ends. She wore her pleated skirt well above the knees, flaunted nylons instead of socks and had a bar stuck through her shirt collar like a sea front Mod. In anybody's terms, attractive. After her, he tried it with Twiggy's younger corpse, Avril. She of the flawless anaemic pallor, and drop-dead-straight albino blonde hair. Margaret could see it now: Avril was an eating disorder waiting to happen, but back then she was just elegance on stilts.

~

Derek was at the bathroom door. She heard him sigh heavily as he manoeuvred himself into the cramped space. She was surprised he hadn't stayed down for a bit to watch the telly.

~

As the term wore on, Hooter worked his way along the entire front row, all the bright, self-conscious young women who were working for a place at university.

Margaret heard them sniggering at the back of their form room, in the rows where she wasn't welcome because she was out with the out-crowd, and they were all definitely in. They made a joke of him, dismissed him as pathetic – "Sleaze ball", "Trouser Twitcher", "Scum-bucket". 'Up the ladder,' he says. 'Just a tadge to your left.' The boys paid no attention.

~

She could hear Derek's pee rattling into the bowl. It seemed as though he was pittling for England. Had he been drinking? But finally he put down the toilet lid, and swore again because he'd let it drop more heavily than he intended.

~

And then it was her turn. A girl not of the front row. Someone who had never had a boyfriend, never been clubbing, never tasted blackcurrant and Coke. Sang in the church choir on Sunday mornings and evenings. Whose one, hard-held ambition was to get into nursing college. 'Could you bring down some more petri dishes, Margaret, please. I think we're going to be short.'

He slipped into the room behind her. She remembered the curious smell of iodine mixed with polish and chalk dust.

'They're up there. Top shelf. Can you reach?'

She climbed the waiting ladder. 'Yes sir.'

'Good girl. Hand them down.'

'She passed him about five dishes.'

On the pretext of reaching up for the next batch, he slid his hand up her skirt and stroked her inner thigh. She faltered on the step.

84

'Are you all right?'

'Yes, sir,' she whispered, looking down at him in fear. Something inside her had stirred. Maybe she was going to wet herself.

He saw that he had unsettled her. 'Then lean just a tadge to your left, and hand me the next lot.' This time he got his hand to her crotch, where he encountered the thick wadding stowed in her pants. She felt ashamed and encumbered. She passed him the next five.

'All right, Margaret. That'll do for today. You can come down. We should be able to manage. Better luck next time.' He smiled.

She tumbled down the steps and fell out of the store-room. She scuttled back to her seat without daring to catch the eye of any of her classmates. All she could see at that moment was that someone had spilled ink on the lab's parquet floor, and that the stain had a green tinge round the edges like the patina on an insect's wing.

~

Water whooshed from the tap into the hand-basin. Derek was trying to clean off the worst of the day's grime. Not enough hot water. No time for a bath. Not enough puff left to pick between his toes. He'd been working every hour God sent. They needed a three piece suite and a washing-machine. At present they were relying on his mother for getting his overalls done. There were always rumours of a three-day working week going around. You had to make hay while the tractor tread lasted.

~

And there was a next time. The next time it was scales, and they were a lot more difficult to shift. She wondered years afterwards, how much effort he used to spend stowing those things up on the top shelf, how many hours a day, a week, he spent setting his trap.

As she was at full stretch on the top rung, he stepped onto the bottom one, slipped a finger deftly inside her body and moved it about as though he were searching for something. She came over faint.

'Are you all right, up there, Margaret?

'I...'

'Come down. I'll get them myself. Maybe I've asked too much of you.'

She scrambled down the ladder and brushed past him.

'Steady as she goes,' he said. He emerged from the store a couple of minutes later, carrying the set of scales carefully, as though it were a new-born baby. The experiment they did had something to do with testing for starch, but the whole thing passed her by. She stayed on her stool with her hands clenched between her knees while the others clustered round Hooter's bench up on the dais and watched him in action. She couldn't think straight, let alone observe and write. For the first time, she had no notes from which to complete her homework.

~

Derek opened the bedroom door and padded in. She made room for him under the quilt. 'Hard day?'

'Ye still awake? As it happens, it was shite.' He wrenched his vest off and dropped it on the floor. 'Still: another day, another dollar, as me grandad used tae say.' He fell heavily onto the mattress, and she bobbed up and down next to him like a cork on a pond.

~

It went on for a while. 'You know I'm just trying to be nice to you,' he'd say. 'Yes sir,' she'd answer.

'Don't call me "sir".'

'No sir.'

'No "sirs" about it.'

But she wasn't sure. The experience troubled her. If someone found out, she was sure all hell would break loose. And yet, it had become a habit she didn't want him to break. Her parents hadn't expected to have a child so late in life, so there was nothing she could discuss with them except who might land the tenor role in the choir's forthcoming rendition of Stainer's *Crucifixion*. She wasn't even sure if the matter warranted discussion. Perhaps it was just something you were meant to wrestle with by yourself as part of growing up. She looked forward to his lessons with excitement and dread. She longed with a terrible fear for the day when he would keep her behind to ask about her missing homework. Which he eventually did.

~

Derek snuggled up behind her, his arm as heavy as a felled tree across her ribs, his broad chest like a stone wall radiating summer heat behind her, his legs folded purposefully into hers. When they were locked together like this, she felt protected against the world. Safe. She caught a whiff of something. She sniffed at his hand.

'What've you been doing?'

Derek shuffled in closer. She felt him begin to harden between her buttocks.

'Got a bit of wire caught in me hand. Right in the fleshy bit. Came off a spindle. Had to put a dab of something on it.'

'Is it all right now? Did you have to have a tetanus?'

'Naw. It's all right. Just a bit sore.'

'Can you wash that stuff off now, then?'

'I've just done that,' he said.

~

She woke with the twang of iodine in her nostrils, and couched in cotton wool. The thing had been no more than a jelly bean, but it had had to go. She was off school for no more than a few days, but when she got back, everything seemed alien. She sat in classes paying attention, but assimilating nothing. The pages of her exercise books remained blank.

Hooter had gone by then. Avril's mother had done the unthinkable, "braying a way in", as she put it, and actually confronting the Headmaster in his lair. Margaret tried to visualise the scene where Avril had voluntarily spilled the beans to her mam, but candour between daughter and mother were unfamiliar to her and a crooked mile from her own wretched situation.

'I telt him what for,' said Avril's mam, briskly recounting the episode to many another mother over many a garden gate. 'Lord High and Mighty! Letten a pervert get his hands on our bairns. Who dae they think we are?'

The girls picked up the term, and with all the triumphalism of the *News of the World*, developed the vitriol further. 'Pervo!', 'Sicko Dicko!', 'The Pervertrator!' they whooped. They declared self-righteously that they'd known all along how dangerous Hooter had been. No-one else said anything. Jimson, the Latin teacher supervised their weekly Biology class and they did nothing but silent revision.

At home, an oppressive silence overhung the house. Biscuits rattled in tins, spoons clinked in saucers and her mother sighed as she did the washing up, but not a word was spoken. At night, the lights were switched off at nine, her father hung his cap on a hook behind the back door and they all went dolefully to their beds, all three lives lived in disgrace.

Margaret failed her Biology exam and did poorly in most of the others. Some of the other girls went on to university. Shelagh even got a place at Oxbridge. First ever from their school. Margaret was lucky to get a job on the production line at the Dainty Dinah Toffee factory.

~

Derek held her closer, stroking her nipple with his thumb.

'Maggie, I've been thinking.' She liked the fact that he called her 'Maggie'. When he first did it, it was like a new and uncomplicated beginning. She was grateful to Derek for loving her, and she did her best to return his affection. 'Dae ye think a bairn would mind if we didn't have a three-piece suite?'

'No,' she said slowly.

'Dae ye think a bairn would mind if we didn't have a washing-machine?'

'It would make life harder for its Ma.'

'But loads of babbies come intae the world without those things, and families get by. Surely the thing is tae want the babbie, not the washing-machine?'

'Well...'

'I'm just so tired of all the bloody graft. Get this, get that. We'll never be done wi' it.'

Margaret stayed silent.

'Maggie,' – he pressed himself in closer between her buttocks, and started fiddling with her with one hand – 'ha'way oppen yer legs, and let's have another go at making the babbie.'

Margaret caught that whiff again. She shrugged her shoulder away from him and rolled over onto her belly. 'No,' she said into her pillow, 'I don't think now's the time.'

The Map of Bihar

The dog was there again when he opened the shutters on his shop. It lay in a hole in the tarmac left by the last heavy rains. Its front paws were crossed over its muzzle and a frond of tail was spread out behind it. It was a stray, but not one of the regular village strays. He had asked around when it first appeared, but no-one recognised it. It wasn't in such bad shape as these things go: pert, velvet ears that fell back to reveal a tawny fleece, a broad white ruff across its chest and a don't-you-dare expression. Like all strays, though, it dwindled away towards its hindquarters as though it had invested so much effort front-of-house, it had been obliged to let things go hang at the rear.

And why had it chosen his shop? There was nothing in it that might interest a dog. Surely it would have been better off further down the hill outside the butcher's, or near the door of the women bakers' co-operative where it might have scrounged a stale chapatti or two. And yet there it was, as though there was some magnetic attachment between it and his front step.

He didn't like having the dog there. He thought it was bad for business. Everyone, at least every Hindu, knew: flesh and foodstuffs didn't mix. He rolled down the top of a sack and lobbed a potato at the dog's flank. The animal flinched, raised its head and looked at him with keen disdain. Then it lowered its muzzle to its paws and resumed its dozing.

He started setting out his wares. He organised the carrots and mooli into pyramids with their tails pointing outwards. He stripped the outer skins from the onions to enhance their purple glow. He selected the largest gobhi for the front of the display, where they would catch the eye, and he interspersed them with bunches of dhania that would provide a good contrast. He was well-practised in the art of presentation. He had learned from his father the knack of raking the display to achieve maximum visual impact, and dousing his produce with water at least a couple of times of day to keep everything looking fresh.

He felt that these were significant factors in his trade. Many people were prepared to walk a little further up the hill, past dingier looking shops, specifically to buy from him. These: and the fact that he was generous with his measures. He certainly bargained with his customers over price, but he never skimped on weights. He kept a box of peas and a few hands of bananas at his side so that he could always make up a shortfall or offer a child a treat. His father had also taught him the wisdom of securing repeat business.

This morning he took his hatchet and sliced open a watermelon then set the segments out on a plate. It was still early in the season, but it looked and tasted good. Most people found it difficult to resist the charms of watermelon, including the westerners.

Behind him, in the house, things were stirring. Onions were frying and he could smell toast. Madhu shouted to say that his breakfast was nearly ready. As he put the finishing touches, Preeti pushed past him and out into the early morning sun.

'Bye, Pa!'

He watched her go. She skipped down the hill, joined by friends from neighbouring cottages. They were dressed identically in their school uniforms, blue-grey salwar kameez with starched white dupatta folded like a set of knives in a box and pinned between the shoulder blades. They all had plaits tied with red ribbons, but – Mukesh prided himself – Preeti's were the thickest and glossiest of all. What was it she had told him the other night about her grades for Algebra and Science? All very well, but as he looked at her now, full of high spirits, he realised suddenly he ought to be thinking about getting her married.

'What married?' said Madhu, when he raised the subject over breakfast. 'She's too young.' He'd tried to approach the matter in a roundabout sort of way because he had a feeling that this was the sort of reaction he was going to get. But, in the end, there was no disguising it. Marriage was not a subject of degrees. Either Preeti was going to be married or she wasn't.

Mukesh chomped on his omelette and toast, feigning a casual air.

'You can't expect to have her here with you all the time. I know she's a good help, especially now that, you know... But we have to start thinking about her future.'

'I *am* thinking about her future,' retorted Madhu stridently. 'She's only partway through Ten Plus One, and her teachers think she's going to do very well. She wants to go on and do something with her life.'

'What can she do, Madhu-ji?' Mukesh reasoned, 'You know we can't afford college fees. Best thing is to try and find a decent match for her.'

Madhu applied the soft pedal.

'Look, no hurry ji. Let her complete her Ten Plus Two. Something may turn up.'

~

Mukesh broached the matter with the barber. He settled into the barber's chair. The barber's lop-sided mirror was propped against the trunk of the jacaranda tree at the top of the street, where he had set it many years ago and where he had plied his trade ever since. If anyone knew what was what, he did.

The blue mist of the jacaranda tree floated high above them and drifted far out into the valley until it merged with the sky. Mukesh tipped his head back until his neck cracked, and breathed the ozone-filled air. 'Ah,' he sighed, as the barber whisked up the lather and began his gentle prattle. He waited until the barber was plying the sopping brush to and fro across his chops, and then began to delineate the problem: 'limited savings...business fair but, on the whole, cash still hard to come by...' The barber swished the razor to and fro along his belt and began carving architectural patterns through the foam. 'The size of dowries these days...Madhu's failing sight... not clear how much longer she'd be able to take in ironing...' The barber made sympathetic noises. 'The girl herself a good proposition – nice-looking, good humoured, good grades – the need to find her a decent boy whose family would settle for very modest means...'

The barber nodded sagely: 'A difficult problem, bhai. You don't want to squander your resources.'

'You hear so many stories,' said Mukesh. 'Greed gets the better of people. The couple not married more than five minutes, and the in-laws start raising the game.'

The barber skilfully negotiated the angle of Mukesh's jaw. 'Oh yes. It can turn ugly. Very ugly. A friend of mine in Rampur clinched a deal for his eldest daughter with a family on the basis of a Maruti 800 Deluxe and a fridge freezer. He knew them only by reputation, but the father was the head of the local panchayat so he thought he'd done very well by her. What d'you know? In no time at all they're insisting on a Mahindra Scorpio special edition with airbags at every corner. In the end, never mind the disgrace and the fact that the girl was too old to get another chance, he had to take her back under his own roof. She was too afraid for her own safety.'

Mukesh squirmed under the towel as the barber wiped the remains of the lather from his face. 'What to do? What to do?' he gasped through the cloth. The barber took up a pair of narrow-bladed scissors, placed a hand on top of Mukesh's head and set about trimming the tuft of coarse hair from his ear lobe. 'The worst are those who plan it, right from the start. Some make an industry of it. Serial marriages in fact...'

Mukesh gave a squeal, and jerked his head in alarm. The barber was emphasising his every fear.

'Stay still, bhai, you don't want me to nick you, do you?'

At last the cloth was whisked away, and cologne smacked about with abandon. As Mukesh placed his few coins on the barber's wooden stand, 'I need help,' he said. The barber beamed. 'Not to worry,' he said, hands on hips. 'All it needs is a bit of careful diplomacy. Let me put out some feelers.'

~

The summer passed slowly. When Mukesh stepped out of the yard before dawn to trundle his cart down to the wholesale market, the air greeted the body like a warm, cocooning blanket. The journey back up the hill with the handle of the cart pressed against his chest, and sacks of produce slumped against one another on the flatbed was agonising. Water leaked copiously from his body. No amount of mopping with the cloth he carried slung across his shoulder made any difference. The veins on his hands thrummed to an exaggerated drumbeat. He lashed his lunghi more tightly round his waist every day.

Work on the Tibetan temple had almost stopped. Large blocks of concrete lay unattended in drifts of grey dust in the courtyard. A bemused Buddha contemplated his lack of disciples. The waft of warm bread from the bakery assailed the senses like a blow from an adversary. As soon as he got the cart back into the yard, Mukesh went straight up to the standpipe at the top of the street and stuck his head under the spout.

The paint on the shutters of the shop blistered and split. As each day progressed, the dog shuffled closer and closer the step, seeking shade, until at last it sat with its bottom in the gutter. Mukesh eventually took pity on it, and started setting out a can of water for it now and then. He may not like it being there, but they were fellow mortals after all, afflicted by the same circumstances.

Business was slow. The yoga centre had closed for the summer months, and there were no westerners around. Still he set out his wares carefully, and did everything to keep them in peak condition. Other than this, the best thing was to sit motionless, mindless, and wait.

Indoors, the women of house lay languidly on their cots. Gallons of mausami juice were drunk. Having finished her Ten Plus One exams, Preeti amused herself with puzzle books, and fiddling with her new cell phone. Occasionally a friend called. Occasionally she called upon a friend.

It was too hot during the day to do any ironing. For this, they had to wait till after dark, when the lamp was on and they could work by its meagre light. Madhu had developed considerable skill in positioning garments onto the ironing board so that they could be tackled without creasing, and looping the cable from the light socket out of the way so that it wouldn't get caught under the iron. She traced her way carefully round each garment, following the seams. But her fingers were always just that bit too close to the hissing plate, causing her to wince now and then and make hissing noises of her own. Customers had started to complain that their collars came back wrinkled, that the creases in their trousers were in the wrong places and that the service was too slow. Even with Preeti's willing help, it was clear that they could not rely on this as a source of steady income and dowry building for very much longer.

Somehow, Mukesh's whiskers were on go-slow, as though they were stultified by the heat. He had little reason to go to the barber's and when he did venture up one day, there was no sign of either the man or his implements. 'Haridwar,' muttered the milk vendor as she passed by.

One day, as he sat in a state of vegetative non-being next to a pile of Himachali mirch, a motorbike roared down the hill. The rider wore a ripped sleeved T-shirt and an aggressive frown. The muscles that stood proud on his upper arms were extensively tattooed. Mukesh yelled in protest as a film of dust settled over his entire stock. He got up, got the water can and washed things down again. No sooner had he finished than bike and rider surged back up the hill on full throttle, leaving a dense trail of fog behind them.

'Haraam zada!' swore Mukesh, wiping the grit from his mouth. He didn't normally pay much attention to the Tibetans, and they didn't have any dealings with him. But he did wonder where the hell refugees got so much money from for large-scale temples and houses that sat in their own grounds, and now motorbikes the size of tanks, the like of which you'd only ever seen in movies. And it was certainly true to say that only someone with wealth could afford to wear their clothes in tatters.

He felt the need to chew the fat with his friend, Kasim. The dog had taken to following him about, and pursued him hopefully down to the butcher's shop, its tangled tail clotted with dirt, and one of its hind legs bumping along behind the other.

'Where the hell did you get that thing from?' laughed the butcher.

'Don't mind it,' said Mukesh crossly. 'It's nothing to do with me. It's independently suspended. It just won't go away.'

Kasim was working on a goat. He had already skinned it and was busy dismembering it. Mukesh stood at a distance, watching with distaste, but unable to avert his eyes as Kasim slid his knife between the bones of ankle, knee and hip, severing tendons as though they were lengths of pyjama string and leaving knuckles of pale blue marble poking through the flesh. 'What's the trouble, bhai?' Kasim threw the dog a hoof which it seized upon gratefully.

Mukesh sat down heavily on the Limca crate which served as the step up to Kasim's shop. 'Sometimes,' he said, 'I feel everything's so hopeless, such a struggle.' He recounted the episode of the young man with the motorbike. Kasim laughed: 'Yes, the matherchode came past here too.' He nodded at the goat. 'Just as well my friend still had her coat on.'

'Where do these lads get all this stuff from?' asked Mukesh. 'Since I was a boy I've sat day and night next to a pile of peas and potatoes, and dragged that barrow up and down the hill till my pants fell off, and I can still barely afford to give my daughter a decent wedding.'

'And you've never had the opportunity to do anything else?'

94

'Not a thing. I thought I was very lucky to inherit my father's business.'

'And do you think lying, cheating or otherwise making a bandit of yourself would help you improve matters?'

Mukesh sighed. 'Even if I thought so, I wouldn't know how.'

'Well there you are then. It's your karam, and you must do your dharam. It's just that their daddyjis are bigger and better off than your daddyji was.'

Mukesh looked hard at Kasim. 'You're a Muslim. I was looking for another point of view.'

'God is he, than whom there is no other. Same principles apply.'

Kasim swapped his knife for a cleaver and began jointing the carcass. 'Don't worry, my friend: it will rain any minute now; the dust will settle; the boy won't trouble us again until next year, and maybe not even then because he'll find another amusement; you'll find a good husband for your daughter, and the world will move on.'

Mukesh sighed again, and hoped fervently that what his friend said was true. At last Kasim gave the cleaver a final flourish and completed his task. 'There is no sword but Zulfiqar, and no hero but Ali!' he pronounced jovially as he rolled his equipment into a cloth and put it away. Mukesh waited until he had seen Kasim wash his hands, then ordered them tea.

Sure enough, the first large drops of rain began to fall as he made his way back up the hill. Women were drawn, whooping, to their windows. Shutters were thrown back. Little boys ran out into the street and tore about like aeroplanes in a dog fight. The air was filled with the smell of baking dust. The dog drew closer to Mukesh for shelter, its dry cork of a nose tickling his shin. There, on their own roof was a laughing Preeti, her long hair flowing in front of one shoulder, her cotton nightdress clinging to her body. Down in the street opposite was the boy with the motorbike, making much of lighting a cigarette under cover of his hands while the engine chortled steadily beneath him. Mukesh sensed, rather than saw, in the dusk that Preeti was flirting. 'Hi Papaji!' she called, suddenly catching sight of him, and trying to recover herself. 'This is just too good, heh neh?'

~

The barber was back. And he had news. The boy's family lived on the far side of town, no more than a couple of local bus rides away. They ran several dry cleaning shops and got quite a bit of business from the military colonies. The boy himself would not play a part in the enterprise, as one of the elder brothers was already overseeing this. He himself had just completed a degree in Tourism Administrational Studies and had managed to get a job in a ticketing agency.

'You can't build a huge empire out of dry-cleaning, no doubt,' said the barber. 'But the family is comfortable and the boy has some education. You could do a lot, lot worse.'

'What do they want in the way of dowry?'

'They've asked for very little. What they've said is they don't want a girl with very modern ways, and that they'd take a dim view of a girl who was very free-talking, or gaddabout. They'll be happy as long as she plays a full role in the household.'

'There'll be no problem there!' exclaimed Mukesh, and he ran home excited to tell Madhu the news.

~

A visit to the boy's family was arranged. The shop stayed shuttered and Preeti was told to go to school as usual.

'We're going to see Neelam Aunty. She has some problem.'

'What problem? Is she ill?'

'Some family thing. Needs talking over. No need to worry.'

~

Things were not quite as lavish as Mukesh had imagined them. The boy's family lived in a jostling suburb within reach of the trunk road. The house was one of many crammed into an area that had seen little in the way of civic amenities, but the scooter-wallah had little trouble finding it. Buffalo bathed forlornly in a litter-filled pond on the other side of the street.

Mukesh and Madhu sat jammed side by side on a heavy wooden settee. The family members surveyed them across a glass-topped coffee table from creaking bamboo chairs that gave them a superior vantage point. Cloths with appliquéd motifs in red and green were strewn liberally about the surfaces. A wooden trunk stood against one wall, and a poster of goddess Lakshmi flapped on another. The room was dark and airless despite the incessant grinding of the ceiling fan. Still, it was clean and bigger than their own; there were no cots in it, and a couple of doors off suggested more accommodation to the side and rear of the property. And, at least, the family could afford a fan.

A range of hard biscuits and deep fried snacks was placed on the table. Tea was fetched and poured into tiny cups.

'Orr lelo.'

'I couldn't possibly.'

'Please.'

'Very generous.'

At every opportunity that presented itself, Madhu grasped Mukesh's arm and hissed: 'Where's the boy? What's he like?' but Mukesh couldn't respond.

In fact, the boy did not appear for some time. Instead, there was some discussion about family circumstances. The short, squat father, affable enough, rubbed his thumb through a wiry eyebrow. 'Time to put one's troubles behind one,' he philosophised. 'We've worked hard and done well, now these boys can get on with it on their own.'

The two sons, slightly taller, but also well-built, sat gruffly in their chairs, their arms folded across their chests and their trousers straining at the seams. Both looked as though they would rather be somewhere else. The business, it turned out, was not several shops but one. But, the eldest son condescended, it had a good location near a crossroads. And anyway, they would be branching out into dyeing soon.

Mukesh took a deep breath and described his own business as "steady". 'People always need to eat, bhai-sahib, no matter what.' No mention was made of the ironing.

The short, squat mother giggled, talked about her sisters, how talented they were, where they had settled and how many children they had. They women cast about in a desultory fashion, trying to trace some common connection between them, but none was found.

Then they were asked about the girl.

'She's very studious,' replied Mukesh. 'She should do well in her exams.' He paused to gauge the response. 'Not to say that she is a career-lady or anything, just that she's a hard worker. Every evening she studies after she's finished helping round the house.'

'So she can cook?'

'Oh yes,' said Madhu. 'Basic dishes of course, but she learns quickly. I couldn't do without her.' She bit her lip and smiled. 'Of course, I'll have to,'

'Is she pretty?'

Mukesh did not wish to overplay his hand.

'Very pretty, but not too pretty. More "nice-looking".' He was getting confused in his effort to appeal to all tastes. Was he really describing the lively girl with the luxurious torrent of hair whom he had seen flirting with biker boy?

A photograph was passed among them. The men muttered. The mother wagged her head from side to side and clicked her tongue: 'Very nice.'

At last the boy appeared. Mukesh wondered if he bore any relation to the rest of the family at all. He was taller than all of them and slender. The belt he wore round his hips could barely be bothered to hold his polyester trousers up. His grey shirt, which had once been white, hung concave against his chest. He wore a ball-point pen clipped in the pocket to give him an air of seriousness. Not that he needed help from the pen. His face was narrow, almost gaunt. The hint of a soft moustache hung around at either end of his upper lip, and in his round brown eyes, where one might have hoped for some kindling of warmth, there was aloofness and perhaps, even, distaste. A thin quiff of dark hair flopped over one side of his forehead.

'Dinesh is doing very well for himself,' said his father, 'holding down a steady job and bringing in a reasonable income every month. He has a good pass degree in his subject, and he has very good prospects. His boss is always saying so.'

Mukesh ventured an enquiry about what the job involved.

'Oh, I have a team of guys working with me over there. As of now there is a lot of trouble-shooting. Sometimes there is a gap in transfer functionality and we have to follow up. Or if there is a lot of cases flown on, we have to deal.' He looked coolly at his nails. 'The business would go down otherwise.'

Somewhat flummoxed by this reply, Mukesh allowed the conversation to move on.

Madhu made some tentative enquiries about where the prospective couple might live, and then, having mulled this matter over for some time, they collectively called it a day.

As they lay in bed that night, Madhu rubbed the knuckles of her husband's spine. She placed her forehead between his shoulder blades. 'Do you think he's the one?'

Mukesh felt cold inside. 'He's as good as we're going to get.'

'Was he handsome?'

'Well...'

'Was he even good-looking?'

'He looked...serious-minded.'

'Oh,' said Madhu. 'He sounded...' she couldn't quite find the word.

'At least he sounds like a hard worker. He's going to be able to provide for her.'

'And was the house...?'

'A damn sight bigger than ours, that's for sure.'

Mukesh pulled the quilt up over his shoulder, making it clear he was going to sleep. Madhu turned her head and allowed herself the luxury of sobbing softly into her pillow.

~

The return match was fixed under the auspices of the barber. Preeti first got wind of it when Madhu proposed a trip into town to one of the main bazaars. 'You need a sari.'

'A sari! Since when have I worn a sari?' asked Preeti in astonishment.

'It's time to start now.'

'I'd be more interested in a pair of trainers.' She had been selected in year ten for the school basket ball team, and had never had a decent pair of shoes to wear.

Madhu looked at her solemnly: 'It'll be a sari. A nice one.'

Suddenly the light started to dawn.

'Oh, no, Mataji!' Preeti wailed. 'How could you do that?'

'It had to be done.'

'Had to be done? What: "Had to be done"?'

'You know how things are here,' said Madhu. 'We've talked about it before. You know how hard things are for your father and all...'

'But I wanted...' Preeti, whose fantasies now featured meeting her husband as one would meet the beloved Krishna; living in a high rise apartment overlooking a city park; working as a research scientist, and/or being a basket ball supremo in the women's international league, sensed that her ship was sailing without her on it. Or, to look at it another way, that she was being bundled onto the wrong ship altogether.

Her first response was fury.

'So what's he like, this Mister Wonderful you've got lined up for me?'

'Very nice. Slim, handsome. Quiet, responsible. He's got a good pass degree in Administration, and works in a ticket office.'

'"A good pass degree"!' Preeti shrieked. 'There's no such thing as "a good pass degree". A pass degree is for those who can't do anything else. He's a duffer, a hopeless duffer working at a desk.'

Madhu was ashamed by her own ignorance. She pulled Preeti close to her bosom and began to stroke her hair.

'Don't worry,' she soothed, 'You won't be far away. And, you never know, he may be willing for you to continue your own studies later on.'

But Preeti could not be consoled. She howled and howled until her tears had soaked the front of Madhu's chemise, and Madhu's own tears trickled cold in the parting of her daughter's hair.

~

Preeti sat sullenly in her pink embroidered sari, her eyes downcast, her cheeks bloated and bruised with weeping. She glanced fleetingly at the boy and found him wanting. The boy's family thought her demeanour becoming in a girl, and showed that she was of a modest disposition. The boy was relieved that she paid him so little attention and that he didn't have to embark on the irksome, not to mention perilous, business of conversation.

The deal was done, a date was set and the barber promised his dues. It was agreed that as soon as Preeti finished her studies the wedding would take place.

~

Business had slumped. The yoga centre was closed. Many of the westerners had contracted amoebic dysentery and gone home, and the owner was busy checking the water filtration system. The Tibetans had opened a large store with western-style fittings at the foot of the hill. This sold some fruit and vegetables as well as groceries and had taken away much of Mukesh's trade.

Only the dog persisted in its attentions. As Mukesh sat lopping disconsolately at a cabbage one morning, he noted that the creature seemed to be rather more out at the elbows than when it had first arrived.

It gnawed incessantly at its rump. When it did so, the lips were drawn back and the teeth vicious. Patches of mottled hide, grey with pink spots, were beginning to appear through the short, dingy coat of its rear end. Its belly was a vulnerable well of flaccid crepe. The fronding on its tail had parted company with its core, and hung in tattered loops.

Mukesh chucked the animal a piece of cabbage stalk. It looked at him listlessly, flapped its tail on the ground once or twice, then lowered its head leaving the tit-bit untouched. At this moment, Mukesh noticed something on his own hand, as though a piece of tissue paper or the wing of a butterfly had stuck there. He pulled back his sleeve to take a better look. There, below the third and fourth knuckles of his left hand, was a small, but nevertheless obvious, white blotch. His heart leapt. No! He adjusted an orange or two on a nearby pile to give the thing time to disappear, and then looked again. Still there. He rubbed it. No difference. His mind spun wildly through a vortex of consequences that would arise should this patch turn out to be what he feared. And yet, time unfolded slowly, allowing him to appreciate in lavish detail the horror of every single implication. He studied the blotch hard. The perimeter was well defined, describing what was almost a diamond shape, with a sizeable nick out of its left-hand margin. It struck him that it had more than a passing resemblance to the maps of the state he had seen in newspapers and on TV. In panic, he threw an arbitrary glance at the dog. It was about to sink its teeth into the base of its tail. He was quick enough to note, though, that its hide bore a pink lozenge remarkably similar to his own.

~

He tried various home remedies – water from a copper vessel left overnight and drunk first thing in the morning; a glass of neem water downed every day – but by the time the kite-flying season had arrived some weeks after his discovery, they had yet to take effect. He did his best to conceal this state of affairs, masking the patch with shoe polish, rubbing earth from the vegetables into the pores of his skin, and keeping his sleeves pulled well down over his hands. He was in a constant state of anxiety about how long these rather pathetic tactics would serve.

The atmosphere at home was strained. Madhu had challenged him to reconsider their decision.

'See how miserable she is.'

'She'll get used to it.'

'Is that what you want for your daughter: to get used to being miserable?'

Mukesh sighed. His shoulders slumped. 'That's not what I meant.'

'I can't bear to see her in this state.'

'Did we have a choice?' demanded Mukesh. 'Weren't we just glad our parents found us for each other?'

'But that was a different age. This is a girl who's good at... good at... Chemistry. I hardly know what Chemistry is.'

'And this is a boy who knows Administrational Studies! They'll get on. They'll work it out.'

'I'm just not sure...'

'Look,' roared Mukesh, 'we have to make her marry him. What chances do you think she has otherwise? It will bring total shame on this family if we break it off now. No-one will look at us again. And we have almost no income. It's now or never.'

Madhu shrank back, unused to such outbursts from her husband.

'Yes,' she whispered, 'you're right.'

'I *am* right!' snapped Mukesh. He was near to tears. He felt rough, and mean and unfair, but he was all too conscious of a ticking clock that Madhu could neither see nor hear.

~

The wedding was fast approaching. A cook had been hired at rock-bottom prices, and the most meagre of awnings hired for the yard. The bride's cheap, tinsel covered sari lay in a trunk in the livingroom.

The patch on Mukesh's hand was pursuing a steady course. It had set off westwards towards his pinkie, as though it were traversing the state of Uttar Pradesh and were now at the threshold of Lucknow. The patch on the dog's flank was progressing in an identical manner.

Mukesh loaded the cart as usual at the wholesale market one day, then left it near the post office, under a nest of telegraph wires. As this was a risky business, he paid a boy a few rupees to mind it. Over the road was an Ayurvedic clinic where he was unlikely to be known. He joined the queue and sat impatiently waiting his turn. He could not afford to be away too long or Madhu would wonder what he was up to. What's more, he would lose much-needed custom at the shop.

Slowly, the patients edged along the benches as they were summoned one by one for their consultations. A desk-fan disturbed the dust near the dispensary. An assistant struggled with fluttering pieces of paper. Tired-looking women soothed restless children. The queue crept forward. A trail of hair-oil along the wall marked its progress, and the progress of many others who had gone before.

At last it was Mukesh's turn. Falteringly, he entered the doctor's cubicle. He undid the rag he had taken to wearing and laid his hand on the table between them, as though it was an object he had found on an archaeological dig.

'Hmmm,' said the doctor. He turned the hand over dispassionately and then turned it back. 'How long has it been like this?'

'Weeks,' said Mukesh. 'Months. But it's getting worse. Steadily.'

'Nothing can be done,' said the doctor dismissively. He took off a large pair of heavy-rimmed spectacles, wiped them slowly on a cloth and put them back on again. It was as though his attention were already on a book he would rather be reading somewhere else.

'Is it leu...?' Mukesh could hardly bring himself to form the word.

'Yes, it's leucoderma. You can expect it to keep spreading, though the pace may vary.'

Mukesh's heart shrivelled.

'Of course, your hands are filthy, and poor hygiene may not help.'

Mukesh looked down, demoralised and ashamed.

'I can give you some powders you can try, but the fact is: no-one knows the cause of this disease, and any "cure" is a fluke.' The doctor unscrewed the top off a fat pen and scrawled something on a slip of paper. 'Hand that in at the dispensary.'

There was a horrible silence, while Mukesh fumblingly gathered up his bandage and scraped back his chair, and the doctor did nothing but watch him. Then Mukesh stumbled out of the cubicle. He didn't bother to hand in the prescription.

~

A single refrain reverberated throughout his body: 'There is no sword but Zulfiqar, and no hero but Ali!' He no longer considered the words: he experienced them as an exhortation originating at some primordial level within him that needed neither definition nor rationale. The solution had presented itself from his subconscious without alternatives.

Now was the time. The patch left Bihar behind and was now heading east towards Kolkata, somewhere in the region of his thumb. If he waited longer, the disease might somehow leap from one hand to the other, and then the situation would be uncontainable.

The shagan would take place six weeks from now, and the nanki-shakk a few days after. Relatives from distant quarters had been notified, and would not be slow in arriving. What's more, he would need time to recover from his "accident". He was acutely aware that if he faltered now, the opportunity would be lost to him forever.

He had rehearsed the action and its consequences a million times in his head. He had practised pushing the cart up the hill with the handle braced against his chest, and steering it down using only one hand. He had hung his scales from the ceiling of the shop so that he no longer needed to hold them up when he was weighing out. He had even practised urinating with one hand held behind his back. And he had considered ruefully how he might hold Madhu in bed. He had no doubt there would be aspects of the trauma that he had failed to anticipate, but still, he was convinced that his plan was feasible. And now was definitely the time.

~

The women had gone to Chor Bazaar to buy trimmings from the haberdasher's stall. Mukesh got up quietly from his place behind two piles of peas and carrots, and set about his preparations. He gathered up his hatchet and his knife and sharpened them carefully on the front step of the shop. In the kitchen he whisked up a very large pitcher of turmeric and milk, and took it through into the yard along with a beaker. He placed a few cardamom pods next to the glass. From the corner of the yard, he fetched a rope that he sometimes used for lashing produce to the cart, a small wooden box and several sacks. He spread the sacks on the ground: he did not wish to make a mess that someone else would have to clean up.

The dog had taken the unprecedented step of following him through the shop into the yard. Because it was a day unlike any other, Mukesh did not trouble himself to shoo it away. He squatted down on the sacking, and fastened the rope round the narrowest part of his wrist. From one or two neighbouring roofs, kites were being flown. He could hear the yelps and shrieks of the boys as they engaged in aerial combat. He scanned the rooftops. There was no-one. In any case, competition was stiff and all eyes would be on the sky. He readjusted the rope. The dog settled in front of him. Jharkhand had been traversed, and the map of three of India's northern-most states was now clearly visible on its flank.

'You,' said Mukesh, 'could have had your uses.' The dog looked at him enquiringly. 'Any dog worth its salt would have helped me pull this tighter.' The dog pricked up an ear, and kept a steady eye on him.

Mukesh was uncertain when to drink the milk, so he gulped down half of it now, and slipped a couple of cardamom pods into his mouth. He laid his forearm along the box, with the sleeve drawn well back. He examined, as he had many times already, the structure of his wrist. He remembered Kasim's knife as it slid between the tendons of the goat's joints, swiftly undoing them. He picked up his own knife and, taking a very deep breath, applied it decisively to the flesh. The blade bit deeply and with ease, carving out its own narrow pink chasm where the walls were, at first, too surprised to bleed. Then the bone came into view. In Mukesh's head there were competing urges: the desire to jump up and flee from himself, and the desire to yell at the top of his voice until someone came and smacked him. And on top of this, came the overwhelming desire to be sick. Biting hard on the inadequate cardamom pods, he wrestled all of these sensations down. 'Hold on, hold on,' he urged himself. 'For her sake, hold on.'

He flung the knife aside. The dog straightened its forelegs and sat alert. He picked up the cleaver. With the practised eye of one who has split many gourds into equal segments, he picked out his spot. Too late now to think about what might have been. Abandoning thought: 'Do it!' he commanded himself.

Darkness knocked him to the ground.

The dog hesitated for a moment, looked round warily, then snatched up the hand, and quickly scrabbled from the yard, taking the map of Bihar with it.

~

The weeks that followed were agonising in every sense. He reeled mentally as well as physically. He still felt the impulse to stretch the missing fingers, to make them grasp, to touch, to provide him with information. The barber had told him on good authority that this sensation would eventually disappear but, as yet, he still struggled to comprehend the change he had inflicted.

Naturally, his accident caused great consternation among their neighbours, who were all keenly aware of what impact such a travesty could have on a working person's livelihood. Many people came to the house to commiserate. And there was a great deal of curiosity about how such an accident could have happened, especially given Mukesh's great experience in using the tools of his trade. But Mukesh feigned being so traumatised by the episode, that he had no clear idea himself, and at last the inquisition died down. Only Madhu continued to badger him, day in day out, about the whys and wherefores. Eventually, swearing her to secrecy, he took her into his confidence.

'Aiyee!' she shrieked, sinking her teeth into the back of her own forearm, after he had explained. 'What have you done?'

'What else could I do? What do you think would have happened if anyone had found out? The boy's family would come running. "You've cheated us. You have a bad disease that might run in the family. Here, take your dirty girl back." And worse still, what if the two of them got married and had children, and then the boy's family found out? What do you think would happen to those children? In any case, it would be the end of things for our daughter. No-one would ever want her as their wife.'

Madhu stood mute at the end of their living room, listening intently to her husband's argument.

'And actually,' added Mukesh, 'they could still find out now, but only if either of us lets it slip. The only thing is: now no-one has any proof!'

When he finished, there was silence for a very long time, then Madhu felt her way gingerly across the room, put her arms around her husband's narrow torso, and gave him the longest hug she had probably ever given him.

~

The wedding went off well, leaving aside the fact that the bride had no enthusiasm for it. When the mendhi artist arrived, it was Preeti's friends who chose the designs. Preeti watched from a distant place while they were applied to her arms and legs.

The few measly strings of lights strung across the front of the shop gave, at least, some sense of celebration. The cook turned out to be worth his money. His puris floated well on the oil, his wadas melted in the mouth and his chana brought back memories of earlier happy days. Madhu held Preeti close before she sent her out into the yard where the guests were assembled. She ran her fingers gently down her daughter's face, trying not to disturb the heavy make-up.

106

'You look beautiful my daughter. I can tell. Very beautiful.'

Preeti returned the embrace mechanically.

As the bride stepped out from the darkness of the room, there were gasps from the aunts, uncles and cousins, for as the lamplight winked on the tinsel and sequins of the cheap sari and gilded the faux ornaments that hung in her thick hair, the bride did, indeed, look very beautiful. The groom, too, had scrubbed up well. In an immense pink turban that flared magnificently at the front, he looked much more of a man and less of a boy than Mukesh remembered him. At the auspicious hour, the couple tied together their chunani and trod their way round the fire. All who remained to observe the ceremony were impressed by how much of an old-style wedding it seemed to be, with the bride never lifting her gaze from her feet and the groom wary and uncertain.

'You see, she wasn't that keen,' confided Madhu to an elderly aunt. 'She wanted to pursue her studies.' The aunt laughed, gripping Madhu's wrist: 'Don't worry, niece. It will only take the first signs of the first child and all of that will be forgotten. You haven't told her birth control, have you?'

'No.'

'Well then, there you are.'

Despite Mukesh's terrible accident, the general view was that it was a time of great happiness for the family. And, the morning after the event, as he watched the bride being bundled into the boy's Hyundai Santro by her new relatives, Mukesh experienced enormous relief. Not only that, he felt some pride in himself. He had pulled it off. It had been a good outcome.

~

In the days after the event, he was hopeful. The household was subdued without Preeti, and they heard little from her, which caused Madhu to fret. But it was well-nigh certain they would hear soon that she was pregnant. The mutilated arm turned out not to be as useless as he had feared, and slowly he began to learn how to perform some of his customary actions if not proficiently, at least awkwardly.

On the business front, things were starting to look up. The Tibetans had over-reached themselves, hiking their prices so high to cover the costs of round-the-clock lighting and refrigeration that many of his former customers had returned. Further up the hill, officials had moved into a

Public Works Inspection bungalow and were slated to be there for months. This had also boosted trade. Then there were rumours that the yoga centre would re-open in the Autumn, and he planned that, when it did, he would introduce a two-tier pricing system to take advantage of the rupees and dollars lying idle in the visitors' foreign purses. His next goal was to scrape together enough cash to pay for the treatment Madhu needed at a proper eye clinic. He was confident that in two or three years' time, they could at least make a start.

The dog had not reappeared, and neither had the hand. Gradually, he stopped thinking about the map of Bihar. Then, one day, when he was up at the standpipe with his head under the spout, something nipped at his ankles. He straightened up, wiping the water from his face, and looked down. There sat a small dog, narrow muzzle, handsome whiskers and a tawny coat. It cocked its head and looked at him enquiringly. Its large, round eyes and intelligent expression were difficult to resist. Mukesh almost bent to stroke it. But then he considered: it was just about the age to be the offspring of... He also spent some moments considering the principle of *ahimsa** and, having done so, he landed a kick right in the dog's flank.

---

* non-violence

The Queen of Campbeltown

There was something wrong with everything in this place. They gave him porridge for breakfast instead of Cornflakes, a grey sludge that looked and tasted as though it had been made out of papier mâché. For dinner, instead of sausages or pies, there was a slice of grey meat in viscous gravy. You chewed it and you got nowhere: you had to let it slither down your throat, and be careful not to cough it up. It came with neeps or cabbage that had a foul texture and a pungent taste. He longed for a Tunnock's teacake for his tea. But what they handed out was musty oatcakes that were about as comforting as old cork mats.

They gave him a new shirt with long sleeves, and socks that he was expected to wear drawn up to the knees. What was the use of all this encasing, he wondered. He wanted his limbs free. He wrested the socks down and the sleeves up at every opportunity.

He had a hard bed to sleep in with a few more on either side. The cover was strapped firmly to the mattress, and he had to prize it open every night to insert himself, like a gift into an envelope. He missed the settee in the corner of the livingroom where his mother would let him wriggle in under a pile of coats. He missed his mother, the antiseptic smell of coal tar soap on her throat, the soft brush of her cardigan on his cheek as she leaned over to stroke his hair.

The days were long, very long, and there was very little to fill them except being bossed about. He had no idea who the folk were who did the bossing. There was a stocky man in a snot-green suit, who sometimes wore a stethoscope, and a pinched-faced woman with a pleated skirt and polished shoes. Between them, they kept the bossing coming thick and fast. There was a scowling woman who ran the kitchen as well, with a lassie to help her. But he'd sometimes seen the lassie getting a clip round the ear. It was best to keep out of the way of the lot of them.

He kept outside in the grounds as much as possible. There was nothing you could do on the gravel court, so he skulked in the shrubbery. He poked in the earth in the looking for bugs and worms, or he crawled in behind the bushes to conceal himself from the house. He tried to make himself a den, but the plants were the sort of plants that had no potential: mahonia, laurel, rhododendron – not that he knew their names. You couldn't climb them, or swing on them, or break their branches off, and they furnished nothing in the way of building materials. There were no bins, bottles, boxes, barrels or broken-down prams either. But then, he thought: what use was a den when he had no-one to share it with? No Danny, or Len, or Jim.

The others here were a dead loss. He hadn't taken to any of them. There was a lad who was too big for his age with bulging cheeks and a dark fringe. But he blew snotters down his nose when he tried to talk, and you could hear him whimpering at night. There was the boy with the lightning-sharp eyes who swung his legs under the meal table. The woman with the skirt was always telling him to stop, but he couldn't help himself, and whenever he got the chance, he'd give you a vicious kick with a studded boot. Then there was the gormless girl who had one of her spectacle lenses blanked out, and sucked her thumb all the time. He missed his pals back home who were good for racing and wrestling and roaming. He missed the swing park with the broken slide where the big lads sometimes came to menace you. He missed the empty tenement with its hanging plaster and its rotting timbers and the fireplace stuck halfway up the wall, and he missed the open ground next to it with its solitary lamp post and heaps of rubble.

He was sitting under a rhododendron bush one morning, stiff with boredom and disorientated by loss, when the butcher's van arrived. The driver got out, and opened the rear doors. 'Is that you, Dougie?' he heard the kitchen woman yell. 'Aye!' called the driver, and he started carting trays of meat through into the house. He whistled intermittently as he went about his business, drawing out the full trays and slotting the empty ones back in. It wasn't a question of whether some action should be taken; it was a question of which action to take. The thing was, "Dougie" had left the high iron gates in the garden wall wide open.

In a flash, he assessed the situation. The van had a rear step. If he rushed out from his cover just as it was leaving, he might be able to jump on and grab the door handle. That way he could get a free ride into town and back to the ferry. It was very tempting, and no more challenging than things he'd done a million times before. But someone might come to the door to see the van off and, in any case, the driver would surely discover him when he got down to close the gate. There was some altercation going on inside the kitchen between them now, the cook and the driver, but it wouldn't go on forever. No, better to make a run for it now.

He scuttled across the gravel and down the lane to where it joined the road. There was a large beech tree at the corner. He hid there to see which way the butcher's van would turn. It seemed an age before it nosed down the lane and made its decision. It turned left. The boy couldn't remember clearly the journey they'd made on the way here, but this confirmed his intuition. He waited until the vehicle had been out of sight for some time then set off himself. It was a while before it occurred to him that the house might have been an early call on the driver's rounds and that the van might now be heading away from the town to continue its deliveries, but it was too late to rethink his options: he was committed.

He strolled on for some time. The pale morning sun was beginning to dispel the dampness from overnight, and now and then insects flitted across his path on erratic errands. The narrow hump-backed road undulated between high hedgerows filled with dog rose, harebells and old man's baccy, all of which were strangers to him. He was amazed at the fecundity of the countryside. If he hadn't been so hard-pressed, he would have stopped to examine the tendrils of purple vetch that scrawled their way up the walls of vegetation. Instead, he concentrated on the road, sometimes following the grooves of black tar worn into the surface by the wheels of infrequent traffic, and sometimes the spine of grey gravel chippings in the middle.

He kept on for what seemed like an age. His legs began to thrum with the repeated action of setting one foot down in front of another, but he was afraid to stop because there was no sign of his destination, and he had no idea how much further it could be. He tried to recall the journey of that first evening, but it was impossible to gauge the distance covered by the vehicle compared with his own effort now.

He began to feel thirsty. The sun was higher now and was beating on his head and shoulders. At last he paused by the gate into a field and sat down on a stone. But immediately he heard the sound of a very heavy animal munching its way towards him on the other side of the hedge. He could hear it swishing its head to and fro through the grass and the thud-

thud of its feet as it shuffled closer one methodical step at a time. He shot to his feet and set off again.

For a long time the road continued to rise and fall. Sometimes he passed under the boughs of crooked trees that thrust out complicated fistfuls of leaves – here dark puddles still lurked in the dips in the tarmac and a dank smell rose from the wayside mulch – but mostly he was out under an open sky with only a trailing cloud here and there to interfere with the sun. A yellow butterfly came and parked for a while on his shirt sleeve. He watched it intently as it adjusted its antennae, but still kept moving.

Then, suddenly, a cottage came into view, the road took an unexpected bend to the right and he found himself walking alongside a low stone wall. On the other side, orange seaweed curdled, rising and falling with the bulky swell of the ocean. Much further away he could see the ferry jetty poking out into the bay. A steamer was heading in towards the shore, its funnels puffing out two black question marks. His heart leaped. His feet were burning now, and his energy was flagging, but he plodded on relentlessly, past the long row of snooty villas that stood up above the shoreline looking blankly out across the bay. He put a spurt on, gauging his own progress against the progress of the vessel. He could not afford to miss this boat.

At last he reached the shops that were at the centre of the town: a barber's; a hardware store; a shop with various kinds of knitting yarn and a handful of dead flies in the window, all rendered peculiar by a translucent orange blind. He turned a corner, made out where the ferry office was, and could see the throng of people waiting to embark. He paused. How to negotiate the tricky business of not having a ticket? The ferry was already shouldering the quay, and a steady stream of passengers was rolling ashore. He made out the letters on the bow, and mouthed them slowly to himself. Not much time to decide upon a strategy for boarding the *Queen of Campbeltown*. In the end, he sauntered down towards the quay with his hands in his trouser pockets as though boarding a ferry were something he did every day of the week. He found it easy to mingle with the crowd. People were in holiday mood, and no-one bothered about what he might be up to. As he got close to the entry gate, he attached himself nonchalantly to the skirts of a woman who was busy marshalling three other children and an awkward pushchair and then, there he was: up the gangway and on board.

112

He wormed his way up the stairs to the foredeck, pushed between the grown-ups and found himself a place by the rail. He gripped the metal tightly. Could it really be that he was going to make it? He cast about furtively, afraid of sighting any adult who might come and place a hand on his shoulder. But then, the vessel shuddered as the engines kicked in; brown water began to skirl beneath the bow; the captain gave three thrilling blasts on the ship's siren, and the boat began its reverse out into the bay.

He kept his grip on the rail, watching the cordon of lace that tethered them to the land gradually fray and then dissolve. Now the shoreline steadily unravelled as the boat pushed the small town further away. Small coves and inlets appeared from nowhere; sailing boats and islets popped out from behind sheltering headlands; buoys bobbed uncertainly beside neglected dinghies, and the slopes behind them began to lose their meaning. Eventually, the boat swung out into the broader reach and adjusted its course. Now, in a slowly shifting panorama, the hills around them stepped boldly out from behind one another then stepped back again in a different order. Further out still, and the water became more important than the land, sea and sky merging ambiguously in the distance. The boy began to breathe more easily. He had his first thoughts of how he would be greeted at home. He imagined the table set, and him sitting in front of it with a celebratory plate of spam fritters and baked beans, after which, he would have a mug of cocoa. The last time he had seen his Ma, she had been crying. He hoped that was all over now.

A girl of about his own age came and stood nearby.

'What's your name?' she said at last. It was something of a challenge, as though if he got it wrong, or she didn't like it, she would poke him in the eye. He considered whether or not to tell her.

'Bobby,' he said. 'My Da called, calls me Robert. What's yours?'

'Elaine.'

They both stood looking for some time into the mysterious portal that had opened up where the sky met the sea.

'Where *is* your Da?' Elaine enquired.

Bobby looked around. A group of people were amusing themselves on the far side of the deck, the men with their arms proprietorially around the women's waists. One man had a box camera and was trying to take a photograph. Another, with slicked-back hair, leaned languidly against the smokestack, drawing on a cigarette.

'He's over there,' he said. 'Having a... having a smoke.'

'Mine's over there,' said Elaine, 'with my Ma.' She gestured in the direction of a couple who were standing quietly by the rail looking in opposite directions. They were very neatly dressed. The woman wore a pale blue hat that looked like a pancake pressed onto the side of her head. The man was lashed so tightly into his long mackintosh that he resembled a constipated bean pole. It seemed unlikely that the pair would ever have anything to say to anyone.

'They're having a row,' Elaine said.

Bobby frowned. It didn't look like a row to him. Rows were when he heard his parents going at it hammer and tongs while he was sitting in the cupboard, or shut in the bathroom.

~

'Where're ye gaen at this time of night?' his mother would start.

'Oot!'

'Oot? Where's oot?'

'I'll mebbie away up Tam's for some craic with the lads.' You could tell his father was being evasive by the way he tried to keep his tone even.

'The lads! The lads!' his mother would yell. 'You've been with the lads all day. Whit mair have the lads got to say for theirselves?' Silence.

'The lad must be awfy geniuses that they have so much tae tell ye.' More silence. His mother found this provocative.

'After some tramp from up the Townheid, mair like,' she would goad. Bobby was curious as to why his father might wish to associate with a down-and-out, but it was a matter which he'd never fathomed, as his father would ignore this too, and then there'd be a scuffle as his mother tried to beat some kind of answer out of him. Sometimes, his father tried a placatory tactic:

'There's nae tramp, Ishbel, nae tramp.'

'Oh aye, that'll be right,' his mother would say sarcastically, and then his father would finally rise to the bait.

'If ye must know, I've jist got tae get oot o' this place tae clear ma heid.'

'Whit? What is it yer heid's sae full of? Are ye busy on the designs for the next Mauritania?'

114

'Man, the fact is, I jist cannae bide in here every night with the curtains drawn, watchin' you destroy yersel with those pills. It's not the reason I married ye. If it wasn't for the wean...'

'They pills is for my nerves, as prescribed by the doctor,' his mother would shriek. 'And if anyone's destroyin' theirsel it isnae me. I'm no' the one with the graveyard cough.' And this was true. Sometimes his father would cough so long and hard it seemed as though his rib cage would crack open, and when he did manage to stop, you could hear his chest still purring, like the chain on a bicycle when you spin the pedals backwards.

Sometimes his mother's attack would collapse into a plea: 'Tak me with you, Rob. Tak me with you,' she would sob. 'I've been stuck in these four walls all day long, wi' not a soul tae talk to, so I have. Do ye wonder that I need some kind of distraction?'

'How can I tak you with me?' his father would say impatiently. 'What about the wean?' And then you would hear him at the coat rack, and the outside door closing and his steps receding along the walkway, along with his cough.

Bobby was still confused about what had happened when his father eventually disappeared. His mother knelt on the floor beside him, her face blotched and swollen. She held his hands, and looked at him keenly, in a way that made the back of his neck creep.

'Your Da's been taken puirly,' she said. 'He's too puirly to come home the now.' He nodded because he could tell that this was something momentous, and he understood even then that life was a tricky business, and that you sometimes had to accommodate things you didn't expect. But the days went by and turned into weeks and still his father didn't come home. And somehow, the moment when he could've asked, 'Will he ever come back?' slipped by unnoticed.

There was a change in his mother. When he came home from school, she was often crouching on the floor weeping, or lying flat out on the bed in some kind of stupor. He scouted round the house looking for food, as his tea was seldom on the table. If there was bread and condensed milk, he would spread a slice thickly for each of them and hand one in to her before he went out to play. At the weekends, he was left to his own devices, unlike in the old days when his father would often take him up to town to see things and meet people. Now he stayed out till well after dark most evenings, playing on the rough ground by the tenement, and there was no-one to call him in. He took to hanging round the chip shop, waiting for the man to clear the batter out of the fryer when he closed up. 'There's two pennorth o' scratchings for ye,' the man would say, handing a poke of newspaper over the counter. At school, he led an enchanted existence, with no-one asking him anything about anything. What he dreaded, though, was meeting any of the women who were their neighbours. 'Is your Ma still bad wi her nerves?' they would ask, and he would shrug because he didn't really know what the question meant, but felt there was something shameful about the answer.

The day the Social came for him, he hadn't been at school. He'd discovered that it didn't make any difference to anyone whether he went or not. He was amusing himself in the livingroom, chasing some Cocoa Puffs round his bowl with a spoon. His mother sat on the settee in a stained summer frock, her head flung back, slowly smoking a cigarette. The wireless was on and Roy Orbison was singing *Dream Baby*. He let the Social in himself. There was a kerfuffle. His mother leaped to her feet. His arm was grabbed. There was some exchange between the two women social workers and his mother.

'No, dinnae tak' him! I cannae manage without him!' his mother cried.

'Yer Ma's no weel,' one of them said to him. 'It's for yer ain good. And hers. The pair of yes ull be back together again in no time, once yer Ma's better.'

And then he was on the other side of the front door, being frog-marched firmly away.

'Bobby! Bobby!' he could still hear the dreadful cry of his mother as they reached the lifts. He felt that cry inside him like the thrill of a raw nerve. He wanted to get back to ease the pain that they both felt.

~

The vessel was ploughing a furrow between low shores now. On the nearer bank you could see meadows where cattle grazed among the buttercups, and pontoons ran down into the water. Here and there, the ribs of broken boats poked through the mud like chocolate-coated fingers. On the opposite bank tiny houses and a couple of pointy grey kirks clung to the water's margins.

Elaine was watching him: 'Ye're looking very queer.'

Bobby shook his head: 'No, I'm all right.'

116

'Yer Da's gone.'

'Oh, has he?'

'He wisnae yer Da, was he? He didnae look out for ye.'

Elaine wasn't short of the full shilling. Her eyes held him like hooks. She wasn't about to let go of the matter. Bobby pursed his lips: 'I'm away to see ma Ma,' he said. 'She's been bad wi' her nerves, but she's better now. They've jist forgotten to come and bring me hame.'

Elaine let her mouth fall open and ran her tongue round inside her cheek: 'What if I tell my Ma and Da?' she said, sensing her power.

Bobby looked at her in horror: 'Naw!' he protested.

At that moment, Elaine's mother unfroze from her statuesque stance and cast about for her daughter. 'Elaine, come here!' she called.

The boat had chosen its destination. It had slowed and was fumbling its way towards the quayside, juddering and complaining. Houses were returning to normal size, and you could see vehicles moving along the waterfront.

'Aw,' said Elaine, 'a cauld wind blowin'.'

Her mother called again: 'Elaine, behave yourself now. Come away from that boy. It's time to get off. I don't want you getting lost.' Elaine threw Bobby a parting glance as she trotted off dutifully across the deck. He saw her mother seize hold of her by the shoulder of her small tweed coat and steer her away.

People formed a great press in their hurry to disembark: eager to enjoy their day out, yet surprisingly eager to get home. Bobby found himself caught up in a scrum of skirts and baskets, shoes and trouser legs. He got swept first towards the wheelhouse, then down towards the lounge, past the toilets and back up another flight of stairs. And ironically, just as he reached the head of the gangway, he came face to face with Elaine. Their eyes locked, and stayed locked for a long moment. Then, 'Hang on,' she said, and grabbed hold of his arm.

They set off down the gangway, along the jetty and up onto the waiting train, Elaine's father out in front, then her mother trailing Elaine, then Elaine trailing him. It was only when her mother and father got settled in their seats in the chuffer that her mother's eye fell on him.

'Where're this boy's parents?' she said, eyeing him critically.

'His Da's just coming. He's just behind. There.' Elaine nodded back down the corridor, beyond her mother's line of vision.

'Well, all right, then,' said her mother grudgingly. 'Just mind what you do.' Bobby noticed that Elaine's father was paying no attention at all. He had opened a small book and was reading.

The two children stood together outside the compartment with their foreheads on the cool glass. The corridor was crammed, with people making their way to and fro waving bottles or leaning on the rail smoking. The windows were thick with condensation. Every now and then Elaine and Bobby rubbed small holes in the mist so that they could watch the backs of buildings sliding past.

'Dae your Ma and Da never speak?' Bobby asked.

'They speak when they're not arguing.'

'Are they still arguing the now?'

'Aye, they've been at it for days. My Da calls it the Cold War.'

'That's a guy queer business,' said Bobby, used to the raucous cut and thrust of his own parents, his mother in particular.

'Aye, my Ma can keep it up forever. She can make the place feel like an igloo.' Elaine lifted her shoulders and shuddered.

'What call is there for that?'

'I dinnae ken. They dinnae tell me.'

The pair of them went back to drawing faces on the window. Bobby drew one of his mother with a perm and a row of big round beads round her neck. He couldn't get her mouth in quite the right place. Elaine drew one of her father, a big, long oblong of a head with pushy-out ears. Then she added a pipe and curly eyelashes, which gave him a startled, saccharine sort of look.

'Does your Da smoke a pipe?' asked Bobby.

'No, but I think he should.' They both giggled. It was the first laugh Bobby had had for weeks.

At last the chuffer chuffed into Central station where it jolted against the platform and blew out its last breath. There was murder polis as everyone tried to get off at the same time. Bobby tumbled out onto the platform with his new-found family. Elaine dragged him through the ticket gate.

'Well,' she said, releasing him, 'cheerio!'

'Aye,' said Bobby, 'cheerio!'

'Best of luck.'

'Aye. Best of luck.'

And once again she was wrenched away from him in her tiny wee coat and her sandals with the daisies cut out on the front as her parents made off in the direction of further transport.

There was something uplifting about Elaine's resilience that stayed with him as he slapped his way along the broad sandstone slabs of Union Street. He wondered where in the town she would be headed, and what like their home would be. But then he lost his bearings for a while and had to concentrate on getting himself home. He was all right once he'd stumbled upon St Enoch which he'd been to with his father on a number of occasions. From there, he steered his way down to the river and felt his way along the bank until he came to the footbridge. Normally, he would have stopped to inspect the water, but by now he was desperate to make landfall. His heart was bobbing in his breast. 'Ma!' he thought, 'Ma!' He longed for the hug she would give him when she opened the door. He imagined snuggling in between the two half fronts of her cardigan, driving his forehead into her midriff. What a surprise it would be for her!

The sky, emptied of sun, was a queer, luminous white. Doorways were darkening and the streets were almost empty. But, once he was over the bridge, he was on his home patch. He knew every bar, every close, every civic building. He started to run, threading this way and that until he reached the open ground, the empty tenement and, behind them, the tall block of flats where they lived. He made for the lifts, but they weren't working. He scuttled up the thirteen flights of steps that took him to the sixth floor. He didn't want anyone to know he was coming: he wanted it to be an unannounced homecoming, so that the joy would be all the greater. But he certainly made a racket as he ricocheted along the walkway, exhausted, out of breath and drunk with anticipation. 'Ma!' he choked. 'Ma!'

At last, he was at their letterbox. He lifted the flap. 'Ma!' he called. 'Ma!' There was no movement. He dropped the flap and rat-rat-tatted with the knocker. No-one came. He lifted the flap again. 'Ma, it's me. Ma!' Still silence. Maybe she was out. What night was it? Maybe she was at the bingo. No, wrong night, but anyway, he couldn't remember the last time she'd been out. Maybe she was asleep. He thumped on the door: 'Ma let me in!' He started whimpering.

Suddenly, the door was jerked open a couple of inches, revealing a thin strip of his mother, clad in a shiny robe. She looked dazed and patted the top of his head gingerly. 'Bobby? Bobby?'

'Let me in, Ma.' Bobby flung himself at her. She fell back under the impact, and the gown slipped from her shoulder. It was clear that she was not wearing underwear. A voice came from behind her.

'Whae is it?' It was a man's voice.

'It's my wean, Bobby.'

'Whit the fuck is he daein' here?'

Bobby pressed the door open further in his struggle to get inside. He could see the man slumped back on the settee – his settee – in dingy vest and trousers, with his fly undone.

'Ye never mentioned weans.'

'I didnae need tae mention weans. They took him awa.'

The man staggered to his feet, knocking over a low table with all kinds of clutter on it. Papers, cans, a plate, pills, a belt, some cutlery, a syringe and a cigarette lighter fell to the floor. The man lumbered towards him, his arms outstretched as though he were driving sheep.

'Now lookee here, sonny Jim. Fuck off! Me and your Ma is busy. We dinnae want you hangin' aboot.'

Bobby looked around bewildered. He waited for his Ma to come to his rescue. She didn't. The man, towering above him had a smell he was not familiar with in his own home and a tattoo he didn't like the look of on his left bicep. He drove Bobby back towards the door.

'Get a move on, kid, or you'll be feeling my boot up your arse.'

'It's all right, Archie. Dinnae fash yersel,' said his mother. 'I'll get him oot. Now, Bobby,' she said in her strictest voice, the one she reserved for when he'd broken something, 'ye'd no business coming back here. Ye ken very well what for they took ye away. So ye'd better get yersel back. Now go on. Shoo! Be a good boy and dinnae come back till ye're telt.'

Bobby allowed himself to be driven backwards until he had stepped over the threshold, and then the door was snapped shut smartly in his face. He crouched there for some time, sometimes tapping on the panel under the letterbox; sometimes lifting the flap and calling in, 'Ma! Ma! Let me in!' but no-one came. Even when he knocked the milk bottles over, no-one came. Eventually, he retreated to a corner of the walkway, where he curled up and tried to sleep. But he could do no more than doze. Beyond a certain point, the sky did not darken. The concrete beneath him was chilly and a cool breeze blew fitfully throughout the night, getting in under the slabs of the parapet and striking through his shirt. He was cold even though he wrenched his sleeves down and yanked his socks up.

The minute he heard the rattle of the milk cart in the street below, he was fully awake. He was off before he could meet the milkman on the stair. He crossed the empty ground and clambered in through a window of the condemned tenement. The place stank of damp plaster spiked with the sharp tang of boozers' piss, and at places the floor gave way directly into the foundations. But if he chose his spot carefully, and had a good look round for stuff later on, maybe he could start building himself a camp.

Moving In

The builder-cum-decorator has arrived with three ladders. One is too long to reach the ceiling; the other two hang from the ceiling, but are too short to reach the floor. He tramples over the curtains and retires to his van to consider what to do. This involves multiple phone calls to friends, family, a bloke in a blanket under Blackfriars Bridge and a man called George.

I lay a trail of biscuits from the van to the front door so that he won't lose his way. He returns some time later with a spirit level, a pot of coving glue and a bristling haircut. The solution is not in view.

He pronounces that he has decided not to mend the crack above the mantelpiece. 'Houses are organic, love,' he avers. 'They breathe. You don't want to get hung up on concepts such as permanence, stasis and perfection. There are no such states. Everyone from Schopenauer on has said the same.' He screws the lid back on a jar of pickles and smokes a fag. 'It's an attractive theory,' I concede, as I peer through the crack and watch two finches fiercely stabbing berries on the euthanasia tree. But one with which I wish to have no truck.

The assistant has been left to his own devices in the living room. The colour charts have been lost down the back of someone's car seat on a trip Up North to see Leyton Orient play Carlisle FC. "Crushed pebble" and "muted moss" are a long way from his mind. He has selected a hideous shade of yellow. Absorbed in his task, he is applying mustard methodically to the ceiling rose. This violent hue strips the paint from the shutters, sets fire to an ashtray and causes the window box to melt. Small children passing in the street whimper forlornly as their Cheese Strings wilt. I eyeball the young man until his twisted denims fade. In return, he eyeballs me. 'Time is money,' he shrugs with the derelict air of the youth trainee, and carries on.

In the hall, the electrician is lying in the cupboard sighing heavily. The wiring he installed on Friday has been done by someone else, most probably some "towel heads". In any case, it's incorrect. 'The trouble is,' he swears, 'these foreign bastards do everything the right way up – they know no better – but centuries of imperialsim have taught us otherwise: they should always be skew-whiff. How else would we maintain our casual air of cultural supremacy?' For days now, he has clumped up and down the cellar stairs between the fuse box and the boiler, but his size eleven boots have obscured his view. Now, thanks to the introduction of an arc light that came his way at a week-end garage sale, he can visualise a solution. That is: start again.

The bathroom tiles arrive. They have been shipped direct from a civic toilet on the seafront at Bridlington, not from the high-class showroom of Seer Green and Jordans where I first encountered them. They are larger than I ordered, but cannot be returned. The tiler is expected at the Casa Mila conference hall on Battló Road the following day, and must get his skates on.

In the kitchen, the cupboards have assembled. They have three legs apiece, none of them the same. The oven is balking at the prospect of being housed. The fridge has too many handles, all of them illegally imported, and the washing machine is stuck on "spin". Lacy knickers and hypo-allergenic socks are chasing each other interminably round the drum. The drawers are in the cupboards, the cupboards are looking bored and the shelves are still in packaging behind the compost bin. The plumber has supplied an Irish sink with two left taps. Unfortunately, their brake discs have gone.

The house is in a conservation zone. Ceilings are being lowered and floors are being raised. Double glazing has been shaved in half, and draft includer fitted. Reason has been suspended, and loiters palely by the door. Thorough-bred Highland woodworm graze laconically on a nineteenth century architrave.

The phone doesn't ring. No-one has thought of calling an engineer. I am dependent on the power of thought and a candle stump to work out where my nearest and dearest might be. Not here, obviously.

'Never marry a man,' my aunt once told me, 'who unpacks the pans before he hangs the pictures.' I am struggling to understand her point. My life partner has gone foraging for saddle soap and a pair of Kookaburra cricket gloves.

123

The cat saunters through the house wearing pyjamas and a balaclava helmet, in anticipation of events to come.

At eleven o'clock, the sofa arrives, having walked all the way from the station. Its bulky exertions have exhausted it. It leans into the wind, panting heavily, and unable to explain itself. It veers into the hall, and lumbers crabwise into the living room. Its teeth are in its arse and its arms are back to front. It gives a crooked smile and tells me it has left three cushions on the train for the benefit of passengers travelling to Croydon, Purley Oaks and beyond.

'What were you playing at?' I yell. 'Outdoing the Gatwick Express?'

The cemetery beckons, but I dare not leave the house in case the coffee table turns up.

A woman with a Primark bag full of shoes and sandals, and a copy of the Apostolic creed appears to help me. She rings the bell and the burglar alarm goes off. She says she's from the Church of Our Lord of Miracles, but faith deserts me and I dare not let her in.

In the street, the security gates are locked. The van bearing the dining chairs and the Casa Pupo rug has taken a wrong turn off the M4, and is currently embroiled in a contraflow near Budleigh Salterton. It may be here next Tuesday, or the Tuesday after. Meanwhile, a tour bus bound for Bruges performs a thirty-six point turn in the drive. Forty members of the Alliance Française, Merton branch, watch less than obliquely while I empty several hundredweight of mouse shit and ancient bottle openers into the dustbin.

I venture into the garden. Someone has walked sideways over the flowerbeds and screwed curtain hooks into the lawn. The bikes have disappeared from the garden shed.

On the upper floor, the empty bathroom is full of angst. The plumber has put the carpenter's nose out of joint. The carpenter has told the plumber to shut his trap. The tumbled travertine has been tossed to buggery, and water trickles down the electric cable into the dining room.

At four thirty, the workmen leave. It starts to rain.

It rains some more.

And then it rains a lot.

The window is open. I close it. It stays open.

There are no biscuits left. I find cream crackers that I cannot remember buying in a jar marked 'Moutarde de Meaux'. I decide to eat them raw, as the deep fat fryer has not turned up and the camping stove's gone missing.

It is half past seven and dark. The gully pot trap beneath the French doors is broken, and the guttering up above has bowed. Rainwater is gushing straight from the roof into the cellar. Men came and dug a hole and did not return. Then they enlarged it. Now it is gaping like an open wound, and the cellar is filling rapidly.

I step outside with an assortment of plastic bags and a shovel to devise some diversionary measure. Clothes are pointless, so I am wearing none. I have clamped a mountaineering lamp to my head, and put my gumboots on.

The phone rings as I perform a gravedigger's manoeuvre.

My friend lost her teeth down a drain in Musselburgh High Street. Sectioned by social workers, she rings me from the Andrew Duncan Clinic where she has been since Maundy Thursday. 'Hello,' she says. Her bed sheets have been folded like the ends of parcels and her pillows plumped. I hear teaspoons clinking, and the sound of chocolate digestives sliding onto a plate. 'It's grim in here,' she says, 'There's nothing to do.'

'You should try it on the outside!' I scream, and slam the phone down on its base.

I start stirring sewage with a stick.

The Menace at the Gate

Her period refused to come. She lay in turmoil beneath the ineffectual ceiling fan. No position brought relief from the heat. After days of tossing and turning and lying in limp sheets, her shoulders and her buttocks were disfigured by the blemishes served up by prickly heat, and the monsoon was still an age away.

Clans of mosquitoes infested the room, convening under the bed, as well as in the adjoining bathroom, where you took your pants down at your peril. Every night, before coming to bed, she fumigated the entire place with Deet, and plastered herself with Odomos. It made no difference. The evil empire persisted in rude good health, while she lay upon the bed like a living sacrifice. Despite a monstrous nightgown and cotton socks that came up almost to her knees, her ankles, wrists and toes were swollen with multiple bites, the flesh ripped raw with scratching.

Her mind was in no better state. Her head was filled with equations that she could not solve. The reek of formaldehyde from the lab was still in her nostrils. She had never guessed when she chose her subjects for Ten Plus, that even Biology, which was her favourite subject, would involve so much chemistry. She thrashed about the bed, struggling with valencies that were at odds with one another, and the chemical description of photosynthesis that she could not complete. At the same time, fragments of the argument her parents had had that morning rattled in her head. They were covering the same old ground. Her mother wanted a beauty parlour, and was asking for a down payment for land. Her father was adamant that no wife of his was going out to work. Over the months that war had been waged across this terrain, the arguments had got worse: her mother more abusive, her father bitterer and meaner. This morning's argument had been conducted with such vitriol that even her brother had been shocked. Not to mention the relatives from the UK who were staying with them.

Anju gathered that business in the state was going down. Everyone was jittery because of the Sikh separatist hostilities that showed no sign of abating. Only last week, people had been dragged off a bus from Chandigarh and shot for no obvious reason. So, of course, her father was right to be cautious. On the other hand, she thought her mother would make a good businesswoman who would have her wits about her, so why hold back? Her father was willing to pay for his daughters' education in the hope that they would become career women, so why not make some investment in his wife? In the meantime, while the matter remained unresolved, the entire household operated in an oppressive atmosphere of unspoken thoughts, unfocused gazes and evasive action when they encountered each other in the living room. She had no idea how things would end.

The words "xylem" and "phloem" drifted through her head tangled up with elements from the periodic table. Then came "cranial enlargement", "thermodynamic equilibrium" and "infantile dementia". A cow sauntered past to buy beauty products at her mother's three-legged market stall. Her father sawed down trees at the corner of the garden to make way for a shamiana. A dog was found to share its genetic origins with a banana. The banana sought an audience with the queen of Punjabi film, Amrita Singh. A balloon drifted off in the direction of Khalistan, taking the film star with it, and leaving her fans behind. No matter how Anju tried, nothing would compute.

She threw herself to the other end of the bed in the hope of finding a breath of air. Now the rattle of water in the cooler was next to her ears, along with the demented roar of its fan. It was like life as she imagined it in an aircraft hangar. She got up and switched the thing off – it served no useful purpose – and launched herself onto her back again. She had begged and pleaded with her parents for a grown-up "pad" away from her obnoxious brother and her feather-brained sister, a place where she could do grown-up things like read novels and listen to film songs. Now that she had it, she could hardly complain about the disadvantages, especially as the room had its own outer door, almost like an apartment. With the cooler off, she heard the motor of the refrigerator kick into action several rooms away, the bottles of water shuddering in the drinks rack. The external screen door banged softly for no apparent reason. And in the back bedroom, her new uncle began to snore like a rutting buffalo.

Things were no better at school, either. In fact, they were worse. She was at that age when she was trying to distance herself from her parents. It was clear they didn't know her any more: they frowned at things she thought were hilarious and read doom, disaster and shortcoming into her every move. Her friends, on the other hand, shared her sense of humour; they took pleasure in the same things as her, whether movies or music; they knew exactly what talents she had and appreciated them. Or that's the way it had been. But, by now, many of her friends had already left school, some for early marriages and some for secretarial training. Meenakshi was even expecting her first child, the gaudiness of her marriage equalled only by her ignorance of matters reproductive. Anju didn't want any of that. She wanted a career she was genuinely interested in, one she could pursue for many years to come, depending on how marriage turned out, and so she'd decided on Immunology, something that would be socially useful. This was what had made her put up so far with the homework, the absolute crateloads of it that she had to drag around every day. This, and having friends to lighten the load.

But now, her best friend, Gurdeep, had discarded her. It would have been better if they had had an argument. An argument is about something, often a misunderstanding, and there's a good chance it can be patched up. But Gurdeep had simply said to her one day, 'Nah, you're just too boring these days. Always self-absorbed; always complaining about things that don't interest anyone else. I want some fun.' And she had turned her attention to a group of Arts students in their year, notably one Kach, a boy with very tight trousers and a quiff of oily hair – a boy they had both despised when they were a year younger. Anju was devastated. It was humiliating. The contagion of rejection spread, and soon she spent her days ploughing a solitary furrow, shunned by the last of her remaining friends. It made break times difficult and it made her school bag twice as heavy.

Her nightdress was stifling. Its gathers added unflattering volume to her body, enlarging her aching breasts, and turning her bloated abdomen into a mound the size of a village pathi. Ribbons of perspiration threaded their way across every surface of her body and collected in its folds.

Suddenly, she leaped up and ripped the nightdress off. And with it, the socks. 'Come on, you mosquitoes!' she cried out silently, as she flung herself across the bed, naked and cruciform. 'What more harm can you do?'

128

But no: no matter how hard she tried to will herself into oblivion, a constant flurry of unrelated items filled her head, like debris caught up in a dust storm, while a peculiar orange glow filled her cranium and pressed at the back of her eyeballs. She felt that at any moment her head might explode. She flailed about desperately in hope of some small respite. Her hips were bruised with twisting and turning on the thin, unforgiving mattress, and mosquitoes screamed shrill descants by her ears. When she had visited a particular chemical equation pointlessly for what seemed like the umpteenth time, 'Enough!' she said, and got up. She wrenched the sheet from the bed and wound it around herself sari-style. She shuffled softly to the door, slid the bolt back gently and stepped out into the garden. Ironic that when her parents had debated giving her the room, they considered how easily someone might get in. It had never occurred to them to think about how readily their daughter might get out.

She stood on the lawn. The grass was oily underfoot. The sunflowers in the borders hung their heads with exhaustion. Nothing stirred. Not even the cicadas that normally hung about in the creeper on the wall. The moon was high and bloated, with a feverish orange stain around it. The pill-box that the Armed Police had constructed on the wall of the Shri Lakshmi Narayan mission, after the separatists had attacked a number of Hindu temples, was deserted. However, further along, at the sentry post next to the gate, a single guard stood on duty. After a while, he gave a muffled cough, and she heard his boots crunch on gravel as he adjusted his weight.

She stood as still as a statue in her makeshift sari. Then, far away, she heard the whistle of the chowkidar on his rounds. Gradually, he came closer, trailing his lathi along a fence. Finally, by the time he got to the end of their lane, she could make out each concussive rattle of the pea in his whistle. The guard shifted his ground, preparing for a diversion. But the chowkidar passed on, intent on his own thoughts, oblivious to the ghost-like figure standing on the lawn. Stick and whistle turned a corner and faded into the distance.

Anju laughed to herself. What kind of a chowkidar was that? He wouldn't see a burglary if it was committed under his nose. She had not been afraid that he might see her, though. She had not been afraid at all. She took a few paces further onto the lawn, and adjusted her sagging "sari" in a way she thought might be more becoming. The guard might, or might not, have been watching her.

A few lanes away, fractious dogs began to squabble, their yelping reverberating from the vast geometry of the blue-black sky. Suddenly the night seemed full of possibilities, offering something very different from the mental drudgery Anju faced on a daily basis; something far away from mind-numbing routine; something exhilarating. She moved as smoothly across the lawn as if she were on castors. Carefully, she lifted the latch on the garden gate and stepped out into the lane. The gravel bit into her feet, sharpening her senses, and she felt a certain thrill at being "out of bounds". She nursed her heavy breasts on her forearm as she held the "sari" close, the nipples standing stiffly to attention. Suddenly, she felt differently about herself: a sense of expansiveness that sat low within her offered itself for fulfilment. This was a far remove from the dead weight she had got used to dragging around.

It was as though the guard had been expecting her. He was young, his facial expression not yet hardened into that of a seasoned officer, but not so young that he didn't know what was required of him. He was eager; brusque but not brutal. She pushed him back against the wall. His uniform was coarse and full of hindrances. Her fast and furtive fingers made short work of them. She waited while he undid his trouser buckle, then she dropped the sheet. His body was narrow, his hips hard. The sex was what they both needed: harsh and hasty. He thrust deep inside her, and she drew hard on him. Her body gave commands she was not familiar with and responded to its own orders. Her mind was nowhere. She clutched him by the shoulders, and raised a knee against the wall to get a better purchase. At her ear she could feel his breath and the softness of a young moustache. When it was over, she hung on to his collar gratefully, and rested her head briefly on his shoulder, but she could not look him in the eye.

Wordlessly, she dragged the sheet back into the garden, and somehow got back into her room without disturbing the household. Now as she lay on the bed, she felt she had already left home. She fell asleep uncovered by the sheet and with no thought for mosquitoes.

The following morning was a strange business. She put on her school uniform – it looked ridiculous – and took it off again. Instead, she put on a modest salwar kameez and went into the dining room. Her parents were busy pretending they weren't rowing, for the benefit of the visitors from the UK, but were clearly on a collision course. Anju couldn't be bothered to try and decipher exactly what was going on. Her mother frowned at her briefly, something about her daughter's appearance catching her attention, but then got distracted by the cold war. Anju buttered herself a piece of toast, smothered it with jam, smiled at her new auntie and uncle and hefted her bag of books out to the school bus.

No-one wanted to sit next to her. She didn't care. As the vehicle wove between the military checkpoints that had been set up all across town, she looked around benignly at her fellow passengers. Too much gossiping! What was there that required so much yakkety-yak? Latest hits and such, she supposed. Whatever it was, it no longer mattered to her. She was in a class of her own now. She smiled inwardly. As the bus trundled along, she opened her bag and slid her textbooks out through the window bars, one by one. She watched small children and dogs run out from ditches and drains to see what gift had been left for them. She felt totally liberated. They, on the other hand, were going to be really disappointed.

She lied her way through the first half of the day: 'Sorry, miss, I think my brother's taken it by mistake', 'Sorry sir, I couldn't finish it: my tooth was paining.' All through some ineffably boring Physics demonstration that involved the use of vernier calipers, she sat looking out through a gap between the buildings at a smudge in the distance where the foothills started up from the plains. One day soon, perhaps, she could be wandering there in the clear mountain air, serenaded by music and caressed by blossom as in the best romantic film scenes. When it came to the practical, she didn't even try to complete it.

In the early afternoon, her euphoria started to dispel. She could hear the thump of munitions and the occasional crack of small arms fire out in the direction of the cantonment. The day was turning muggy again. Even minus the school uniform, she felt hot and bothered. Slowly, it dawned on her that without money she was going nowhere; without passing her exams, she would be unable to go to college, and if she did not graduate and become a professional lady who earned money, then she would be parcelled off to some local buddhu whom, knowing her father, she might have very little say in choosing.

And what if her period never came? What if, after nine months, her body exploded and gave forth a baby? She, better than anyone, should have been able to guard against this possibility. The ins and outs of the human reproductive system were on their curriculum. How could she have been so stupid?

She sat up late that night, listening to old film songs on her radio. Or rather, not listening, but gripped by terror as plaintive melodies lilted by, one after another. She didn't know the first thing about having a baby. She didn't want a baby. She couldn't imagine herself in such a situation. The whole business of garnering another being from within yourself and pushing it out into the world was too grotesque. But before she even got to that, there was the matter of how she would break the shameful truth to her parents. They would be appalled, and their fury would be boundless. She would have ruined things for them. They would become social outcasts, unwelcome in every outpost of their family, and she would be some ugly pariah, hated by herself as well as by everyone else. The truth was unspeakable. She couldn't do it: she couldn't tell her parents. She would rather die.

There was nothing to do but wait, and that meant strapping on the uniform again; figuring out how to catch up with her homework and trying to get hold of the textbooks she had discarded at a point in the school year when they couldn't easily be replaced.

The days passed wretchedly, and the nights too, with the fan battering against the ceiling and the cooler keeping up its incessant din. Her body was not complying with the laws of nature. It did nothing. Except, perhaps, inflate: the waistband of her school skirt got so tight, she felt faint when she bent over, and her bra bit into her flesh like the rope on a cotton bale. Her ankles had lost their definition, and her toes were like little loqats. As the days ticked by, her sense of dread increased.

Meanwhile, her mother had noticed the logjam in proceedings. She threatened Anju with a visit to the doctor's.

'I can't go. I can't miss school. We're doing important stuff.'

'This is important stuff. You can't let matters like these drag on. They need to be sorted out. Otherwise, you don't know what all problems you'll have in the future.'

'I hate it,' said Anju. 'You can't see him in private. You have to sit there and tell him all personal stuff in front of half the town. Last time I heard a woman telling him all about her discharge. It was disgusting.'

'Grow up!' said her mother. 'Everyone has such problems. You're no different. He's a good homoeopath. He cured you overnight when you were tiny and had whooping cough. And he treats the police horses for free.'

Anju snorted in disdain. 'I'm not going!'

But finally, her mother did get her way. One morning Anju found her braced in the frame of the external door, barring her way.

'Right, madam, you can put your school bag down. We're not having this tamasha any longer. We're going to the doctor's.'

They set off across town in a rickshaw. Although she'd applied an avalanche of talcum powder to herself, Anju's cleavage was already wet and her palms clammy. 'Now,' said her mother, 'when we get there, speak out. Leave nothing out.' Anju hung her head. She didn't think so.

But when they arrived at the surgery, they found the whole place in turmoil. The yard that served as the waiting room was filled with a jostling throng of distraught people. Men were shouting and women wailing. Someone was waving a crutch over someone else's head. A woman in a yellow sari was kneeling in the garden, tearing at her hair. The crooked plastic chairs normally used to seat the patients in orderly rows were in disarray, and some had been knocked to the ground. Patients were jammed in the doorway to the doctor's consulting room trying to elbow their way in past each other. 'What's going on?' asked Anju's mother. Eventually, she had to grab the arm of an elderly mali in a dirty shirt. 'What's happened?' She hung on to his arm, insisting on an answer.

But the cry went up from elsewhere: 'They've killed him! The bastards have killed him! Straight through the head!' The hubbub grew. Everyone wanted to see with their own eyes; to know for sure. What were the sick to do without their healer? How would the lame walk and the blind see?

And Anju and her mother were no different from the rest. But it was some time, in all the confusion, before they could fight their way to the consulting room door. And there the doctor lay behind his desk, his head protruding at one end, a sock and shoe at the other, the face that had been formed in friendly greeting now starting to look tired. An indecent orifice gaped at the centre of his forehead in the position of the third eye. Anju wiped her hand across her mouth, and felt her throat was dry. Her mother started to bleat.

That evening, the family abandoned their usual practice of sitting out on the porch after dinner, trying to catch the last breath of the day. It felt too dangerous. The servant had gone home early to avoid the curfew, and Anju's brother had sent word to say he'd been kept late at college and would lie low with a friend. The three of them – mother, father, and daughter – huddled in the claustrophobic living room with their UK

133

relatives, with the fan whirring and the curtains flapping, lamenting the death of the doctor.

'So generous,' sobbed Anju's mother. 'Always a kind word. So good with the little ones.'

'What I don't understand,' said Anju's English auntie, 'is why anyone would want to kill a doctor.'

'They're saying in the market it was that business with the horses,' said her father.

'So now horses are their enemy?' her mother wailed.

'They said because he helped the Armed Police he was fraternising with the enemy.'

'Ludicrous!' declared Anju's mother. 'Have people no com-passion?'

They sat together for some time pondering the whys and wherefores of the turmoil that was unfolding all around them. Anju wondered what her alien auntie made of it all. They had bribed government officials to get her a permit to enter the state. Anju wondered if she would have come at all, if she had known what she was letting herself in for. With her short hair and knee-length skirts, she looked lost and completely out of place.

Anju went to bed early in her separate apartment. It had been a narrow escape for her, but at what price? She lay on her back with the light on, watching the ceiling fan clank round. Where would it all end?

In fact, it was English Auntie's alien qualities that meant that Anju felt some affinity with her. Just once or twice, in odd moments over the breakfast table, for example, she was tempted to turn to her for help. She would begin to form the words of some English sentences in her head, and then English Auntie would catch her eye and smile, and ask her some banal question about her day at school or her interests, and Anju would freeze, stammer a word or two and drop her eyes. Except once, that is: when English Auntie asked if she had any boyfriends. Anju saw her mother's head snap round on its neck. 'My God, no!' Anju declared. 'No, never.' She had enough words available in her English vocabulary for that.

The end of month tests came round. Anju did worse than everyone except she herself expected, and uncomfortable enquiries were launched over the dinner table. Her father, briefly and uncharacteristically sympathetic, conjectured that her poor performance might be due to her anxieties about the ongoing conflict, or a rumour that had been going around that some schools might close because of the troubles. Only Anju knew different. She promised to try harder, but her head was so packed with cotton wool that she couldn't think straight, and her fat fingers were too stiff to produce a decent diagram. Haggard, nauseous and with black patches under her eyes due to lack of sleep, she slogged to school every day like a manual labourer with a penchant for alcohol.

The newspapers were full of menace and desperate deeds. Pak was threatening to make incursions into Kashmir, and the separatists were threatening to make Punjab into a no-go area. Twenty people in Kurukshetra were seriously ill in hospital because they had drunk contaminated milk, and a headless torso had been found in a ditch in Kapurthala. Three ten year-old children from Khanna's Model Town had hanged themselves from a ceiling fan. Two sisters and a cousin all gone in one fell swoop, afraid that they would disgrace their parents in the end of year exams. Closer to home, the Armed Police had brought in customised agricultural machines with high-rise wheels to flush out terrorists hiding in among the sugar cane.

Anju pored over the photograph of the children's sad little corpses. How she admired them for what they had done! What courage and logistical planning it had taken to pull this off. How she longed for such a release! Time was running out for her. The business with the doctor had, after all, been a deferment and not a solution. She had already been considering whether her own careful plan would involve phenol, the rat poison under the kitchen sink, the painkillers her mother kept in a drawer to treat a recurring back problem, or the razor her father used every day. And now the children had given her another idea. She decided to give herself until the weekend when things would be easier to arrange.

That Friday night, she fell into bed exhausted, after struggling with a series of velocity-time graphs and the laws of thermodynamics. She was wiped out, vanquished, had nothing left to offer. She was asleep before she could remember to switch off the radio. While singers crooned softly throughout the night, and the terrorists crept through the fields towards the next victims on their list, her body thought things over and decided to free itself from the grip of inertia. The first blood it released leaked quietly from between her thighs. Anju sighed and turned over in her deep, dreamless sleep.

By the time morning came, a dark stain with gelatinous deposits had soaked the sheet, and smeared itself across her body. For the first time, she did not regard this as a nuisance. She stuffed the sheet into a bucket of Rin, and and went out joyfully to the market to eat as much falooda as she could manage.

On Monday morning, in Biology, she handled the slides for a series of experiments on the cell structure of plants so deftly that it won praise from her teacher. Later on she produced a depiction of the chloroplast with such accurate attention to detail that it was reminiscent of a Mughal miniature. She was back on form!

No-one commented on her change of mood. Things at home continued in the usual vein, but she got into one or two conversations with girls in Plus Two who were preparing to go to medical college, and this raised some interesting options she had not considered. Eventually, end-of-year exams came. She sat them and acquitted herself well. Then, they were on vacation, and though she kicked about at a loose end with nothing to do and no-one to do it with – it was too risky even to contemplate a trip to either the cinema or the bazaar, for example – it was not a bad experience. She knew that when school resumed, she would be giving her full attention to the Ampère versus Biot-Savart problem, and her study of the musculoskeletal system. In the meantime, she amused herself reading *Wuthering Heights,* and *The Broken Bridge* by Jagdish Vaidya.

The monsoon broke, and swept through the land, washing it clean of dissent and destruction. One night, in Ropar district, the Armed Police harvested twenty terrorists, and finished them off. No questions asked either by state or by central government. There was a collective sigh of relief in many quarters. The pillbox on the temple wall was dismantled. The sentry box where the young guard had stood was already crumbling. The Armed Police went back to barracks. The family's British relatives caught their flight back home. Anju started preparing her application for college. She had shifted her focus from Immunology to Reproductive Health and Population Management.

Washing Machine Wars

With two immaculately laminated fingernails, Mrs Çelik drew back the ornate voile panel at her bedroom window. A large removal truck was parked at the kerb with the tailgate down. Two white men were rummaging about, readying themselves to do the business. One of them stamped out a cigarette on the pavement.

'Huh, they're in my disabled parking bay,' said Mrs Çelik pouting. Nevertheless, she felt a small thrill of satisfaction at the fact that this gave her an excellent vantage point.

'Well?' said Aysel. They had been awaiting the arrival of their new neighbours for some weeks now.

'Stop pushing! I don't want them to see me.'

'Well, though?'

'There's no sign of them yet. It's just their furniture. Looks like their bedroom stuff.'

'What is it? What've they got?'

'Limed oak headboard and bedside cabinets. I've never cared for that. Looks worn out before you start. Oh, and a dressing table.'

'Let me see!'

'Nothing to see. They've taken it in. Go make me a cup of tea,' Mrs Çelik commanded.

Aysel swept off downstairs affecting a huff. In such matters, her mother could not be defied.

~

The Çeliks were veterans when it came to vetting neighbours. In their early years there had been an elderly white couple who lived like sloths behind sagging curtains. Whenever their back door opened, there was a waft of steamed cabbage and suet dumplings, as though the house were emitting a bad fart that had been a long time in the making. Their bin was full of Fray Bentos tins. Their garden, on the other hand, was full of raspberry canes that had run amok, crab apple trees that went untended and ornamental currant bushes that no-one was interested in.

I don't know why they're called white people,' said Aslan, one of Mrs Çelik's older boys, 'because they're grey.' He was right. The old man got greyer and greyer, till eventually they glimpsed him no more. Then one day, a hearse turned up, the old woman went down the front path in a previously unseen hat and they gathered that matters were drawing to a conclusion. A few months later, the woman herself disappeared, her demise evident only from the accumulation of pizza leaflets in her porch. Only their cat remained, lamenting plaintively on the kitchen windowsill then, cutting its losses, it too departed the neighbourhood.

Word about the empty house evidently got around. One morning, as Mrs Çelik went to fetch in the milk, a dark shadow loomed in the glass panes of the front door. Mrs Çelik opened the door with caution. She wasn't expecting a parcel, and the meters had recently been read.

'Eh, hello there.'

Mrs Çelik glared at the man's dilapidated shoes on her gleaming porch. 'Hello.'

'Can I come in, now?'

The man was wearing an overcoat that was in bad shape, and he himself looked even worse, with straggling hair, unshaven jowls and a couple of front teeth missing.

Mrs Çelik blinked.

'Is this not the place with the...er...with the spare room going for a person such as myself?'

Mrs Çelik shook her head emphatically.

'Ah. Oh well, then. Maybe I've got the wrong number. Sorry to have troubled you missus.'

And that was how Mrs Çelik discovered that the neighbouring house had become a squat.

'There was an Irishman on the step!' she screamed down the phone to her sister-in-law in Potters Bar. 'An Irishman!'

The Çeliks couldn't make any sense of the squatters. They painted the doors and window frames orange and daubed the walls of the kitchen black. In the garden they built a compost bin that attracted rats. They made several attempts to grow things, but never quite pulled it off. On

138

summer days, people lay for hours in the undergrowth, smoking miscellaneous substances and gazing at the sky. Cannibalised pushchairs and supermarket trolleys accumulated steadily outside the front door. Then, all of a sudden, all this stopped, and the house was empty once again.

A builder had bought the property. Skips had been lodged on the pavement for weeks and there had been the clanging of scaffolding props and jangling of clamps while the roof and been stripped and refurbished and the doors and windows replaced. Now it looked like one of the more desirable residences on the street. The *For Sale* signs had gone up and been taken down again. The Çeliks waited impatiently for a glimpse of their new neighbours. After all these years, they felt they deserved something – someone – better.

~

Aysel returned with the tea. She took her mother's place at the front of the bay window, as her mother held two lesser nails aloft and sipped.

'Ooh! What's that now?'

'Three-piece suite,' said Mrs.Çelik, 'with coffee table. Look, only cloth. Brown colour.' She raised her upper lip slightly above the hot tea.

'Oh, here comes their telly,' cried Aysel, and they both craned forward.

'Small. Thirty-two inch,' said Mrs.Çelik drily. On the roof of her own house was a satellite dish the size of Jodrell Bank, with its receivers trained on Eutelsat, while her living-room housed a screen the size of a double duvet, which Hasan, her eldest, had wangled from somewhere.

On the one hand, it was quite a satisfactory turn of events. Obviously, the people moving in were a family of modest means and were unlikely to present any challenges. On the other hand, it was disappointing: all the indications were that they were not Mrs Çelik's social equals. She was about to vouchsafe some of this to Aysel, when a car drew in behind the van, a long, black saloon.

'A Mercedes!' declared Aysel.

'Yes, but old,' said Mrs Çelik. 'See the registration.'

The driver opened his door and got out. He was a short, brown-skinned man in a tired brown suit. He wore heavy-rimmed spectacles and his black hair was oiled flat across the top of his head. He padded round the rear of the vehicle and opened the door on the passenger side. A baggy green trouser leg dangling a cream-coloured mule was extended to the pavement. Then gradually, a short, plump woman in a fawn cardigan extruded herself from the car. She looked up and down the street and beamed, patting smooth the knot of hair on the top of her head. Then she led her husband into the house.

'Ah, well,' sighed Mrs Çelik, as Aysel dropped the curtain. 'At least they're not blacks.'

~

Diplomatic relations were soon established, albeit tentatively, over the fence. The new neighbour was evidently interested in gardening. 'Your garden is so full of flowers,' she said to Mrs Çelik, 'so...well organised, so...colourful.' She surveyed the wall of couch grass that dominated her own domain: 'I think I might put a circular patio here and a herbaceous border there.'

Mrs Çelik looked at her sceptically. 'Twenty-five years it's taken to bring this soil up to scratch. You have to be turning it over, giving it compost all the time. The first thing you need to do once you get the weeds out is put down lots of lime.' But still, she proffered a clutch of nameless tubers by way of encouragement.

'Gardening is very hard work,' said Reenu Gupta when her husband came home from work a few days later, after several thwarted attempts on the wilderness. 'I can't do it on my own.'

Hari subsided behind the newspaper. 'Can't we get it paved over, and save all the bother?'

'Nooo. I want an English-style garden, with roses and creepers and trellises.'

'Where do you get these ideas from?' said Hari, who spent most of his day administering drugs and verbal solace on the closed ward of a local mental hospital.

Reenu got them from the Adult Education centre she attended to fine-tune her written English. It had opened her eyes to all sorts of things. Sometimes they did comprehension exercises based on articles from magazines like *Home and Garden* or *Beautiful Bathrooms*. Eventually, she'd started reading these things for herself. One of her ambitions was to visit Sissinghurst to see the garden of Vita Sackville West. Another was to go to the Lost Gardens of Heligan, though she wasn't quite sure how they could be lost when obviously they'd been found. One day, when her own garden was in full bloom, perhaps she could have a kitty party, like they did back home, and she and her friends could sit and drink sweet lassi on a shaded patio.

In the end, they hired a workman to turn the ground over with a rotavator, to construct the patio and to lay a rectangle of earth to lawn.

~

One thing was evident, and that was that the Guptas weren't Muslims. Every morning, with the back door open, Reenu played a recording of some interminable droning chant that drove Mrs Çelik to distraction. Then, in the living room window, she had set a carved figurine, presumably of some deity, waving its legs and arms about. This was a far cry from the vase of blousy silk peonies that adorned Mrs Çelik's own windowsill. Nevertheless, Mrs Çelik kept a tight lip in the interests of harmony.

One summer evening when Hari was in the mood for something chatt-patta*, Reenu decided to make samosas. She rolled out the pastry, set the karahi to heat and mixed the filling. As she hummed along to the Gayatri Mantra which was, as usual, playing on a loop in the kitchen, a noble thought suddenly struck her, so she doubled the quantities and made a second batch, especially for the Çeliks. She handed this offering over the fence in a basket lined with kitchen roll. After all, what could be better than breaking bread with your neighbours?

The following evening, Mrs Çelik responded with feta cheese and spinach gözleme, served on a flowery plate with a paper doily. 'These are very tasty,' said Hari, licking his lips.

'Yes, but not too tasty, I hope,' said Reenu warily. 'They *are* made by Muslims.'

'Now, now,' said Hari, with mild amusement.

The following week, after giving the matter some thought, Reenu decided to go into bat with chana and batura. She got the dahi-impregnated dough just right, and the bread billowed in the pan. 'Call them now!' she urged her son, Jaikishan, who happened to be at home from university. 'I don't want them to go hard.' The two items were handed over triumphantly in stainless steel dishes, along with a bowl of tamarind sauce.

---

* Tasty enough to make you smack your lips

141

Mrs Çelik lay low for a little while and then retaliated with an array of cold meze on a compartmentalised wooden tray. 'Very nice for the hot weather,' she said.

'Ha,' said Reenu indoors, 'cold food! Anyone could make that.' She mounted an assault the next day with lobia and vegetable kofta, probably the best she'd ever made. Almost at once, Mrs Çelik launched a broadside of braised chicken drumsticks with a side dish of green beans and walnuts.

'Oh my God,' said Reenu, 'they haven't realised that we don't eat meat! We'll just have to bin it all.'

Jaikishan eyed the drumsticks with longing. If he'd been with his university friends, he might have washed a few of those down with a pint of lager. As it was, he watched them slide into the pedal bin.

Soon, both families were eating two meals a night, whether they wanted them or not. The exchange of food was fast and furious. There were one or two items for the more experienced epicure that caused the recipients to turn their noses up in disgust. And there was the occasional cultural deviation too. One day, Reenu sent over a Black Forest gateau. 'Just a little something from Delia,' she simpered. 'Oh,' gasped Aysel, her eyes wide with lust, 'my mum could never make that: she can't read English.' Mrs Çelik shot her a look that nearly curdled the cream. But despite these little faux pas, each cook felt the other was rather good... and resented her for it.

'This has to stop,' said Hari, whose belly was beginning to bulge uncomfortably over the waistband of his trousers. By now he was taking bundles of cooked food to work for lunch and distributing them among his colleagues. 'You know there's something disturbed about this behaviour. And I'm speaking here as one who has a professional interest in such matters.' But neither of the women could stand down and, in fact, Mrs Çelik was planning to raise the stakes to an unprecedented level.

Over an entire Saturday, the Guptas were subjected to the sound of building works, the smell of cigarette smoke and the raucous voice of Hasan on his mobile phone – 'Three parts sand... Yeah, yeah... My mum says... Naw... Yeah... I've effin' done that... OK, then...' – but they couldn't make out what was going on.

'Oh, for goodness sake!' Hari said on Sunday morning – he was sick of Reenu stalking inquisitively about the house and trying to peer over the fence – 'Let's go out. It's not exactly as though they're building a conservatory without planning permission, is it? It can't be that important. If it's something we need to know about, they'll tell us.' Reenu wasn't so sure, but she thought the matter over.

'I'll go out if we can go to IKEA to look at fitted kitchens,' she said. Hari blithely agreed.

When they returned a few hours later contentedly hauling a few carrier bags of unplanned purchases, they were mystified to see a thin haze of smoke drifting between the two houses. 'Dunno what that is,' said Hari, 'somebody burning off their garden refuse, maybe,' but he was distracted by the prospect of a cup of tea. However, once they'd dropped the bags in the hall and gone through into the kitchen, it was impossible to ignore the clouds of dark smoke billowing over the fence, and once they opened the back door, they couldn't ignore the smell of singed carcass either. Reenu banged the door shut quickly:

'Oh my God,' she said, 'they've built a barbecue! They're grilling meat!'

And so it was: not a trolley-thing that you could push about the garden and station in some obscure corner, but a whopping great structure of bricks and mortar that was evidently intended to be a permanent feature, backing onto the Guptas' garden and facing the Çeliks' back door.

Hari and Reenu cowered in their kitchen, not knowing what to do. The prospect of being in close proximity to charring flesh was repellent to both of them. If this was going to be a feature of Çeliks' way of life, then they would have to say something about it. At the same time, it occurred to them that barbecuing meat was probably a cultural norm that the Çeliks were committed to. In which case, it was going to be very difficult to confront them about it.

'You can't just let it go, Pa,' said Jaikishan.'

Reenu looked at Hari with narrowed eyes. He had always been a passive man, immersed in books and newspapers. Sometimes this was a good thing, and sometimes it wasn't. 'Your father can't do: he's too much a gentleman,' she said witheringly. 'He won't be able to stand up to those loud-mouth boys. They'll make a monkey out of him.'

Despite the slur, Hari was grateful for the get-out clause. He knew that his wife was correct.

'What about you?' Reenu asked Jaikishan. 'You could always talk to Hasan.'

'Me? I don't think so, Ma. I don't even live here anymore.'

'Oh, I see,' said Reenu bitterly. 'So now it comes down to the woman of the house to do the dirty job.'

They were still debating this half an hour later when they were interrupted by shouting. It was Hasan calling them over. Gingerly, taking a deep breath, and drawing her kameez down purposefully over her bosom, Reenu opened the door. There stood Hasan, balancing an enormous tray of kebabs on top of the fence. The platter was edged with vine leaves, and glistening chillies protruded from between the chunks of meat. At Hasan's elbow stood Mrs Çelik, dignified and proud.

Reenu stepped forward and cleared her throat.

'This is most kind of you, Mrs Çelik,' she said, 'very generous. But, I'm afraid...' – there was an awkward pause – 'there's no-one in our family who actually eats meat.' Her neighbours regarded her blankly.

'It's our religion, you see. We're not allowed... We're forbidden... Scripture says...'

Slowly, the penny dropped. 'We have plenty chicken here,' Mrs Çelik said, gesturing at the platter.

Reenu held up her palm as though she were stopping traffic. 'No. I'm sorry. Not even chicken.'

Mrs Çelik's face fell. Her expression turned slowly from one of hurt to one of anger, as it occurred to her to wonder what had happened to some of the previous dishes she had donated.

'Well, there you go!' said Hasan, and he withdrew the platter from the top of the fence. 'Too good for Ma's kebabs. Fancy fuckin' that!' The two of them retreated and slammed their kitchen door. Reenu was left standing in her flowerbed without having even broached the underlying issue of the barbecue. She could hear the Çeliks stamping about their own house, Hasan's bass voice, full of menace, rumbling from room to room like thunder and Mrs Çelik's running the full gamut of histrionics like a diva rehearsing for a first night.

The remainder of the summer passed with the Guptas penned in their house on sunny days with the doors and windows sealed shut, while the Çeliks ardently fanned the flames of their barbecue. A nostril-rasping haze hung in the gap between the two houses on many days. Reenu took to tending her plants in the early hours of the morning before the Çeliks were up.

~

Slowly, the seasons turned, and the two gardens emptied of their vegetation. Drizzle hung in the trees in the neighbouring park. Temperamental breezes wandered between the houses, causing the gates to clang at unexpected hours. Foxes stalked across Reenu's lawn on their way to somewhere more amenable. While Reenu spent her time attending classes and drawing up designs for her border, Mrs Çelik introduced another layer of flounces to the bedroom windows and installed a doorbell that played the Harry Lime theme.

It was Mrs Çelik who eventually broke the ice. After all these years, the short days of winter still depressed her and made her long for home. While Reenu had her classmates for company, Mrs Çelik's only daytime companions were the characters of the soaps she followed on Turkish TV. But even she eventually lost patience with their antics. And so, when the first snowdrops and muscari paradoxum pushed their heads through the earth, she ventured out into the garden to get a breath of fresh air and found herself speaking to her neighbour.

'How are you? How are you keeping? How is your family? How is your mother?'

Reenu was pleased enough to answer. As a matter of fact, she'd been concerned for some time about her mother's health, so it was an easy topic of conversation.

Mrs Çelik listened attentively: 'What can you do? So far from home it is very difficult. I, myself, have many problems. Only God knows how long life will last. All we can do is pray.'

There was no disputing this, and so Reenu nodded sagely.

'You know, my dear,' Mrs Çelik added, her eye still focused philosophically on the middle distance. 'You should not grow so many of these bluebells. They take all the goodness from the soil.'

And so, horticultural combat was commenced.

~

Reenu tried her hand with lilies, peonies and lupins – all the things she understood to be part of an English country garden – while Mrs Çelik concentrated her energies on oleander, hibiscus and figs. The two women had very different ideas about how a garden should look. Reenu's vision was that plants should cascade, mingle, entwine. Mrs Çelik, on the other hand, had assimilated the Ottoman principles of symmetry and order. She aspired to perfect cultivars displayed in splendid isolation in beds of extreme geometry. Reenu tried everything she'd read about organic techniques, letting borage run rampant in the border, and adding crab apples to her compost heap. Next door, Mrs Çelik had Hasan spread a thick carpet of illicit Irish peat over all her flowerbeds, which Aysel then peppered with slug-slaying pellets.

When there were really crucial tasks to be done, then Mrs Çelik would remove her shellac fingernails and come out into the garden to do the work herself. If visitors from Potters Bar were expected, she took out the vacuum cleaner and hoovered the lawn. For if there was one thing Mrs Çelik could not abide, it was untidiness.

In the first few years, the odds favoured Mrs Çelik. Many of the things Reenu planted in the autumn failed to materialise in spring. And, as it turned out, the summers were unusually hot. Reenu looked on in dismay as her foxgloves took fright, and her honeysuckle was reduced to a bunch of kindling hanging on its frame. From June onwards, the earth hardened and grasped the roots of weeds so brutally that she couldn't get them out. Fissures appeared in her lawn. Every year, a hosepipe ban was imposed and, mindful of the colour of her skin, Reenu was afraid to contravene it. Despite her best efforts with the watering can, the lawn went bald in patches, as though it had alopecia.

There were no such qualms on the other side of the fence, where water trickled soothingly throughout the summer months through pipes and tubes, in a manner reminiscent of the bustans of Baghdad, and where a rotating spray played lavishly over the lawn every single evening. From early spring until well on into autumn, the Çelik garden was rife with colour. Parrot tulips and petunias; gladioli grandiflori and dahlias the size of dinner plates turned on, off; on, off; one after another, like some carefully orchestrated programme of illumination. Mrs Çelik looked out from a rear window on the lamentable collection of spindly sticks that represented her neighbour's efforts and felt a quiet satisfaction.

But then fortunes changed. Airstreams shifted mid-Atlantic bringing seasons that were mellow and moist, providing warmth and nourishment at exactly the times when Reenu's plants needed them. Her clematis took off and leapt along the fence; her rose bushes were crowded with handfuls of exquisite blooms filled with folded petals; ferns unfurled by the water feature, and even the wisteria managed to dangle twelve purple lanterns on the rear wall. Reenu was beside herself with joy.

146

Everything was running wild in just the tasteful way she'd anticipated. Mrs Çelik frowned. This was not the sort of thing she cared for at all.

Reenu was reading again. If only she could find something exceptional to take the final place in her border, it would confirm her supremacy. She trawled catalogues of rare plants looking for something that Mrs Çelik would not be able to trump. She sat in the kitchen one morning, with her reading spectacles on, thumbing through the latest catalogue.

'I just can't find what I'm looking for,' she said.

Hari snapped the top onto his lunch box: 'Has it ever occurred to you to wonder why these things are in a rare plant catalogue in the first place? It's because no bugger can grow them!'

But Reenu was not to be deterred. She set off for the college library with renewed determination.

Mrs Çelik stood by the kitchen window, tapping her fingernails on the work surface. All that verdant plant life writhing and seething in her neighbour's garden really irked her. Nor did she like the fact that much of it had begun to writhe and seethe in her direction. She looked at the cloak of clematis armandii that was making a leggy advance upon her barbecue. Something would have to be done. She went to the cupboard under the stairs to look for tools.

When Reenu saw the mess, she sank her head into a tasselled cushion on their settee and keened like a heifer caught in a wire fence. And then she was furious. Several years of work, not to mention growth, decimated by her neurotic neighbour! She resolved never to speak to the Çeliks again. Hari, on the other hand, took an administrator's approach. He got a solicitor's letter drawn up, warning the Çeliks of legal action if there were any further instances of malicious damage.

Hasan was nonplussed. 'What the fuck is this?' he said, struggling with the word "malicious". 'What the helluvyou done, Ma? We don't want no police or nothing sniffing around here.' Mrs Çelik was abashed. She was used to being the one who threw her weight about with officialdom and who generally got her way. This was an altogether different tack that she had never experienced. They took advice from Potters Bar. 'Better keep your heads down,' said the Potters Bar confederacy. 'Play it cool.' And so they did, for a considerable length of time.

~

Some years passed, and it was summer once again. It was an uneasy, brooding sort of season, with flash flooding up and down the country. But things other than the Jet Stream seemed to be adrift. The weekends spilled over into the weekdays, with people out in the park at the wrong hours of the night, and the constant cry of emergency vehicles carting people off to A and E. Sometimes, in the early hours of the morning, the police helicopter would come and station itself over their gardens, its rotor blades thwacking the sky in a tremendous din, its beam strafing the entire street seeking out someone or something the residents were unaware of. It seemed that no-one was asleep.

And things were afoot in the Çelik household. Everyone had flown the coop, apart from Aysel, though Hasan occasionally visited at weekends. It was Mrs Çelik's chance to get things exactly as she wanted them. She started with a new glass and steel extractor hood for the cooker. Reenu noticed the packing next to the dustbin. She looked around her own kitchen, remembering the visit to IKEA that had come to nothing. 'You know,' she said to Hari, 'our kitchen could do with a facelift.'

Janmashtami* was only a few weeks away, which put Reenu in a beneficent frame of mind. Suppose she could get the kitchen sorted out; perhaps the time had come at last for her to hold the first celebration in her home to which she and Hari could invite all their friends. Not a kitty party as such, but something bigger, for which she would do all the catering. She barely formulated the thought: 'and to which I might even invite Mrs Çelik'.

They bought a 240 litre cabinet freezer. 'Just for party things and such,' she explained to a startled Mrs Çelik over the fence as she revealed the plan without actually proffering an invitation.

'In this life we are nowhere without our friends and family,' growled Mrs Çelik with feeling. 'God knows.' Later that day, she got Aysel to go to Argos, and order the largest American-style fridge-freezer they had in stock. It had a horizontal bottle rack and water and ice dispensers. The repayment instalments would stretch far into the future and use up a large part of her weekly benefits payment.

---

* Celebration of the birth of Lord Krishna

148

Reenu considered the situation. All in all, she was pleased that diplomatic relations had been resumed. It didn't do not to be on good terms with your neighbours. It wasn't in keeping with the spirit of the Gita. But she was dead-heading roses in her garden on the day the men installed the American-style fridge-freezer, and she could glimpse the newcomer through the Çeliks' kitchen window. It was about the size of a double wardrobe, and twice as beautiful. Reenu inhaled sharply. She could feel saliva at the back of her throat. She was falling in love.

'So much cleaning, nah?' All that stainless steel,' she said to Mrs Çelik. 'How will you get all the finger prints off?' This presented no challenge at all to Mrs Çelik, who cleaned everything in her kitchen twice a day with antibacterial spray. Still, the barb went home and gave Mrs Çelik pause for thought. The following day, while Reenu was up in town assessing the features of various dual fuel ranges, she sent Aysel down to Comet for a George Foreman grill.

Reenu's new range was spectacular. It had seven burners, two fan-assisted ovens and a griddle plate, and its surfaces were of sleek, black enamel. Mrs Çelik waited several days, until the new appliance had made itself at home, and then appeared in her garden with Aysel in attendance. She placed her fuschia-coloured finger tips along the fence, and called for Reenu.

'Of course, my dear,' she said when Reenu appeared, 'you must do exactly as you please but, you know, Indian cookery has too much deep fat frying. You must look after your health.' She beckoned Aysel over, and Aysel presented Reenu with the George Foreman grill.

Hari was stumped: 'I don't get what you two women are playing at,' he said. 'Our houses are emptying of children, and here are you filling them up with the largest appliances on the market, as though you were preparing to fuel the Indian Army. And,' he said, pointing at George Foreman, 'how many fancy pieces of equipment do you need? What happened to bowls and spoons?'

'Hmm,' Reenu didn't bother to answer him. She knew that he would start bleating on soon about his modest salary, and rightly so. She felt guilty about his willingness to indulge her. But still, she needed to decide how to counter this latest neighbourly offensive, and now his last comment had inspired her.

The following day, she borrowed Jaikishan's laptop and visited Amazon. After much scrolling up and down, she clicked in an order for

149

Gary's Glorious Gateaux, a cornucopia of recipes by a well-known masterchef. What's more, she arranged to have the book delivered right into the heart of the Çelik household, haste-post-haste, with a message of goodwill and a wish that the work would provide her neighbour with many pleasurable hours of reading. Satisfied, she turned her attention to researching washing machines.

When Hasan called in on Saturday, his mother was in bad shape. She was lying stretched out full-length on the settee in the living-room, still in her dressing gown, although it was five o' clock. When Hasan touched her, she emitted a low, pained moan.

'What is it, Ma? Is it your back?'

Mrs Çelik moaned again. Hasan looked at Aysel. Aysel shook her head.

'Has she seen the Doc?'

'Doc's been.'

'What did he say?'

'He gave her sleeping pills.'

'Sleeping pills? What the hell's wrong with her?'

Aysel showed him the book and filled in the details. 'They know she can't read it.'

'Bastards!' shouted Hasan. 'Look, Ma,' he tried to pull his mother up by the shoulder to get her into a sitting position, 'they're not worth it.' Mrs Çelik started howling, the howls punctuated by unearthly yelps. The hairs stood up on the back of Hasan's neck.

'Look Ma,' he said again, 'don't worry. I'll sort it. I'll see to it. I really will.' He cradled his mother awkwardly until, at last, the howling subsided and, instead, she made snuffling noises on the front of his t-shirt.

'You calm down, take it easy. I'll see to them. Now, let me get you something to cheer you up. Come on, now. Anything you like. I can get it. I'm in with a good bloke now. He don't make no promises he can't keep.'

Aysel brought tea and biscuits through, and Mrs Çelik sat and looked thoughtful for a while as they consumed them. At last she whispered, as she adjusted her coaster under her saucer, 'LG six motion washing machine.'

'What?' said Hasan.

'LG washing machine, with six different motions for different washes, 11kg size drum.'

'OK, Ma. Gottit. Whatever you say.'

Hari came home from work two days later with tales of conflagration in Croydon and looting in Lewisham. The Guptas turned the television on. He wasn't wrong. The whole of the country seemed to be seething with unrest. In the Çelik household, Aysel and Mrs Çelik witnessed some of it on Turkish TV. Word was getting out about Britain's Big Society.

Hasan delivered his mother's washing machine. It came without packing. All the work he had been doing at the gym paid off, and he was able to lift it out of his car and carry it into the house single-handed. Then he arranged for one of his mates to come and plumb it in. Mrs Çelik sat in the kitchen, nursing a cup of her finest coffee, and admiring the latest thing in household chic. She felt fragile, but on the mend. She might try and have a shower later in the day.

That same afternoon, a delivery van drew up in the street. It disgorged a domestic appliance onto the pavement. Reenu was standing alongside, hopping from one foot to another with eager anticipation. In her bedroom, Mrs Çelik had just managed to get dressed. She drew back the voile panel that hung at the window. She recognised at once what the new appliance was – an 11kg LG washing machine, with six different motions. She was on the phone to Hasan immediately. It was a very loud and troubled call.

~

The Guptas wandered out into their garden in the early evening. Hari was sipping a glass of tea and held a chana papri between his fingers. Reenu was wondering if they might need to hire chairs for their impending Janmashtami do. All at once, the Çeliks' kitchen door burst open and Hasan came out. He made a grunting noise that might have been a greeting, and then there was some banging and scraping. Suddenly, he appeared, head and shoulders above the fence.

'Here,' he said, 'you lot! We're sick to death of you. You've been nothing but trouble since day one.' He was holding some object the Guptas struggled to come to terms with. Hari wondered at first if it might be the nozzle of a high-pressure hose like the one he used for cleaning the patio, but then thought maybe not. 'You've nearly driven my mum off her trolley, you bloody Hindu bastards,' Hasan went on. 'And I'm going teach you an effin' lesson so you won't ever effin' do it again.'

He swivelled the snub, snug, snout of a mini Uzi, the favoured weapon of enforcers everywhere, over the fence till it was pointing directly at Hari's legs. In the strange moment that followed, they all noted the wall of sound that wafted from the town centre less than a mile away, the sound of a crowd having its way with civil liberties. Then Hasan let loose a spattering of bullets. Hari dropped to his knees, looking surprised. His glass smashed into tinkling pieces on the patio tiles. Reenu let out a shout of alarm.

Hasan swivelled the barrel again, raising the nose of the submachine gun a little higher. 'And you, you bitch...' he said, 'the best is for you.' This time the Uzi was pointing right at the centre of Reenu's chest.

Veil

I first came to when I felt your fingers smooth the channel between my buttocks. Long, deft strokes you made, purposefully but not with force, so that my slow, inert flesh conceded willingly. You held my attention with your steady work. I caught my breath, and lingered somewhere between darkness and light each time you reached into the heavy fatigues slung low about my hips and paused.

I waited while you stroked my belly. Your hands swept to and fro between the blades of my pelvis emphasising a gentle undulation that was obvious but not overblown. Deftly, and without fear, you opened the dark eye at the centre of my abdomen and looked coolly in. I liked your unhurried and yet thoughtful gaze. You made time, plenty of time, to hover, dipping your fingers tenderly in the pools of curving shadow that lay where flesh met bone. I had no thought of what your next move might be, only feared that I might lose my senses once again.

Your fingers unfurled my ribs one by one. I inhaled, arching upwards and to one side, the bones more apparent through the flesh here than there. The hollows of my armpits opened to welcome you: they shouted for your attention. You coaxed my breasts to fullness. The nipples – small, precise, precocious – rose to meet you. I gave myself into your hands. My back prickled at your touch. My shoulder blades flexed like wings. I fluttered with desire.

My wiry arms were raised and folded. In a slow and languorous dance that kept us intertwined for hours, you clothed sinew with substance. Long, slender muscles stirred beneath my flesh. You gave me a necklace that I took as a token of your love. When, at last, I felt your breath on my face, I could wait no longer: I opened my eyes.

From behind the thin gauze you had so carefully constructed around my head and forearms, I searched for your face. I found your patient, clever eyes, soft as stoats. As you stepped around me, I glimpsed a foam of golden hair, and white skin flecked with copper. I craved your kiss. I could barely conceal my passion for your touch. My face twisted with pleasure behind my veil.

You slathered me from head to hip with water. You caressed me fulsomely until I knew I must gleam like a beacon of sensuality. I willed you to go further: to seek within, to coalesce with the gentle but insistent tongue of flame you had kindled.

I discover longing.

~

I can hear voices. I have been sealed and seared and moved. Now there are two people talking in front of me. One of them is you. I half open my eyes.

'The men had difficulty getting her down the stairs.'

'Well, well done them. I think this is just the place to put her. It's time we had a focal point in this room.'

You nod.

'The place has been modernised so many times and not very well. The walls have always stayed blank, and we've never really shown off our students' work. But so many people meet here, we ought to show them what can be achieved. We should try to inspire them.'

You nod again.

'You must be very pleased with her.'

'Well,' you hesitate, 'I feel I've managed to say something of what I wanted to say, though you can always think afterwards of different approaches you could taken.'

A little arrow enters my heart. For you, I have unequivocal love.

'Well, I think you've done extraordinarily well. You've really managed to capture something there. That moment of sexual anticipation, you know... I'm pleased to have her with us. And I'm not surprised at all you've won a scholarship. You absolutely deserve it. She'll remind us of you long after you've gone.'

My heart stirs again with this brittle news. From the slit between my arms, I watch the two of you drift away towards the hazy end of the room, you with your unkempt beauty and trailing clothes and a small dapper woman in a tartan suit, who is no match for you. The door swings idly after you are gone.

I discover betrayal.

~

There are rows of chairs set out in the room. They have been here since early morning. Now they are gradually filling up, and the noise level is rising.

There's a man in the second row wearing a brightly coloured woollen hat. 'Oh man,' he says breathlessly. 'Where de hell dat ting come from?' The younger, hatless man next to him smirks salaciously.

'A real dog, man!' shouts a man in the front row. 'Just let her come down my way on a Friday night. We could do something real cool, bro!'

There's laughter all round. But this triggers a response from a black woman in an extravagant head tie and extensive earrings.

'I don't know what kind of a gender equality programme you have running at your centre, my brother, but I don't think I would rate it very highly.'

'Ach, you women! You need to loosen up a bit,' says the man in the second row. 'It's just a joke.' The men snigger at the double entendre.

'Well I think Faith's right,' says another woman. 'There ain't no such thing as a joke when it comes to this subject. Where you bin the last ten years when you supposed to bin training? Here we are workin' with young people, trying to persuade them to respeck each other, and explaining the importance of safe sexual behaviour and here you are runnin' off at the mouth like a dog with a bone. It's disgustin' and you're disgustin'. I don't know how that piece of pornography got here, but I'm covering it up.' And so saying she gets up, stomps to the front of the room in her baggy pants and wobbling shirt and slaps two pieces of adhesive paper – red adhesive paper! – across my nipples.

A sputtering of applause runs round the room. I am mortified. I am thankful that my face is covered and that no-one can tell I am trying to blush. Who knows what might have happened next, but at this point, Tartan Suit puts in an appearance. Silence falls. She marches to the front of the room, turns her back on me, unseeing, and begins a peroration. I do my best to hang on to my dignity until the gathering is over and everyone has departed.

Later you come to me. You remove the invidious stickers. You speak to me softly as you place a small, beautifully calligraphed notice on the wall: *This is a piece of artwork. You may hold any view about it that you choose, but please do not deface it in any way.*

I discover humiliation.

~

Today the sun is out. Patterns of light and shade flither across the floor. I am filled with optimism. Perhaps you will visit me soon. But here are two people whose mood is not so light. Two women stand before me, Tartan Suit, and another one of similar build in a fawn cardigan.

'I just don't think it's appropriate.'

'Why? It's been produced by a student who has done very well for herself.'

'It's the subject.'

'Well I know there's an element of sexuality about it, but I think it's a wonderfully uncomplicated representation of the female torso. I love the smooth furrows of the ribs on that side. See? And that groove just above the trousers. It says something to me about this young woman just discovering and celebrating her sexual identity. See the way she's just drawing up her T-shirt, but hasn't quite got it off. A sort of "coming out" moment. Don't you get that?'

'As a matter of fact, it's the breasts.'

'Eh?'

'Putting it here doesn't show any sensitivity.'

'What do you mean?'

The second woman twists her hands in the pockets of her cardigan and looks wretched.

'Well, there are women who've experienced breast cancer, you know.'

'You're not saying you...'

'No, not me. But we've got one member of staff who's off sick at the moment having chemo because she's had a breast removed. How is she going to feel when she comes back and sees this? And for all we know, there may be others among our students in a similar situation.'

Tartan Suit looks taken aback.

'I must say, I've never thought of it from that point of view.'

156

'Well I think you should,' asserts the cardigan wearer, making the most of her advantage.

'But,' says Tartan Suit slowly, 'if we follow that line of argument, it means we couldn't show pictures of cute little kittens either, just in case someone's cute little kitten has been run over by a bus.'

'Now you're just taking things too far.' The cardigan wearer is bristling.

'No. I'm genuinely struggling to see the difference.'

'If you want to show it, put it somewhere where only the Art students can see it. Stuff like this isn't to everybody's taste.'

'Oh?'

'In fact,' says the cardigan wearer, tears boiling in her eyes, 'displaying stuff like this is just another of your ridiculous ideas we could all do without.' She turns on her heel and makes for the door.

'So you're saying it would be OK to display it in the coal hole,' Tartan Suit calls after her. Then she turns back to me. 'Or maybe you're saying you'd rather display me in the coal hole,' she says sadly.

I discover disillusionment.

~

Now we have a ring of low chairs. And an unsteady three-legged stand with a pad of paper on it. Alongside me there's a table covered with a cloth, and cups and saucers set out in rows. A young woman brings in two silver canisters and some biscuits and leaves them next to the cups. Rain is snaking down the windows and the lights are on even though it's mid morning. People start to arrive in dribs and drabs. They shake their outer clothes off and leave them at the far end of the room. Some attempt to shake the cold off themselves. Someone goes to the stand, wrestles with it for a bit, and then writes on the pad in large, uneven print, *Planning Meeting Equality and Diversity Conference* and then, underneath *Aims, Objectives*. No-one is keen to sit down. Some come to the table and make themselves drinks. Two men – white – fall into conversation close by me. One is not so slender. His belly hangs over his trouser belt. His hair is thinning. He wears heavy rimmed spectacles. The other – thin, ginger, a few red pimples poking through stooks of beard – looks undernourished.

'Freezing out there.' The larger one jangles a spoon in his cup.

'You're not wrong there.' The ginger one brushes biscuit crumbs from the front of his Fair Isle jumper.

'Bit off the beaten track.'

'Yeah. But not a bad venue. Plenty of space – and cheap. Adam thought of it.'

'What goes on here, then? Is it a council building?'

'Oh yeah,' the ginger one ventures authoritatively. 'Night classes. My wife used to do tapestry here. Some pretty decent tack she turned out as well.'

The two of them fall silent for a while then 'Will your lot show their faces at this conference, d'you think?' asks the larger one. 'Social Work aren't you?'

'Oh, yeah. They know that in our line of work you can't afford to put a foot wrong these days.'

The larger one sighs. His spectacles take on a gloomy cast. 'I have to be on the case all the time with my lot: "What the eff has this got to do with me?" they say. "I'm on the effin' trucks all day. All I see is bins and the effin' incinerator. Who am I going to equalise?".' He pauses for a moment and then leans forward confidentially. 'I dunno what they'll make of that.' He jerks his head up in my direction. 'She can come round my house any time for night classes with titties like that.'

'Ah.' The ginger one is only slightly phased. 'Whatever floats your boat. I suppose it's Art.'

They are busy contemplating this point when the door at the far end of the room swings open with force, unleashing a small tornado. A tall, gaunt man with a briefcase tucked under his arm steps into the room.

'Morning, everyone. Sorry I'm late. Caught in the traffic.'

He strides down the room amid a flurry of copious mackintosh.

'I'll just grab a coffee, and then we can start.'

He makes for the table, then veers right as his eyes fall on me.

He stops right in front of me. He glares up. I can see his eager-beaver eyes, and the hollows of his cheeks. His skin glistens from the rain and his dark, sleek hair is wet.

'Good God!' he cries.

He's wearing a badge on a clip. It says, 'Adam Curtiss, Equalities Officer.'

'No-one told me this was here when I made the bookings.'

He's forgotten the coffee.

'Well, we can't be having this!'

He performs a tight pirouette.

158

'The Muslims will go apeshit!'

After he's been gone for a while, an emissary is sent after him. When she reappears, the group gathers its stuff together and leaves in ragged formation. Coffee cups are abandoned on the floor and windowsills. The intended objectives of the equality and diversity conference remain undeclared.

I discover outrage.

~

A group of women, six or seven of them in assorted garb – nylon saris, floor length coats and flowered headscarves, salwar kameez – huddle over a central table. They have exercise books in front of them and murmur quietly as they consider the exercise they have been set. Periodically they drive their biros or pencils into the page sighing with the mental effort. A woman with gun-metal hair and a grey complexion wanders around the periphery of the group, peering between people's shoulders, and diving in here and there with a comment or a question. 'Good, Anima, good!' 'Oh, wait now, Shruti, what sort of ending would you expect to have on a word like that? N-o-o. That's right.'

The women labour on until their teacher goes to fetch more papers from her shopping bag. Suddenly Anima, who is sitting closest to me in a long brown coat and dappled headscarf, loses her concentration. She throws down her pencil and looks round the room impatiently, seeking something to distract her. She finds it. She sucks her teeth, and segues into a language it takes me a moment or two to attune to.

'Hey, Keka, I bet you wished you looked like that after your four babies.'

Keka also throws down her pen and swivels round to see the object of Anima's attention.

She clicks her tongue. 'You have some cheek. How d'you know I don't look like that? As a matter of fact that's exactly how I look.'

The others laugh. An older woman sighs: 'Look at her,' she says wistfully. 'I can remember when it was just like that. Waiting for your husband to turn up. Waiting for him to undress you. Wanting to please him. Tingling everywhere. I was so innocent when I married him. I looked to him for everything.' She starts to croon softly in a low, melifluous voice: 'Gungat ke patt khol re tohe piya milange.'

The others look at her blankly.

'What?' says Keka.

'Hindi?' says Anima.

'Yah, "Open the flap of your sari and you will see your lover."'

'Careful, Madhu,' says Keka, 'you'll embarrass our young sister.'

A young woman at the end of the table, her pale oval faced encased in a tightly folded headscarf, looks down her long straight nose and blushes comprehensively.

'What? It's only a religious poem by the blessed Mira. My neighbour in Lalabazar sang it all the time. Anyway, young sister will find out for herself sooner or later. All sweetness and light today, all dryness and dust tomorrow. I can tell you since what's-her-face wife number two showed up six years ago that's been the end of sweetness and light for me.'

'Count yourself lucky!' says Anima. 'I'm worn out with it. I've told that motherfucker of mine he can go and stick his stick somewhere else.'

They all laugh loudly.

The teacher, in her low-heeled shoes and drabbly skirt, pads back to the table. Madhu draws the pallu of her sari forward and pulls it down till it obscures much of her face.

'Now,' says the teacher – she places a pile of papers in the centre of the table –'how are we doing? How have you been getting on making up those sentences with the adverbs of frequency in them? Let's hear one from you, Shruti.'

'My cousins always come round at the weekend,' reads the young woman bound in the headscarf.

'Good. "My cousins always come round at the weekend." And what do your cousins always do when they come round?'

The young woman pauses for a moment.

'They always play music.'

'Good. "They always play music."' The young woman looks down demurely and allows herself a small smile.

'Anima?'

'I usually go the market on Saturdays,' says Anima confidently.

'Good. "I usually go to the market on Saturdays".'

'Madhu?'

'My sons like to go to the cinema.'

The others look at Madhu hard.

We can all tell that she's got it wrong.

There's a pause.

'No-o-o, not quite. Have another think.'

Madhu bows her head a little further towards the table. It's impossible for me to see her face at all now, but I can see the pale tips of her brown fingers planted doggedly along the edge of her sari as she props up her head with her hand and hopes for enlightenment.

There's a long and uncomfortable pause. It's evident to us all that she's not going to get it.

'We're talking about adverbs of frequency,' says the teacher gently. Things like "sometimes", "usually", "often", "always". We know your sons like to go to the cinema, but do they go sometimes, usu..."

'Often!' shouts Madhu triumphantly. 'They often go to the cinema.'

There's a collective sigh of relief.

'Good. That's the idea. "They often go to the cinema." Keku?'

'My husband sometimes does the housework,' says Keku primly.

Anima snorts.

'Good,' says the teacher.

'The bastard never lifts a finger,' murmurs Anima in her other language, 'except for you know what.'

The others shuffle in their chairs, suppressing their laughter.

Keku glares at her.

'Is something wrong, Anima?'

'I think she's made a mistake. I think it should be "My husband never does the housework".'

'It's right,' hisses Keku. 'He sometimes does the housework. He can make mogo chips.'

'Well,' says the teacher, 'men not doing the housework is a very common problem. Probably universal. So if he sometimes makes mogo chips, you're a very lucky woman.'

Anima and Keku raise their eyebrows at one another in mock defiance, and the teacher hands out the next exercise.

I discover the dry dust of second class citizenship.

~

For days now there have been comings and goings. Tables have been set up and draped in colourful cloths, and items of curious shapes – many of which I cannot discern clearly – have been set out on them. Notices have been stuck to the walls and pictures pinned to boards. Coloured streamers

161

– purple and green – drift from the light fittings. This morning, while the windows are still grey, the door flaps open and two women with lots of bags and several small children deposit themselves in a pile at the end of the room. One of the women draws a gadget from a bag and, working it steadily, begins to form brightly coloured globes that bounce and float erratically. The children are delighted. They charge round the room, setting the globes off in different directions, losing them, finding them and fighting over them. Soon, a host of green and purple globes is hugging the ceiling.

The weather brightens. More women arrive. Women of every description: careworn and youthful, dark-skinned and light, festooned in colour and clad in darkness. There are small children everywhere. The noise level steadily rises.

Suddenly, I see Tartan Suit thrusting her way through the crowd. She takes up her usual place with her back to me. 'Welcome,' she says, 'to this celebration of International Women's Day.' She talks at some length about why it's important, and about how the many exhibits round the room show just how talented women are, and what wonderful things they can achieve given the chance. She builds it all to a terrific climax, at which moment a huge cake is brought in and placed on a table beside her. The cake is a delicate shade of mauve and tied with a green ribbon. 'Made by our own students,' says Tartan Suit. She takes the knife that is offered and digs into the cake with a flourish. There is applause all round, followed immediately by an immense hubbub.

The day is filled with an ever-shifting montage of women drawing forth images from paper, printing complex patterns onto cloth, fashioning elaborate confections of beads and wire, and much more besides. While some women show great skill, it seems to be the first opportunity for others to make their mark on proceedings. The delight they show at their small achievements is touching.

At intervals throughout the day there is music: raucous and insistent, low and plaintive, loud and affirmative. The women leave what they are doing to listen, clap and dance. And everywhere there is the smell of food, a glorious mélange of sweetness and spice. Large portions of food are consumed with enthusiasm. Spoons and forks are abandoned in favour of fingers. Clothes are spoiled and paper plates dropped.

Towards the end of the afternoon, when the room has started to empty and the air has become stale, two elderly women catch my eye.

162

They make a slow progress round the room, examining the items on the walls. As they approach me, I see that one has strands of iron-grey hair pulled away from her face and folded into a pancake on top of her head. She wears spectacles that rule a heavy line across her face. The other is shorter. She has a frank, business-like expression, and vigorous white hair that halts abruptly where it meets her jaw line.

They stand, faces upturned, examining me for some time.

'Would you just look at that,' says the one with white hair at last. 'If I had'nae seen it masel I would not have credited it.'

The pancake one is wearing a close-fitting coat that seems to make her uncomfortable. I can hear her breathing heavily.

'Me neither,' she pants. 'It's an outrage.'

'What do they mean by putting it here?'

'The other stuff's bad enough...'

'...what with the no perspective...'

'...and the muddy colours, painted with a dishcloth dipped in shit...'

'...but this?'

'It's just an outrage.'

They reflect for a moment.

'And what is it she's wearing exactly?' says Pancake Woman.

'It's a string vest,' says her friend.

'It's a sack.'

'I don't think it's a sack. It's a string vest. Maybe a bag.'

'So here we are,' says Pancake woman bitterly, 'in this year of Our Lord, after decades of arguing against the objectification of women, a statue of a woman with a bag over her head.'

'And on International Women's Day.'

'After all the work we've done for women's equality in this town, sitting on committees and working parties night after night...'

'Aye. Arguing the case for dignity in the workplace and equality before the law.'

'Calling on every last relative to babysit so you could get to their bloody meetings in the first place.'

'It's not on, Zelda.'

'You're right, Maeve. It's not.'

They look at each other.

'I'm not going to let it pass,' says Zelda.

'What're you going to do?

'Write to the Leader of the Council.'
'Well, that'll work.'
'So if it doesn't, we'll take...'
They chant together: 'Direct action!'
I discover self-loathing.

~

It's dark outside. The lights are on in here. The caretaker is stacking the chairs and hoovering up the last of the crumbs. I've seen him often before, this man: thin, slightly stooped with a few straps of dark hair plastered onto the narrow dome of his skull. He plies the hose of the vacuum cleaner steadily to and fro. As he approaches, the cylinder of the machine follows him erratically across the carpet. Occasionally he turns, and boots it along the ground. When he reaches me, he stops suddenly, straightens up, clicks a switch and drops the tube. It makes a "boink" as it hits the floor. He steps back, folds his arms and looks at me critically in the silence. It's the first time he has ever done such a thing.

Then he reaches up, and briefly fingers the necklace you gave me.

'Dog tag!' he says to himself.

I can hear the air in his nostrils. His mouth curves unpleasantly.

'Fuckin' dog tag. Cunt! Cunt needs showing.'

With some fumbling, he reaches into a pocket in the centre of his overall and begins to draw out the handle of some tool. I assume that it is an implement of his trade, for cleaning or hammering, perhaps.

'I'll show her.'

But in fact, the implement won't come. It's stuck. The caretaker pulls harder. Still no joy.

He works the handle this way and that. 'Show – her – what – it – means – to – be – in – combat – fuckin' – slag.'

He develops a look of ferocious concentration. He hunches his shoulders and drops his head. He redoubles his efforts. The air leaks from him now in small gasps: oof-oof-oof. There are no longer any words.

It is at this point it occurs to me that this is something different from a work-related task, a menial chore. I am a party to something I should not be a party to. I wish desperately to remove myself, but cannot stir. I am fascinated but horrified. Finally, a judder passes through the man's frame. He clutches himself and groans. He stays hunched over for some time, then hastily stuffs the implement back into his pocket. Without glancing back at me, he scuttles out of the room.

I discover hatred.

~

We are in some mausoleum of detritus. The caretaker and another man grappled me down the stairs and into the freezing outdoors. I wished to extend my neck and project a well-directed arc of spittle at the caretaker for daring to lay a finger on me, but couldn't. The pair of them heaved me into the back of the small vehicle you used to bring us here. We jolted and twisted our way to this destination. Shadows moved across my vision, grey on grey, but I could make out nothing of our journey. A chill seeped into the vehicle along every metal seam and through every pane of glass. At my base was a grey plastic box that you used to keep me wedged in place.

The speech Tartan Suit had given to mark the end of the year had been plain enough. All students had done well and they took with them her every good wish for their future. In addition you would take with you this piece of work which, she regretted, she could no longer accommodate. The time she needed to devote to continually defending me was more than she could cope with in the course of her ordinary duties. She was sure I would find a good, and more amenable, home.

And so I stand here, surrounded by iron-walled containers, wondering what you have in mind for me. A thin drizzle starts to fall. To my left I have a partial view of the maw of a container. It is piled high with broken furniture, a lamp-stand with a buckled shade and a pink plastic animal with its legs locked in a perpetual gallop. To my right is a lop-sided stack of white metal boxes, with doors missing or hanging forlornly from their hinges.

You have your back towards me. The back door of the vehicle is raised and you are busy with the plastic box. When you turn towards me, you have a metal bar, bent at right-angles, in your hand. I cannot read the look in your eyes. Perhaps bitterness, perhaps contempt. The rain dampens your face and is forming glinting beads that are caught in your hair. I long to tell you that nothing matters because my passion for you still burns. But you draw back your arm.

The first blow falls in my belly, riving open my too-solid flesh and offering my carefully contrived innards to the dismal air. I reel at the shock and can barely gather my senses. Your second blow is vicious. You emit a shriek as you deliver it. As I topple backwards, the veil falls from eyes.

Finally, discovered, I see what I am worth.

The Work of Lesser-Known Artists

'Fucking toast! Fucking toaster!' The time was up, but the lever stayed down and the toast hadn't appeared. The thing had jammed again. Patti seized the machine, turned it upside down and gave it a vigorous shake. A shower of blackened crumbs sprayed across the draining board and bounced onto her grey work skirt. She dusted them off the thin, ungiving fabric with the back of her hand. The stuff had already acquired bobbles after just a few turns in the dryer. 'Get yourself in here. Now!' she yelled. A door thumped at the end of the passage. Patti had used the "f" word so often recently that her upper teeth had begun to settle in readiness in a groove on her lower lip. 'I said now!' she bellowed. She waggled a knife blade in the slots of the toaster, and finally prised out two crumpled slices of unevenly singed carbohydrate.

The kitchen door opened.

'Your tea's made, and there's your toast,' Patti pointed. Shevonne eyed the carboniferous remains momentarily then levered open the biscuit tin and swept half a dozen coconut fingers straight into the mouth of her shoulder bag.

'Tea?' enquired Patti.

Shevonne shrugged. 'Get can,' she said.

'That's not a good use of your pocket money.'

'So?'

Patti felt her upper lip prickle. Shevonne had turned into a belligerent teenager completely unlike the good-natured child Patti had been used to. She resented everything her mother did – or didn't – do. Entirely morose at home, she was a completely different creature once she got outside with her friends. On more than one occasion Patti had spotted a gaggle of them dragging each other about the paved court of the shopping mall, assaulting one another in that contemporary urban patois

167

that was the verbal equivalent of pepper spray. Shevonne, Patti noted, had been at the heart of affairs. The fact was, Patti didn't know how to handle her. Her only strategy was patience, and that was in increasingly short supply. She wondered how many more years she would have to endure before Shevonne evolved into someone half decent.

And then there was the matter of what Shevonne was wearing. Just what was the school's policy on uniform these days? Patti struggled to remember the most recent circular. Surely the stretch-velour tracksuit that left the navel uncovered was well beyond the limits? Shevonne was not built the way her mother had been at the same age. Patti was a hefty woman now, but in her youth she'd been straight up and down. Shevonne, on the other hand, was already well developed, a legacy perhaps, of all those matriarchs on Leroy's side of the family. Her bosom was large, and her buttocks gyrated like two boulders in a bag when she walked. She had heavy thighs that made her belly look as though it was in retreat, and a compact pubic area that formed a narrow, downward arrow in between. Her body could be read as one simple message, and that was: an invitation to try your hand. This was a message the tracksuit did nothing to repudiate.

Patti started to form words that would broach the subject, but then the radio spoke: Five to eight. No time to deal with this now. She would have to try and remember to bring it up later. She rammed a plastic box containing an already-weary sandwich into her shopping bag and then stuffed in a couple of carriers. She would need to get to the market in her lunch break. And the post office. She ran through the list of things she needed: vegetables of course, pan scourers, a bra for herself – oh! – and some cooking apples. She was planning on doing something with them tonight for dessert. 'Right,' she said. 'Out!' She shooed Shevonne out onto the landing then, following closely on her heels, slammed the door of their flat behind them.

~

A crush of anxious people fidgeted at the bus stop. The numbers on the overhead indicator board tickered by, seemingly at random. Six minutes, four, eighteen, two. Crouch End, Friern Barnet, Holloway. None of them was what she needed. She'd already been late three times this month thanks to breakdowns, stoppages and diversions. She couldn't afford to be late again: her appraisal was looming. To take her mind off the consequences of a "does not meet expectations" rating, she stared at the overflowing rubbish bin next to the bus stop. It had been an unusually long summer with a gritty heat that got into your pores and a blustering breeze that brought no relief. The discarded chicken carcasses, crushed cans and greasy cartons, a testimony to the previous evening in the inner city, were already stinking. Splotches of chewing gum spattered the paving, and a potpourri of prematurely crushed autumn leaves and cigarette butts whirled intermittently in the gutter. Patti blinked. She could already feel perspiration creeping between her bargain basement canerows.

She wasn't late, but only by good luck. She took up her place in an upper salon next to Exhibit One. Ivan sloped past her, well off the beaten track for Mediaeval Armour.

'Whazzup?' she said.

'Researching a novel. Arthurian legend meets Australian outback. It's all up here.' Ivan tapped the side of his head where the long, knotted scar scythed through his greasy locks.

'Look forward to hearing more about it,' Patti said. Ivan disappeared.

There were only a handful of early morning pensioners doing the rounds, making the most of their exhibition passes. Patti would have liked to have sat down after her gruelling journey – she'd had to stand all the way on the lower deck, and already her ankles were beginning to inflate – but that had been forbidden. Since that chap had made off in broad daylight with a Persian amphora and an Anglo-Saxon comb there'd been a change of regime. The fact that he'd been caught trying to sell the stuff on eBay had made matters worse. It had made the top managers look utter damn fools. So now you were supposed to stand all day looking as though you were "on your toes". Patti eyed the stool that still stood by the entrance to the room. Perhaps she could just slide one buttock on?

There had been other changes too. They'd all been issued with "walkie-talkies" and were supposed to use them to transmit surveillance messages to each other. The old, reactionary trade unionists and the young, avant-garde postgraduates talking to each other in alphabet spaghetti: *Alpha, Foxtrot, Charlie. Come in, come in. Bacon sandwiches now available at the Monmouth Street entrance.* Within about a fortnight, eighteen handsets had either been stolen in mysterious circumstances or accidentally dropped down stairwells.

169

Then there was the uniform. The new Head of Customer Service had come from some northern constabulary, nothing to do with Art at all, and decreed that their kit needed an overhaul. Now they were all dressed like members of the Metropolitan Police force. The women wore blazers with jaunty cravats that clipped on under the collars of their polyester shirts. The ill-fitting blazers were bad enough, but worst of all were the shirts which were far too thin, freezing in winter and broiling in summer, and which revealed every detail of your underwear. The young women turned this to their advantage, wearing elaborately corniced balcony bras to instigate flirtation with the visitors. But for larger-chested, older women like Patti, it was a nightmare. She didn't like being on display: people were supposed to be looking at the Art, not at her. And she somehow felt that unruly breasts might let her down – that their conduct was being appraised as well as hers. What she needed was some serious breast management.

The trickle of visitors gained a steady momentum. She was patrolling a temporary exhibition: *The Works of Lesser-Known Artists: Surrealism Revisited*. She stood in front of the introductory panel, reading again some of the smart-smart stuff that was written there. The six featured artists were: Gérard de Forcalquier, Pascal Thierry, Guy Sans-Sens, Florent de Haute Ville, Jean-Paul Gascon and Emile de Vouvray. All had been featured in or contributed to a little-known journal called *La Fenêtre Ouverte*. There was much about life on the edge and the years the artists had spent in fevered introspection in clubs and cafés. One of them had committed suicide and another had attempted it. Alongside was a portrait of them, a group of po-faced men in horse-hair suits and starched collars doing things they thought were witty with bananas. The text ended with a quote from an actor: 'Surrealism is not a style. It is the cry of a mind turning back on itself...' Patti sucked her teeth. She had her doubts.

Two pensioners approached. 'We're puzzled by this painting,' they said. Patti followed them over to the painting in question, a series of dotted lines, attenuated eyebrows and unfinished business entitled, *Un Portrait de Madame F. et Son Chien*. 'Where's the dog?' asked the elderly woman. 'Only, we've got a terrier, and we can't see it,' said the man. There was no bloody dog. Patti pointed at a ball of scribble floating in the bottom right-hand corner. 'Some critics think this is the dog,' she said. 'If you look carefully you can just make out marks that might be eyes and a tail.' The pensioners were satisfied. They thanked her and moved on.

When she'd landed this job, she'd been filled with enthusiasm. It was such a change from working in the dry cleaner's, keeping track of tickets and inhaling petroleum fumes all day long. Not to mention the string of other worthless jobs she'd had, cleaning offices, serving behind bars and working on the switchboard at Duke's Taxi Cabs. She'd really thought she'd be able to make good use of the diploma, Art and Counter-Culture, that she'd embarked on years ago at Goldsmiths, and which she'd had to abandon when she'd fallen pregnant with Shevonne. She'd even considered resuming her studies, perhaps doing a couple of evening classes in Art History to improve her job satisfaction and increase her promotion prospects. In reality, she'd had to work such long hours to make a living, aspiration had begun to wither on the vine. Régime change had finished it off.

A teacher arrived with a party of Spanish school children. What the heck were they going to make of some of this stuff? The teacher caught her eye. 'Don't worry,' she said, 'I've got workbooks for them.'

Patti followed them round at a slow pace, revisiting works she'd looked at many times before: in the middle of the room, a series of spinning discs and spindles that played the music of Varèse when you pressed a button, plus a rotating dentist's chair complete with patient, a concoction of papier-mâché, wire and some unsavoury scraps of synthetic fur. Every time the chair passed a trigger point, the patient's mouth opened to 180 degrees and he emitted a terrible scream – the kids might like that at least. Then the paintings on the walls: a tree with segments of a female torso hanging from it like handbags; a woman with a tuning fork for a nose and a kipper for a mouth; a whale-shaped blob on stilts that Thierry had entitled *Sous La Mamelle de Ma Mère*, and a creature of Gascon's imagining that was half-woman, half-scissors, the finger grips representing her ovaries, the blades the extraordinarily long lips of her vulva. What was wrong with these men? What explained the fact that they seemed to know so little about women and appreciate them even less?

She felt a particular hatred for *La Rêve d'une Négresse Verte* by de Haute Ville. With its vibrant colours, the work dominated one end of the room. It depicted the head and shoulders of woman with features similar to her own, set against a tropical backdrop. The woman's eyes were closed. But she had substance only as far up as her lower lip. After that, her head became a spiral of vegetable peel, opening up ever wider, to reveal the landscape behind her, until it trailed off into the sky. In other words: the woman was empty-headed. Patti stood glaring at the piece for a good ten minutes. Then she became aware that the cluster of people behind her was growing, so she moved on to let them get a better view.

The whole thing depressed her. She was standing fuming by the fire extinguisher, inventing a few titles for alternative art works of her own – *Husband Takes the Piss*, *Six Meat Dumplings Orbit Ceiling Fan*, and *Suitcase Contemplates a Rubbish Chute* – when she felt her mobile phone tremble in her pocket. It was a text: *Shevonne is not in school today. This is an unauthorised absence.* What? This was a new development. Not Shevonne absenting herself: that had happened often enough. But the fact that the school could, would dare to, invade her privacy by text. When had she even given them her mobile phone number? She struggled to read the rest of the message. *Secretary of State for Education... legal requirement... parental responsibility... subject to fine...* Dear God, how would she pay any fine? She could barely afford margarine to scrape onto their bread and off it again. Fuck the Secretary of State for Education! Just what was she supposed to do to get her truculent adolescent through the school gate every day? It was hard enough getting her out of the house. Her heart sank at the prospect of the evening of ugliness that lay ahead. She would get home knackered, and then she would have to confront Shevonne not just about the tracksuit, but about the matter of skiving off again. This time all the more serious because of the prospect of a fine.

She spent her break in the staff restroom, when she would much rather have listened to Ivan rambling on about his novel, trying unsuccessfully to contact her daughter. She slipped a chocolate Penguin into her mouth, and followed it with another. With a couple of minutes to go, Eileen from Oriental Textiles plonked herself down next to her.

'Thought you were trying to cut down?'

'Now never seems to be the right time,' said Patti. 'Soon I won't be able to get this skirt on.'

'Friggin' uniform,' commented Eileen, who had opted for the trousered version of the outfit. I've got gay women all over me like flies on shit.'

Back on the floor, Patti cruised past Forcalquier's sculpture, *Motion Perpétuelle*, an assemblage of female body parts with no head that, cleverly, could be fucked from every angle. *Fragmentation, dismemberment; dismemberment, reassembly: the cycle is interminable*

172

and inevitable, the caption read. She was watching Japanese students assiduously copying this down when her handset crackled.

'Beat Seventeen, come in, come in.'

'Yes. Hello, I'm here.'

'Beat Seventeen?'

'Yes, yes.'

'You should use the proper form of address.'

'Can't remember it,' said Patti sullenly.

The person on the other end clicked her tongue. 'Delta Five and Delta Six would like to see you now. Beat Twenty-One will relieve you.' Lorraine and Ursula, the Queens of Mean of staff supervision, two bright young appointees who were another feature of régime change, and who took their new-found responsibilities far too seriously. One of their greatest acts of altruism was nailing Stanley, the shop steward, on a disciplinary charge, within six months of his retirement. Now he was sitting at home, suspended, sweating about whether or not he was going to get his pension.

What could this be about? Ah, perhaps it was the request for Christmas leave she'd put in weeks ago. It would be a big family do in Kingston, and probably the last chance she'd have to see her dying father. She'd already taken out a loan and bought the air tickets before the prices got way beyond her.

She rushed down darkened corridors in the basement to find the pair of them.

'Hello, Patti,' said Lorraine silkily from behind the desk they shared. Patti smiled brightly, if somewhat unconvincingly. 'What it is: we need you to work Sunday.'

That knocked the smile off Patti's face. 'I've already worked five in a row.'

'Can't be helped,' cooed Lorraine, brushing something invisible off the lapel of her narrow jacket, and flicking her sleek brown hair over her shoulder. 'There'll be a big party in for a special event.'

Patti decided to take a stand. 'No, really. I have things to see to at home, and I need to spend some time with my daughter. Ask someone else.'

'We know you need the money,' said Lorraine, stiffening. 'You should be grateful for the opportunity. We don't offer it to everyone. And what's more,' she said, 'Ursula saw you sitting down this morning.' Ursula pursed her perfectly pink lips and nodded.

'I only…' began Patti, remembering the one buttock.

'Backside in contact with surface of chair,' said Ursula brusquely. 'It's called sitting down. If you don't work this Sunday, we'll put it on your record.' With her long pastel fingernails she picked at a corner of the buff-coloured folder in front of her.

'Jeez-us!' the word squeezed out from between Patti's teeth. 'And what about my Christmas leave?'

'We haven't made our minds up yet,' said Ursula.

'Time's getting on,' whispered Patti.

'Mmmm,' said Lorraine, languidly. 'Still thinking it over.'

~

'Cha! What bitches!' fumed Patti as she rushed through the back streets at lunch time. 'Let them kiss mi backside!' Still, she couldn't afford to dwell on the morning's incident. She needed to get to the market as fast as possible. There was a chap at the far end who specialised in underwear for the larger woman. She made straight for him.

'I want something with plenty of reinforcement,' she said.

'As in "Send reinforcements, we're going to a dance?"'

'Eh? No.' On another occasion, she might have had a joke with him, but today she was too hard-pressed to appreciate the levity.

'Never mind, love. It was probably before your time,' said the trader. He rummaged among the hangers on his rail and brought out an item to show her. He removed the cellophane wrapper. The bra was a bastion of buttresses, broad straps and ample cup coverage yet, somehow, it still managed a feminine appearance. Patti sized it up.

'Got it in red as well, if you fancy a bit of passion,' said the trader. He raised a flirtatious eyebrow.

Patti looked at him witheringly. 'Black's perfect. How much?'

'Tenner.'

'Eight.'

'Two for eighteen.'

She couldn't afford two. She would have to take one and wash it out every night. She got the original for nine.

She fought her way back between the backsides and baby buggies of people who had more time on their hands to do their shopping than she did, queued at the fruit and vegetable stall and took on a load of apples, carrots and bananas, and then set a course for the last leg – destination post office – to pick up her Child Benefit. Just as she passed the homeware stall with its pyramids of pans, teetering towers of Pyrex and boxes of knock-off washing-up liquid, the trader got up on his perch and started his pitch:

'The most useful thing in your kitchen. Quality German steel. Opens bottles, opens cans. Will core an apple. Will peel a potato. Quick as a flash.' He held up a complicated looking object. It had a corer at one end, and a bottle opener at the other. But, cleverly, the bottle opener had an additional prong for puncturing cans. The trader flourished the item for effect. 'Look here!' he said, then eviscerated a cooking apple. 'Come on, now, only a dozen of these left.'

Patti stopped in her tracks. The very thing! *And* it had a pink plastic toggle on it.

'One for four-fifty, two for seven. Buy one for yourself, buy one for your mate, buy one for your daughter.'

The magic words! A novelty gadget like that would certainly appeal to Shevonne. It might even persuade her to give a hand with making the dinner, and then they could get talking, and then...

Patti pushed her way to the front of the gathering. She fumbled in her purse and flashed the guy a fiver. A gadget was quickly handed over. It was too much of a challenge to get it into her bag, so she dropped it into the pocket of her blazer. Result! Now, heaving to, she steered her way towards the post office.

The atmosphere in the post office was oppressive. The place was full, but the Indian couple behind the counter ran it with all the languid hauteur of colonial bureaucracy, taking a dead-weight of time to do anything. The long queue inched painfully towards the counter amid sighs and coughs, and women menacing their fractious children.

Patti nudged her bags along the floor with the side of her shoe. Her feet felt like jars of potted salmon now, and she moved her weight from one foot to another to try and relieve the burning sensation. She had her eyes on the clock above the counter. The pointers were jerking round steadily towards the witching hour when her lunch break would be over and she would, once again, be at risk of reprisals. 'Come on, come on!' she muttered. A smoker with a lot of tar on his chest embarked on a long cough that sounded like the rattle of maracas. A toddler got entangled in the tape that was supposed to keep the customers in order, and set up a loud, penetrating wail. Patti considered leaving the matter for another day. But she couldn't: she couldn't last without the money. She would have to take her chances.

The pointer on the clock jerked another notch and wobbled. The door swung open. A man in a wheelchair glided in and, deftly manoeuvring the controls on the armrest, circumvented the queue and made for the counter. The man had no legs, just flaps of trouser folded up and safety-pinned. He looked untroubled either by his condition or the winding ribbon of people.

'For Chrissake!' thought Patti, clenching her hands. 'If that bastard thinks he's getting served before me, he can think again. I'll rip his arms off.' Then she caught herself mid-sentiment. She had just completed her NVQ module in Equality and Diversity. Where had all that gone then? What was life doing to her? She was losing sight of herself. She spent every waking moment struggling to hold things together. She had no time for anything: no time for herself, no time for her daughter and now, no time even for compassion. Her whole existence was absurd. And what did it amount to? Nothing.

The man in the wheelchair took a couple of information leaflets and a form and veered out again. There was a collective sigh.

At last, with the press of people behind her, it was Patti's turn to wash up at the counter. She rested there like a beached whale while she felt inside her shoulder bag. The man behind the grille looked over his spectacles at her and parted his lips in what wasn't exactly a smile. 'Child Benefit,' Patti said. She pushed her hand deeper into her bag. The small wallet that held her payment card wasn't in its usual place. There was a pocket she kept especially for that, but it wasn't there. The man raised an eyebrow and moved his pen from one side of his blotting pad to the other. Now Patti felt around frantically. She could hear muttering and the impatient shuffling of feet behind her. Sweat broke out on the back of her neck. She panicked. She started to turn her bag out.

'It's here. I know it's here.'

'Aw, come on,' someone said, as a set of keys fell out and a lipstick rolled across the floor, 'shift your arse.'

She fled.

She stood at the crossing on the busy main road waiting for the lights to change, with her ton-weight carrier bags wrenching her arms from their sockets. She had no explanation for what had just happened. That wallet was never anywhere else but in her bag. So had it moved into the fifth dimension, or was she losing her marbles? An immense truck thundered past creating a downdraft that nearly knocked her over, sand-blasting her face with grit and pulling tears from the corners of her eyes. Now she was out of money and almost out of time.

She got into the back door of the gallery with seconds to spare. She swiped herself in, rammed her shopping into her locker and slung her walkie-talkie back on her shoulder. Her sandwich remained wilting in its box. She should really be back upstairs by now, but she was desperate for a wee.

The wee cost her valuable minutes and back on the beat among *The Works of Lesser-Known Artists* Ivan, who'd been holding the fort, was champing at the bit.

'Sorry, mate. I've had an awful lunch time.'

'You and me both,' he said. 'It's hell in here.'

The place was packed. An ill-tempered throng of seasoned exhibition-goers stuck their elbows in each other's sides and flung their jackets in each other's faces, as they jostled for viewing positions. The benches were full of people resting their feet and refusing to budge. College students were crouched on the floor in positions of submission, sketching in their notebooks, hoping that accuracy of observation would enhance their grade profile at some point down the line. The temperature had soared, and the place smelled of many varieties of sweat. Why hadn't management decided on regulated entry for such a prestigious exhibition? But then that was the policy these days: 'Stack 'em up, sell 'em high'.

Patti did a slow round of the room, thwarting a couple of children intent on sticking their fingers into the fuckable sculpture, and giving directions to a young couple with unintelligible English who seemed to be in the wrong gallery altogether. The dental patient was howling his head off and the Varèse was jangling away relentlessly.

Patti approached *La Rêve d'une Négresse Verte*. The riven eyes of the woman in the picture seemed to be closed in prayer, asking mutely for release from her torture. For a moment, as she stood there in her boil-in-the-bag blazer and cling-film shirt, with her feet puffed up over the edges of her shoes and perspiration trickling down over the rolls of fat on her back, Patti joined her in a plea for liberation. Then her handset made a noise like the sound of chips entering the fryer.

'Beat Seventeen, come in, come in.'

'Yes. What?'

'I said, "Beat Seventeen..."'

'I know what you said. And I said, "What?"'

'It's Delta Five here.'

'I know it's Delta Five. What do you want?'

'You should say, "How can I help you?"'

'How can I help you, Lorraine?' How old was she again?

'You were late this afternoon.'

'I wasn't late. Check the time clock.'

'Delta Six saw you. You were late onto the beat.'

'I had to go to the toilet, that's all.' She was forty-five and she was trying to justify having a wee.

'Well, anyway, we've made our minds up.'

Patti stayed silent.

'I said we've made our minds up.'

'Oh?' Patti knew what was coming.

'We've decided No. We can't give you the time off at Christmas.'

'You can't give me time off to see a man who's dying?'

'No. The rosters are very tight. Later in the year would suit us better.'

'Did you not hear what I said?' Patti started. 'I...' then she snapped the phone off. What was the point? Suddenly, both hope and hopelessness dropped away from her like barrels rolling overboard into a tranquil sea. She had nothing to lose and there was nothing she could gain. Instead, a force that she had never known before stepped into her shoes, and swept through her like a tidal wave. Time expanded. Like an off-spin bowler coming in from the Vauxhall end, she took her arm right back in her awkward jacket, and flung the handset with full force onto the floor. It shattered, sending bits of plastic skittering between people's shoes. But in the midst of bedlam, only a few people close at hand noticed this aberration... and moved on.

Now she placed herself squarely in front of the painting. She watched herself stand strong, indomitable and tall. She had never felt so powerful. She was raised up! Whether through the mysteries of obeah or of God Almighty Himself, she did not know. But, oh Lord, she was raised up! Somewhere in the background, a small, fearful, submissive self was wittering away neurotically. Her strong self dismissed it. Coolly, she

178

fingered the gadget in her blazer pocket, testing the prong against her thumb. This thing had been purpose-built for the job in hand, and she knew exactly what to do.

She stepped over the rope that kept the pictures from the public. She sank the fang firmly into the canvas, and drew a strong diagonal right to left across the picture. She followed it with another and then another. Then others, left to right. The woman with the peeled cranium fell with relief from her frame in fragments that rolled slowly to the floor. The ripping sensation that reached through the blade and up into Patti's arm was wonderful; the scorching, tearing sound was glorious. Truly, she had stepped beyond herself into a world of pure sensation. 'Lord, let me stay in this place of exaltation forever. Let me stay forever.'

But now she felt strong hands hauling her arms roughly behind her back, and heard the thrill of alarms all around. At the edges of her vision, there were faces frowning in disapproval.

~

She sat in the Director's office. The apple corer-bottle opener thing had, rather unwisely, been left unattended on the desk. She had stopped crying now, but the front of her shirt was wet. Her cravat was missing. She closed her eyes. All she felt was that she felt nothing. 'Surrealism is not a style. It is the cry of a mind turning back on itself.' In her mind's eye, she saw a darkened salon hung with pictures: a cluster of palm trees dripping shadow; a white torrent slicing through a dense green forest; a bowl of orchids in an airy room. She turned from one exhibit to another, studying the detail. Just because the gallery was in her head, did that mean it wasn't real? She waited for some man to come and tell her.

~The End~